THE WORLD'S DEADLIEST MEN . . .

Errol ran hard across the parking lot, head back, the knife blade flashing as he sprinted for the safety of the quay.

Kleiner rested the pistol butt firmly in the palm of his left hand, aimed carefully at the jinking form, and fired once . . . twice. A giant hand lifted Errol forward, off his feet, hands flailing, headlong across the hood of a car, smashing him into the windshield before he cartwheeled out of sight, leaving a drift of dust to float up into the slanting shafts of light.

In the stillness, Simon could distinctly hear the blood pounding in his ears. He watched as Kleiner felt around with his feet for the ejected cartridges, picked them up, and put them in his pocket, easing the hammer forward before handing the pistol back to Simon.

"You are something else," Simon said at last, spacing the words carefully.

"So are you," Kleiner said. "We both are."

"[Quarry is] detached, cerebral, occasionally tender but usually just plain lethal, cloaked in moral ambiguities, and seldom less than utterly fascinating."
—*ALA Booklist*

Books by Robin Hunter

The Fourth Angel
The London Connection
Quarry's Contract

Published by POCKET BOOKS

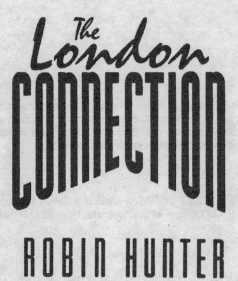

The London CONNECTION

ROBIN HUNTER

POCKET BOOKS

New York   London   Toronto   Sydney   Tokyo   Singapore

This book is a work of fiction. Names, characters, places and
incidents are either the product of the author's imagination or
are used fictitiously. Any resemblance to actual events or locales
or persons, living or dead, is entirely coincidental.

POCKET BOOKS, a division of Simon & Schuster Inc.
1230 Avenue of the Americas, New York, NY 10020

PROLOGUE

Violence is a part of Cay Dorado. Violence created the place. That volcanic cone that grew out of the sea millennia ago, to rumble and erupt down the centuries, finally blew apart sometime in the fourteenth century, creating that deep encircled bay that has made the island's fame, and to some extent, its fortune. When the Spanish explorer Vasco Nuñez de Balboa chanced on Cay Dorado in 1513, the jungle had already repossessed the steep slopes of the mountains, and the pounding Caribbean Sea had long since washed away the volcanic ash along the shore, replacing it with those long golden sandspits that caused Balboa to give the island that evocative, romantic name. He careened his ships in the bay and rested his crews ashore before leaving the seriously ill behind with one ship and sailing on across the Gulf of Darien to Panama and that peak from which he, and not "stout Cortez," first glimpsed the Pacific Ocean. When he returned to Cay Dorado six months later, he found the *Santa Maria de la Trinidad* wrecked upon the shore, and most of his men dead of yellow fever.

The Spanish colonized Cay Dorado in a fitful fashion over the next hundred years, but by the middle of the seventeenth century it had become a haven for English pirates and French buccaneers, who preyed on the Spanish galleons along the Mosquito Coast and took their prisoners and booty back to Cay Dorado, where, according to one ransomed prisoner, they had turned the shanties of what later became Caytown into "the next best thing to a hell on earth." In that respect, at least, nothing much has changed down the centuries.

The French threw out the pirates in 1739, and Caytown Harbor became a thriving and prosperous colonial port, a slave market, and a center for the trade in sugar and rum produced by the great plantations that flourished on the terraced slopes of the mountains. During the Seven Years' War, the British made their first landing on the islands, losing half a company of men in the initial assault and the best part of two battalions to sickness and drunkenness during the three years they remained in occupation. After the Treaty of Paris in 1763, Cay Dorado reverted to the French, but in 1789 the long-suffering slaves revolted against their owners, slaughtering many of the planters and driving those who survived off the island, they hoped forever. The planters returned after six months, accompanied by an army, and the Slaves' Revolt was bloodily suppressed. French rule was finally terminated in June 1805, during the middle years of the Napoleonic Wars, when Admiral Lord Nelson, flying his flag on HMS *Victory,* bombarded Caytown for half an hour, then landed marines without further opposition and hoisted the Union flag. The British were to remain on the island for the next 159 years, a century and a half, offering the most sustained period of tranquillity the islands have yet to enjoy.

During this time, the population grew and diversified. The basic mix of Spanish, African, French, and Latino people, which might loosely be called Creole, received periodic injections from the ruling British, who occupied the upper levels of island society but fornicated enthusiastically among the lower orders. The women of Cay Dorado are noted for their beauty, the men for their cheerfulness, indolence, and capacity for rum, so what with one thing and another, Cay Dorado was a happy place. Trouble, such as it was, came from America; the southern tip of Florida is just 167 miles away, and during the American Civil War, Cay

Dorado sheltered gun-runners carrying munitions for the beleaguered Confederacy, even enduring a two-month blockade by Northern warships until the British West India Squadron came up from Antigua and forced them away. For one brief moment in 1863, it even looked as if Cay Dorado might provide the spark that ignited a war between Britain and the United States.

American influence and American dollars lie heavily on all the islands of the Caribbean, and their weight grows with proximity. Much of this is to the good, but when the U.S. government passed the Volstead Act in 1920 and ushered in Prohibition, the gangsters arrived on Cay Dorado to run booze across the short sea route to Florida. Once ashore, they never really left. When the island gained independence from Britain in 1964, Mob activities multiplied, notably in the opening and running of gambling casinos, funded by Mob money and run by mobsters for mobsters. Within two years of independence, gambling and prostitution were the island's principal sources of foreign exchange.

The first prime minister (later president) of Cay Dorado, Sir Lancelot Spurling, gained power by the simplest of methods—he asked for it. During the fifties and sixties, the British were hastily divesting themselves of an empire they no longer had the energy or the money to maintain, and when Spurling founded the Progressive Independent Party in 1959 on returning from the University of Georgia, he found them more than anxious to treat with him. Spurling has—had—no more intelligence than most politicians, but he knew enough to gain power, and soon gathered enough support to maintain himself in office. Besides, he had certain natural advantages. He was black, like 93 percent of the island's population; he was well educated; and above all, he was popular. The Spurlings were a well-to-do Doradan family, owning shops, a hotel, several bars, and virtually controlling the souvenir trade, while in his younger, slimmer days, Lancelot had played cricket for Cay Dorado, carrying his bat for 115 runs in that glorious final game when they won the Caribbean Cup. When he stood for election on an independence ticket in 1962, he could hardly lose.

He was cunning enough not to make it all look too easy. There were various riots of a small and genial kind, and it took considerable effort before Spurling finally gained that essential qualification for any Independence Hero and provoked the British into arresting him. He served three months in Caytown Jail under a liberal detention order, and emerged a martyr of the people. From that time on, independence negotiations went on as merrily as a wedding feast. Spurling's PIP gained forty-seven of the fifty seats in the island's first election; a minor British royal arrived to watch the Union flag come down; and with almost audible sighs of relief, the British left. Three years later, they were back.

Half the problem was economic. Cay Dorado is simply not a large enough unit to support a growing population with rising expectations, but then that is true of many Caribbean islands. One answer might have been to federate, and during the Independence Decade, 1955–66, many islands tried to do this, at least to begin with. Then those in power discovered all the magical properties that went with the title of president or prime minister: large mansions, state visits, seats at the UN, expenses-paid trips to all kinds of countries, chances to hobnob with the great and the good, plus unlimited opportunities to rant and rave at other, larger powers. This is heady stuff for any politician. Even without the added perks of reliable graft and (if the shit should ever hit the fan) a Lear jet to the foreign home and the well-stocked Swiss bank account, being prime minister of a small Third World country is not a bad row to hoe. Hardly anyone resigns.

Even so, most of the islands have done well enough over the years, their problems eased, if not ended, by massive injections of overseas aid, soaring inflation, and continual emigration. Unfortunately, Cay Dorado had the added burden of President-for-Life Lancelot Spurling, and that extra weight proved crushing. Most dictators enjoy a honeymoon period with their electorate, however brief, or are cautious enough at the start, but Spurling had been training for this role for most of his life, and as one British politician put it sourly, "He hardly waited a second before putting his trotters in the trough." It takes a talent almost amounting to genius to ruin the economy of an entire country in thirty-four months, but Spurling managed it. Within that short space of time, he also contrived to make "Papa Doc" Duvalier's regime in Haiti look almost enlightened, for Mob muscle was available to kick the shit out of anyone who got in Spurling's way.

Addressing an unsophisticated electorate, simplicity had always been the hallmark of Spurling's policy, and so it was here. He wasted no time covering up his activities or concocting elaborate scams; he simply stole. He stole from the Treasury and the Taxation Office. This was easy, for his brother was finance minister and his brother-in-law chief inspector of revenue. He levied funds from developers, he imposed a payroll tax on the workers and a sales tax on souvenirs. Nothing changed hands in Cay Dorado without a percentage—a large percentage—going into the president's pocket. Foreign investors began to stay away in droves, and those already there swiftly left. Spurling began large-scale graft by appropriating the farewell gift of the departing British, a goodly sum intended to put a new wing on the Prince Charles and Princess Anne Cottage Hospital in Caytown. (This name accounts for the fact that never having seen storks or gooseberry bushes, small Doradan children believe that babies come from C & A's.) Having got his hand in the till with that one, Spurling developed a real genius for making off with foreign loans, so much so that when the appropriate U.S. Senate committee sat to consider his request for a fresh transfusion of aid, one of the senators remarked, "We might as well send the check straight to Zurich and cut out the middleman."

Cay Dorado might have survived graft, even on Spurling's massive scale, but for a factor that no one could control. The bottom fell out of the sugar market. Within months, Cay Dorado's fragile economy slid after it. Schools shut, the

C & A ran out of drugs, Public Services collapsed as the staff went unpaid, the IMF and World Bank officials arrived, blanched, and departed. Chaos reigned. Spurling had survived up to now, his popularity more or less intact, by the well-worn political expedient of passing the buck. He went on Channel 1 of Radio Dorado from time to time and blamed all the island's woes on the British, who, it now appeared, had taken the family jewels with them on departure. "If you don't have all those good things I promised you before Independence," he told his long-suffering countrymen, "don't blame me. Blame those imperialist colonial exploiters." Unfortunately for Spurling, this gambit misfired. Some of the younger elements from the youth wing of the PIP fell on a party of British visitors ashore from a cruise ship and beat them up with clubs and machetes. That did the tourist trade no good at all, and Spurling lost his last reliable source of hard currency. A month later, the Doradans finally took to the streets. After three nights of rioting, Spurling invoked the Anglo-Dorado Aid and Defense Treaty; cursing, the British complied. A rifle company of 2 Para arrived fresh from patrolling the streets of Belfast and put a stop to the riots without firing a shot or breaking a single head. They just stood three-deep across Independence Square, looking mean. The British Army withdrew after three weeks, and was replaced with a contingent of British bobbies, who found little crime on Cay Dorado outside the walls of Government House and were photographed by half the world's press, wearing their helmets while paddling in the sea.

Behind the scenes, though, hard words were being said and real work was being done. Spurling sat back and said nothing, while the British took his administration apart, cleaned it up, and put it back together. The British couldn't do much to stop the graft, but they told him to be more discreet about it. They also contracted to buy the sugar crop at prices well above market rates, raised and trained a company of local men for the defense force, and departed once again, leaving Spurling somewhat chastened but still in the saddle. After all, who else was there?

Growing ever more seedy, Cay Dorado stumbled on for the next decade or so, slipping faster and faster into the hands of the Mob. It became a tax haven for fraudsters, a center for laundering Mafia money. In the thirty or so tall buildings that together form Independence Square, there are no fewer than 158 banks, some of which no one in the streets below will ever have heard of. Mafia money, gambling, prostitution, and a 2 percent tax on currency exchange kept the island from bankruptcy, with the sugar-crop revenue topping up the kitty from time to time. Then, in the midseventies, two further, final blows finished the island off. Britain joined the Common Market and had to buy her sugar in Europe, and the American public discovered cocaine.

MIAMI 1989

Larry Teal was on short finals when he saw the little knot of men and cars waiting by the hangar. For a moment, he even thought of shoving the throttles through the gate and pulling away to land somewhere else. Then he thought, What the hell; I've dumped the junk as arranged two miles down the glide path, and customs has rummaged me before and found zilch. Fuck 'em.

He put on more flap, pulled back on the stick, and put the cargo plane down on the runway, gentle as a first kiss, snapping off switches as the aircraft rumbled down the track, then reversed the thrust to slow the bird down, gunned the port engines to turn her onto the peri-track, and rolled gently up to the hangar and the waiting men and cars. One of the cars was a Dade County green-and-white, and even through his insect-specked windshield, Larry could see that all the men out there were grinning. He didn't like that.

Still, when you've been around a bit, flown six tours in Nam, seen the world, and carried responsibility, you don't scare easily. Larry let them wait, running up the engines, the prop wash blasting across the yellow grass, taking time to unstrap, gather up his flight bag, and get out of his seat.

When he did swing stiffly out the door, he had a smile on his face, and his hands were almost steady.

"Well, this is nice," he said, looking about him. "A reception committee . . . have I won a prize, or what?"

"Something like that," said one of the men, a civilian in a rumpled suit who was half leaning, half sitting on the hood of a beat-up Chevy. "You are Mr. Teal? Mr. Larry Teal?"

"That's me," Larry said cheerfully. "Larry Teal, pilot of the year. You name it, I'll fly it. Now who the hell are you, and what is all this?"

The man sniffed and took another pull at his cigar. "My name's Sinker . . . local agent for the DEA."

"Are you now," Larry said. "So?"

"That's the Drug Enforcement Administration."

"I know what the hell the DEA is," said Larry, disgusted, "but what the hell do you want with me? I thought maybe you was customs, but if you wanna search Old Betsy here, feel free. You won't find shit . . . of any kind."

The man grinned. "Well, no, I don't suppose we will," he said. "Usually fly an empty plane about, do you, Mr. Teal? Unusual, isn't it? And expensive?"

"I'm an eccentric millionaire," Larry said.

"Maybe you are at that," Sinker said. "Anyway, forget the aircraft. I want to show you something." He turned, sliding off the hood to stroll round to the back of the car, jerking his head for Larry to follow as the other men closed in, trailing along behind. When he got to the trunk, Larry at his elbow, he fumbled in his pocket for the keys, unlocked the lid, and swung it up. "Take a peek," he invited.

A peek was enough for Larry; maybe more than enough. Packed in there were the half-dozen grubby, heavy-duty polyethylene sacks he had dropped into the swamp a few miles away—and there they were, wet, muddy, draped with weeds, and very, very valuable. At a guess, that trunk held about $6 million worth of uncut cocaine.

"Shit!" Larry said.

"It is, and you're in it," Sinker said.

"Now wait!"

There was a movement, a stepping back, a cocking of pistols. Suddenly, the grins were gone, and Larry found himself in a grim-faced circle, hard eyes over gunsights.

"Put your hands on the roof of the car and spread 'em," Sinker said. "And you, read him his rights."

Ten minutes later, Larry was sitting in the back of the green-and-white, speeding down the road to Miami, the DEA man sitting comfortably at his side. Larry wasn't comfortable. It's not easy to sit comfortably when your hands are cuffed behind you.

"Can we talk about this?" he asked.

Sinker was studying the glowing tip of his cigar, and took his time answering.

"We might," he said at last, "but you are between a rock and a hard place, my man. You live too high on the hog, Larry, and it sticks out. We've been watching you for months, flying in and out, seeing what you were up to. When you dumped that load, we were waiting for it, and we got here before you'd switched flight paths. You should have changed your methods, but then, why spoil a winning combination, eh? Where were you taking the dope, Larry?"

"Can we cut a deal?" Larry asked. "I know a lot of people, big people, people with plans. This is not just a nickels-and-dimes run I'm on here. This is a mission for the top brass. Believe me."

Sinker leaned forward to hammer on the wire mesh and tell the driver to pull over and stop.

"Okay, Larry," he said, when the driver had stepped out to take a leak by the front wheel. "Who are these top brass?"

Larry gulped. "This is just you and me?" he said.

"Spill it, Larry," Sinker said. "And spill it now. Once you're booked, it's open house on you. Who are you flying the junk for?"

Larry took another swallow at the lump in his throat, and then went for it.

"Only the carriage trade," he said. "I fly dope for the Cartel."

Sinker whistled softly. "Do you now," he said. "Then maybe we can do a deal after all."

LONDON 1989

The big difference between Simon Quarry and Klaus Kleiner was that Kleiner actually liked killing people. Quarry only did it if provoked. Commander John Catton of Scotland Yard's Special Branch looked up from the files and thought about that difference for a moment, letting his eyes brood on the gilded turret of Big Ben's tower, soaring high above the roofs of the Palace of Westminster. As he looked, the big hand slipped across to mark the hour, and the great bell began to boom, the sound of eleven strokes drifting across the rooftops into Catton's office. When they had stopped, he pulled his eyes away from the view and returned them to the files on his desk.

Quarry was back. Three years ago, he had vanished from London, leaving behind a few bodies and a great deal of confusion. Last month he had surfaced in Italy, up to his old tricks apparently; and now he was back. Catton read through the reports from the Milan Questura yet again, making a mental note that the ones gunned down were no great loss, and then shuffled them swiftly into Quarry's fat file, turning his attention to the man across the room who was busy emptying filing cabinets and stacking a selection of their contents on the table between them.

"All that stuff we are throwing out has to be burned as well as shredded, Tom," he said. "You'd be amazed at what some people can do with a little patience and a lot of glue. What time did Mr. Yates call?"

"About ten, sir."

"And he definitely wants us to pick up Quarry?"

"Not officially . . . nothing heavy. Just for a chat. Said if you could persuade Quarry to join you for lunch, that would do the trick."

Catton thought about that. "Hmm. If it's just social, why doesn't he ask the man himself? They used to be friends. It does nothing for my image here if I'm seen hobnobbing with Kleiner's hired killer."

"Oh yes . . . that's another thing. Mr. Yates wants to see the Kleiner file. He's sending over a docket."

"Not a chance," Catton said firmly. "Special Branch files are not open to view . . . ever."

"It's a docket signed by the Home Secretary, sir. Heavy metal."

A look of annoyance shot across Catton's face. "Bloody man! He's always up to some damned game, always interfering with other people's work. Every time I shake hands with Yates, I feel like counting my fingers to see if he's made off with any." Catton brooded out the window again. "I'd like to see him manipulate Klaus Kleiner though," he added thoughtfully.

The sergeant shoved a stack of files aside and hitched his leg up on the edge of the desk, stopping for a breather.

"Who is this Kleiner bloke? What's his game?"

Catton took another look out of the window before answering. "It depends on who you talk to," he said at last. "If you're in business, he's a titan. Rich, powerful, well connected, companies all over the world. If you're in politics, he's a . . . what? A right-wing liberal . . . if you could define Genghis Khan as a liberal. He backs politicians who win elections, whatever their politics. He has a yacht or two, a couple of planes, an island in the Caribbean . . . you name it."

"But why is he in our files?"

"Maybe I'll let *you* read the file, Tom. He is in here because he has links with ETA in Spain, the Basque terrorist movement, and because he set off a lot of hard action in Italy a couple of years back when his daughter got kidnapped. Some rich men play polo, Kleiner likes hitting people. Now, he's got some kind of connection going with Simon Quarry and my old boss here, Philip Wintle. Frankly, I don't know what his game is. But I intend to find out."

"It won't be crooked if Mr. Wintle's in it."

"It may not be crooked, but it can still be illegal," Catton pointed out. "Where is Quarry now?"

11

"At the hospital, sir, visiting Mr. Wintle. He goes there every day, sometimes morning and evening, sometimes with Miss Fiori, sometimes alone. Today, he's alone. I got the bulletin you asked for. It seems Mr. Wintle's on the mend."

"Good . . . and Miss Fiori? Where's she?"

"In Knightsbridge, shopping. Gates is with her. He radioed in just before you came in. Said he could follow her all day. She's very easy on the eye, sir, and speaks very good English."

Catton smiled. "She practically is English. She went to school and university here. Among his other talents, Quarry seems to have the knack of acquiring beautiful foreign women. When he was last here, he had an American lady in tow. Equally dishy but blond. Personally, I prefer brunettes."

Tom grinned. "And how is Miss Hitchcock, sir?"

"Very well. Yes? What is it?"

A brown-coated porter stood in the doorway, one hand on a trolley, looking around the room. "I was detailed to help you move, Commander. But . . ." He took another look around. "You've got a lot of furniture here, and it won't all go into your new office. Not with you two as well. Too small."

"It won't have to," Catton said. "All we need are those two empty cabinets, the ones over there with the combination locks. The rest stay here for my successor."

When the man had trundled the cabinets away, Catton returned to the files on his desk, leafing again through the telex messages, sorting them into little piles. The one covering the wounded Philip Wintle (with requests for airport clearance, an ambulance to rush him to the hospital) could now be torn up. Others concerned Kleiner, still in Milan, clearing away the wreckage of this last business, liquidating Luigi Fiori's criminal empire. And now, Simon Quarry and Fiori's daughter, Lucia, were here in London, and Alec Yates, the Prince of Darkness, wanted to meet Quarry for lunch. Catton thought that was curious. He looked up at his sergeant, taking Quarry's photo from the file and holding it out across his desk, face forward.

"Look at this, Tom," he said. "Remember him?"

"Not really," said the sergeant, looking at the photograph. "It was all too quick. He doesn't look, well, what he is. It's quite a nice face really. He's quite a pleasant-looking bloke."

"I believe Quarry is pleasant enough, unless you cross him," Catton said, "and then he can turn unpleasant remarkably quickly."

The sergeant thought this one over for a moment. "I wonder what Mr. Yates wants to see him for."

"God knows. But I'm sure he'll tell us, sooner or later. Lock those files away, then go and bring the car round. We had better go and pick up Mr. Quarry before he slips away again."

When the sergeant had gone, Catton shuffled the piles of reports into the top drawer of his desk and locked it. He was halfway to his feet when he hesitated and dropped back into his chair, reaching down to unlock the bottom drawer, peering in. A .38 automatic pistol lay inside, tucked into a hip holster. Catton picked it up, hefting the weight in his hand for a moment, thinking.

"No," he said to himself, softly. "That's not necessary. Quarry's not like that." He dropped the pistol back into the drawer, turned the key, and then, dropping it into his pocket, he got up and left.

═══1═══

Simon Quarry came out of the hospital, down two steps onto the wide, empty pavement of Beaumont Street, and stood there for a moment, sniffing the fresh morning air, letting his eyes drift absently about the street. The man was still there, hovering on the far side of the road. It was a crisp, glorious day, the cloud-littered sky a clear blue above the London rooftops, midmorning shoppers strolling toward Oxford Street, the traffic just a distant hum; a day for walking, or for losing a tail. With an hour still to go before lunch, Simon turned left and headed at a brisk pace for Hyde Park. If the bloodhound came sniffing after him, that would be a good place to sort him out.

"Mr. Quarry?" The sudden voice at his elbow made him turn sharply, veering away to the railings, stepping back a stride to look at the burly young man who had come up so quietly behind him. Simon shot a glance across the street, but the first man was just standing there, staring across at them quite openly. No problem there, so Simon switched a hard look onto the one in front.

"Who are you, and what do you want?" Simon kept his tone even. "Where did you spring from, anyway?"

"Just over there, sir . . . gentleman in the car would like a word. It won't take a moment, and we'd consider it a favor."

Simon flicked a harder look at the man before him, then another toward the black car waiting by the curb. He hesitated briefly, then strode across to it, the man at his heels. As they approached, the rear door swung wide open, and Simon put one hand on the roof and bent forward to lean in. A man was sitting well forward in the back seat, leaning toward him, holding the door wide and smiling pleasantly.

"Well?" Simon said shortly. "As I've asked your chum here, who are you, and what do you want?"

"Good morning, Mr. Quarry," the man said cheerfully. "I'm sorry we had to ambush you in the street like this. My name is Catton, Commander John Catton, from the Special Branch at Scotland Yard, and I'd appreciate a moment of your time."

Simon looked down at him for a moment, his body half in and half out of the car, still hesitating. The other man stood behind him, one hand on the car roof, keeping just out of earshot.

"Have you got a warrant card?" Simon asked at last.

"Yes, of course."

"Then let's see it," said Simon, holding out his hand, "and tell this man of yours to stay where I can see him. I don't like people at my back."

While Catton reached into his breast pocket and took out his wallet, the other man opened the front door of the car and slid in behind the wheel. Catton produced the card, Simon looked at it for a moment, comparing face and photograph, then nodded briefly and handed it back.

"All right, Commander, so you're a Scotland Yard officer. So far, so good. What can I do for you?"

"Well, it's rather complicated. If you can spare the time, I thought we might have lunch," Catton said pleasantly. "Then I can explain myself fully, and we can get to know each other better."

"Really?" Simon's tone was ironic. "Why should we want to know each other better? Some other time, perhaps. I already have a lunch engagement." He straightened up and began to close the car door.

"I'm sure you have," said Catton quickly, shifting across in his seat. "No doubt with Miss Fiori. At the moment, she's in Harrods, buying up the food hall, but I'm sure she'll understand. Harris . . ." Catton leaned forward to tap the driver on the shoulder. "Can you get a message to Miss Fiori? Tell them to let her know that there has been a slight change of plan and Mr. Quarry will meet her for tea at . . . where? Brown's Hotel? That is where you are staying? At . . . shall we say four o'clock? Will that be convenient, Mr. Quarry? Someone wants to meet you, and I need to talk to you. I'd rather not make it official, so this way will be easier and much less embarrassing for us both."

Simon looked down at Catton, his face set, nodding his head slightly, thinking, wondering what was going on, where all this was leading. Then he shrugged.

"Well, why not?" he said, waving Catton back across the seat and getting into the car. "Tell Miss Fiori I'll meet her at Brown's at four. You're an impertinent bastard, Catton, I'll say that for you. Are you allowed to do this? I just hope all this is worthwhile . . . worth *your* while, that is. I don't think we have anything to talk about."

"I apologize for being so insistent," Catton said, "but you do tend to slip away. Here today, gone tomorrow, it's hard to keep up with you. Actually, it's a mutual friend of ours who insists on buying lunch, so you will be doing a favor to us both by agreeing to come, and killing two birds with one stone, if you'll forgive the expression."

"Really?" Simon grunted, settling into his seat as the car pulled away from the curb. "I didn't know we had any mutual friends."

"One or two. This one is Alec Yates, of the Foreign and Commonwealth Office, or so we are led to believe. I think you know him rather well."

"Yates!" Simon almost spat out the name, his tone rising a note. "Alec Yates is no friend of mine, as you must very well know. If you know as much as you seem to, you'll also know he once tried to have me killed. I'd rather give Yates a very wide berth."

"Well, a lot of water has flowed under the bridge since you were last in town," Catton said mildly, "and no doubt he had his reasons. Alec Yates is a very pragmatic character—

ends tend to interest him rather more than means. But let's leave him for the moment; how is Philip Wintle? Now I come to think of it, that makes our second mutual friend. Philip has always spoken of you very warmly, Mr. Quarry, which is rather surprising, considering what he is—or was—and what you were—or are."

Simon ignored the thought behind that last comment. "All things considered, he's rather perky," he said. "When I left him just now, he was fully conscious, sitting up in bed and calling for food. That must be a good sign. It's been two weeks since the shooting, and he's recovering fast. He should be out and about in ten days or so."

"I'm pleased to hear it," Catton said. "Actually, I slipped in to see him last night when you and Miss Fiori were out at dinner, and the doctor said he was much better. I know your sudden flight from Italy was necessary, but after four bullets in the chest, it took a lot out of him. He's not a young man."

Simon shifted sideways in his seat, and the two men looked directly at one another, each trying to size the other up. Catton was a lanky, fair-haired man in his midthirties, with gray eyes set in a pleasant, intelligent face. Elegantly suited, black shoes gleaming, with a hint of white shirt cuffs jutting below his sleeves, Catton looked like nobody's fool, and policeman or not, Simon found himself liking him. Feeling more relaxed, he sat back as the car circled Marble Arch and turned down Park Lane, willing to let Catton carry the conversational ball, content to wait and watch the pretty girls heading through the traffic for lunchtime in the park.

Catton found Simon Quarry rather older than he had expected. There was plenty of gray in his hair now, more than he could remember even from recent photos, but he looked fit and alert, with sharp eyes set in a tanned face, his expression glinting with that ironic look that Catton remembered well. It was the look of someone who knew how to take care of himself, who would give nothing away.

"Philip has spoken very highly of you, Commander," Simon said. "So, who knows, maybe I would like the chance to know you better. I'll even endure Alec Yates for a while and strive to be polite. Where are we meeting him?"

The car had turned off Park Lane now, and was moving slowly down Mount Street, heading into Mayfair, cruising gently between long lines of parked cars.

"Just along here, at the Connaught," Catton said. "Yates said you used to like lunching here in the old days. It costs a fortune, but he's paying, so we can do ourselves rather well. Pull over, Tom, and stop here. You might like to shake hands with Sergeant Harris, Mr. Quarry—he's another old acquaintance."

"Really?" The surprise in Simon's voice was genuine. "I can't recall . . ."

"Sergeant Harris—Detective Constable Harris, as he was then—was driving my car in Stratford-on-Avon some years ago when some person unknown killed the head of the Green Jihad, who was sitting almost where you are now, in the back seat of a car very like this one. Harris got a clutch of buckshot in the shoulder, some broken fingers, and accelerated promotion. It has worked out rather well for him."

"Oh . . . I see," said Simon, leaning over the back of the front seat to offer his hand. "I hope you're all right now, Sergeant Harris . . . and no hard feelings?"

"Yes, sir, thank you," said Harris, turning to take Simon Quarry's hand in a firm grip, "and no hard feelings at all."

"Oh well . . . good," Simon said. "Thank you."

Alec Yates was waiting for them in the bar. He looked exactly as Simon remembered him, dark, autocratic, urbane, slippery. Even his pinstriped three-piece suit seemed familiar, darkly evocative of the bad old days, but his manner was warm, even effusive. As Catton ushered Simon in, he sprang up from his chair and came striding across to meet them, hands outstretched, smiling widely.

"Simon! My dear fellow! How nice to see you. It's been far too long. Well done, John, but then I told you he'd come. And how are you, Simon? You're looking well, very well."

"I'm fine," Simon said dryly. "I look after myself. How are you?"

"Well, living in the sunshine on Majorca must be marvelous . . . do you sail, or is it tramping in the hills? You were a great walker, I remember. I, alas, can only sit at a desk . . ." Yates flowed on, keeping up a stream of small talk until they were sitting in front of menus at a corner of the bar, contemplating their drinks.

"I thought we'd order here, then go straight in," said Yates, dropping his voice and looking around for a waiter. "The dining room is quiet until about noon, but then it fills up, so I've asked for a quiet table at the back, somewhere we can talk. Is that all right with you, Simon?"

"That's fine with me," Simon said shortly. "But what do you want to talk about? Which one of you two am I supposed to be meeting? Or is this lunch purely social after all?"

"Well, not quite. I need a little advice," Yates said. "But it was my idea. John happened to know where you were, and he wanted to meet you anyway. But there is no problem here, Simon. Nothing for you to worry about."

"I'm glad to hear it," Simon said. He had already decided that since Yates was paying and Catton was interesting, he might as well make an effort to be friendly. Simon had noticed that while Catton's manner with Yates was friendly and polite, it was not remotely deferential. If Catton was not running errands for Yates, that was something else in his favor. "This is all very nice," he said, putting his glass down on the bar and looking around. "In some ways, it's good to be back. I hadn't realized how much I missed England until I got home again."

"Do you miss England much?" Catton asked curiously, the glass half raised to his lips. "It's been, what . . . nearly three years since you left? No thoughts of returning? No regrets about leaving?"

"Did I have a choice? But no, not really. Only the jokes," said Simon, looking out of the window at the blossom-hung trees in the square. "You don't hear many good jokes in Majorca. The English sense of humor doesn't seem to travel. Otherwise, I don't miss England much. But when we were coming in to land over the Thames Valley last week, I noticed how green it all is, not a bit like Spain, where it's all burnt off and dusty. Still, all in all, I prefer the warm

20

weather. I don't like the litter, or the dirt, or the crowds, but on a day like today, London takes a lot of beating."

"You should try Italy," Yates said smoothly. "The problems are even worse over there. Or so I have heard."

"I have tried Italy," Simon said. "I know about the problems over there."

"We know you do," said Catton, looking down into his glass. There was silence for a while, a silence that began to drag, killing off the friendly mood.

"So you have no thoughts about coming back?" Yates inquired pleasantly, veering away from the awkward silence. "Although you have retained an interest in your publishing business, and you still have property here."

Simon wondered when they would get to the point, but he kept it going. "I rent my flat to the Japanese embassy, and I have only a financial interest in the publishing business," he said. "Lucia and I had dinner with the managing director last night. You remember Ruth, don't you, Alec? She seems to be coping very well, and was discreetly anxious that I should *not* come back and start interfering. I discreetly told her that I don't intend to. I'm quite content to be the sleeping partner."

"She must be doing very well indeed if the Quarry Press can afford to wine and dine their sleeping partner at the Gavroche," Catton conceded. "That dinner party last night must have cost a fortune."

That produced another pause, while Simon and Yates slowly digested this remark, Simon twirling his empty glass between his fingers, the ice tinkling, his eyes resting on Catton's face.

"I see," he said at last, half-amused. "So you were there too, were you? I didn't spot your man until this morning. You put the matter most delicately, Mr. Catton, but it gives me an uneasy feeling between the shoulder blades to know I'm being watched and followed about."

"Well," said Catton, deciding to get on with it, "let me tell you how it looks from my side. Some years ago, you started shooting Arabs, all over London. We knew why you did it, but that's not really allowed, Mr. Quarry, however strong your motive. Then you vanished for a couple of years, only to pop up again last month, shooting people in Milan for Klaus Kleiner. I've had dealings with Mr. Kleiner before, and he's another one who takes a very cavalier approach to the law. Then last week you come whistling into Heathrow in Kleiner's private jet with a beautiful lady and a wounded man on board, a man who turns out to be my old boss at Scotland Yard, Philip Wintle. Now, if you were me, wouldn't that interest you?"

Simon smiled. "Perhaps. But I'm not you, and you can't prove at least the first half of what you have just said—or can you? Frankly?"

"Frankly, no," said Catton, picking up his drink. "If I could, our meeting would be under very different circumstances."

"Of course we still keep tabs on you," Yates said soothingly. "You can hardly blame us. After the Jihad business, no one is quite sure what you will get up to next. As to this business in Milan, we are particularly interested because you have been working with Klaus Kleiner. Kleiner is a power in the world, and with you and Wintle on his team, he could have considerable potential for whatever schemes he has in mind. Don't look too surprised, Simon. The Western intelligence community is pretty close-knit. We keep each other informed of events, and they soon let us know what was happening in Milan. Now, Kleiner has got together with you and Philip Wintle, who was once one of our people. I didn't know you were that friendly with Wintle, but no doubt he knew what he was doing. As to this Kleiner business, did you volunteer, or were you simply helping Philip, as he says? John interviewed Philip last night."

"The only reason I got drawn into Kleiner's Italian business was because of Philip," Simon said. "I don't look for trouble, as you know. In fact, I go a long way to avoid it. Look, why am I here? What do you want with me?"

"First things first," Catton put in bluntly. "Are you armed?"

"What—right now?"

"Yes, frankly."

22

"No. Not at this minute. But since we're being frank and open with each other, if you look under the front seat of my car, you will find a Browning Hi-Power with a full clip in the butt. I'd like you to leave it there. It soothes my nerves."

Catton shook his head ruefully. "That's very naughty, Mr. Quarry. How did you get it in? We screened your baggage very carefully at the airport. Or did you pick it up here? You can keep it, but I'd really like to know how you got it."

Simon shifted a little in his chair and smiled slightly. "Well, what the hell, why not? It was on the stretcher, under Philip's blankets. We didn't think anyone would look there. On the ambulance ride to the hospital, Lucia put the pistol in her bag. I hired a car at Heathrow, followed her to the hospital, and picked up the pistol there."

Yates decided to change the subject. "Look, let's order and then go through," he said. "We've got a lot to talk about, and there is not a lot of time. However, just to bring you up to date, Simon, we don't give a damn about what you did here years ago, or what went on in Milan last month. That's all history. We have another problem at the moment, and we may need your help. We certainly need your advice—so let's get on with it."

Nothing much was said during the first two courses. They sat at the back of the dining room, chatting of this and that as the room filled and emptied, with the busy lunchtime crowd coming and going. It was not until the port and cheese arrived and the nearby tables were emptying that Yates finally got to the point.

"Right," he said, pushing his chair back, leaning forward, and looking across at Simon. "Would you like to tell us what your plans are now?"

"I don't have any particular plans," Simon said. "As soon as he is fit to travel, I'm going to take Philip and Lucia back to my home in Majorca and cultivate my garden. I fancy a quiet life with two people I rather care for."

"What about Kleiner's plans?" Catton asked intently. "What is he up to?"

"You'd better ask Kleiner."

"We shall," Yates said, "unless he tells us first. Last time he came and told us that he wanted to zap the men who kidnapped his daughter. Just to be helpful, we told him about you, and now he has done what he set out to do, and you helped him do it. What now?"

"I'm glad it was you who shopped me to Kleiner," Simon said. "I thought it was Philip, and that bothered me."

"No, don't blame Philip, it was me," Catton said. "Kleiner is very hot on drugs. His daughter went on the loose after she was kidnapped, and ended up here in London, hitting the heroin. We found her too late, but when he went after the Italians and needed some muscle, we thought of you. What Kleiner wants, Kleiner gets. That's one of the rules."

"I noticed that in Italy. But even from the Special Branch?" asked Simon, raising a surprised eyebrow. "Don't you usually report to the Home Secretary, or directly to the Prime Minister? Can Klaus Kleiner command that much clout?"

"Why not?" Yates put in. "A man who can open factories and create four thousand jobs in a marginal Tory seat just before a crucial by-election can get just about anything he wants from the government. Believe me, Simon, Klaus Kleiner has plenty of clout."

"To get to the point of all this," said Catton, pushing away his coffee cup, "Alec feels that we have a problem which may interest Kleiner, and he'd like your opinion. However, just to keep the record straight, I'm also involved, or I soon will be, and I'm dead against briefing civilians on police business. But that's not my problem at the moment . . . Alec?"

Alec Yates smoothed his hair back sleekly over his ears, looking from one to the other before replying. "We have a new situation developing, and we want it stopped," he said. "We have information that the South American group who control about eighty percent of the world's cocaine traffic are mounting a major push into Britain. We may also have a political problem with the Americans in one of our Caribbean dependencies, caused by the same drug ring. Now, it's well known that Kleiner hates dopers. He has his own security company, KSI, which Wintle runs for him, and he has stated quite openly that he wants to get into our act. It's all a bit messy at the moment, but there is a possibility—I put it no higher at the moment—that Kleiner's help might, or could, be useful at some stage in the future. I'd like to explore the matter a little further, while keeping my options open."

"I am sure you would," said Simon, "but if you want Kleiner's help, why not let him in? Chasing dope fiends might stop him bothering other people."

Yates pointed a finger at Catton. "John doesn't like it."

Simon switched his eyes to Catton and smiled. "I don't blame him."

"I don't want free-lance gunmen interfering in our affairs," Catton said shortly. "We are already tackling the drug problem. We have the customs and excise, we have the Drug Squad at the Yard, we have regional squads in the provinces, and plenty of police on the street. We don't need Kleiner, especially after what the pair of you got up to in Milan. Besides, it's not our way—you know that, Alec."

"Yes, but we still have a drug problem," Yates said smoothly, "and it's growing. When I heard Kleiner had linked up with you and Philip Wintle, and then when you turned up here . . . well! It sounded as if the Old Firm was back in business and looking for work. John will have enough on his hands here, but the drug people are based abroad, beyond his jurisdiction. I wonder if they might interest you? Unless you have some other target in mind?"

"Not a chance," Simon said. "I neither know nor care about the drug trade. I don't think Philip does either. Drugs are Kleiner's craze, and he is very welcome to it. The man is not quite sane, you know."

"Well, wait a moment," Yates continued. "Last year, after his daughter died, Kleiner was very keen to involve himself with our drug problems. Naturally, at the time we turned him down. As John said, we have our own resources, but in the last few weeks three things have happened which may—I repeat, may—be relevant to his offer. Just remember that Kleiner has both clout and international connections. He also has tremendous motivation, and no one can tie his hands politically. The man does what he wants."

Yates paused to pour himself another cup of coffee, offering the pot to the others, his eyebrows raised inquiringly. They pushed their cups forward, watching while he poured, saying nothing until their cups were full.

"Well, get on with it," said Simon, taking back his cup. "What's happened?"

"Firstly, the PM has been on one of her periodic trips to Washington. As always, she has returned full of ideas; foreign travel seems to inspire her. You may recall she got very excited about litter after a short trip to Israel. We all got lectures and bigger wastepaper baskets. This time she has returned very excited over drugs. It is a serious problem here, but nothing like as bad as it is in the States—not yet."

"Not yet," Catton agreed. "Maybe not ever."

"That's right," Yates concurred. "Maybe—but not yet. That is one reason why you are going there, to look it over. Anyway, as is her way, the PM decided to set up a task force—after the Falklands War, it's a name she likes— because, although they, like us, have countless agencies combating drug traffickers, that's what the Yanks have done. They now have a special task force, reporting directly to the President and controlled by the Vice President. Apparently, the poor devil doesn't have anything else to do. The PM told me to investigate ways of setting one up here."

"So?"

"Well, when I am told to consider ways of establishing a special task force, naturally I drag my feet a little. Unlike the Vice President of the USA, I have plenty to do, and besides, the PM's enthusiasms do not always last. We have not heard a lot about her Anti-Litter Drive for the last year or so. However, obviously I have to do something, so I put out feelers and gathered certain information. As a result, I came up with two worrying bits of news. Have you ever heard of a man called Larry Teal?"

"No," Simon said. "Who's he?"

"Or Cay Dorado?"

Simon thought for a moment. "It's an island in the Caribbean . . . quite small. Tell me about Mr. Teal."

"Mr. Teal is a former TWA pilot. More recently, he has become one of the most successful drug smugglers in the Western world. His personal assets are said to exceed thirty million dollars, and he has gathered most of that in the last two years flying cocaine into the USA from South America."

"Lucky man," Simon said.

"Indeed. However, his luck has run out. He has been arrested, and now faces several terms of life imprisonment if he comes to trial. To reduce the effects of his misfortune, Mr. Teal has been cooperating closely with the DEA—that's the Americans' Drug Enforcement Administration—and some of the information he has given them is relevant to us. In his . . . what shall we call it—confession? statement? . . . Mr. Teal alleges that the Medellín Cartel intend to expand their operation out of the U.S. and South America into Europe, specifically into the U.K. If so, that is very worrying indeed."

"Who or what is the Medellín Cartel?"

"Medellín is a town in Colombia. The Medellín Cartel, also called the Colombian Cartel, controls the world's cocaine trade. Most of their production goes to the USA, where the cocaine trade is currently estimated to have an annual turnover of around eighteen billion dollars. That's eighteen *thousand million* dollars, Simon. It would pay for our defense budget twice over."

"That seems to be serious money," Simon conceded.

"Indeed it is. Larry Teal's information was relayed to me by the DEA officer at the U.S. embassy here in London, and I put it on my file for the PM. Then, two days ago, when I was happily engaged in reading about your exploits in Milan, the DEA man gave me a call. He was just leaving for Madrid to request and arrange the extradition to the USA of a man the DEA have long wanted to interview. This man claims to be in Spain buying Muira bulls, fighting bulls, for the South American circuit, but he was picked up dining with a group of people Scotland Yard would very much like to interview back here. All were East End villains currently living on the Costa del Crime—and that makes interesting point number two, for the man the Spanish police picked up was Jorge Orchoa."

"And who, pray, is Jorge Orchoa?"

Alec Yates smiled suddenly. "Jorge Orchoa, my dear Simon, is the head of the Medellín Cartel."

There was a sudden stillness round their table, letting the noise from the few remaining diners break in on them. It was Simon's turn to lean across and refill their cups, glancing briefly at Catton's calm, noncommittal face before he spoke.

"I can see where all this is heading," he said at last, "and I can see your problem, but what has all this got to do with Kleiner and me?"

"Good question," Catton said.

"John is a policeman," Yates said, "but the international drug trade won't be cracked by the bobbies on the beat. I've learned a lot about it in the last couple of months, and the more I learn, the more worried I get, especially about that part of it, the major part, which is controlled by the Cartel. Cartel people are rich, well connected, and dangerous."

"Ah . . . like Kleiner," said Simon, nodding.

"That's exactly what I thought," Yates said. "Maybe Kleiner is a match for the Colombian Cartel. Consider the situation pragmatically. Just to begin with, he has one hell of a motivation . . . drug pushers killed his daughter. He has suggested drastic action against them before. That business with his daughter led me to think of you, and then I discover, somewhat to my surprise, that you and Kleiner are already connected. Since the Jihad business, I've been wary of your connections. I thought we should talk, so I had a word with John, and here we are."

"I knew nothing about all this," Catton said to Quarry, "but now I know why we three are here, and I still don't like it."

Simon ignored him, still brooding over his coffee cup. "One of the first things Philip Wintle told me about Kleiner was that he was insane on the subject of drugs. He said that given the chance, Kleiner would ban aspirin. And Kleiner is a dangerous bastard, you can take my word for that. I've seen him in action, and it's not a pretty sight."

"It's a more complicated story than just the little I've told you," Yates said. "I'm for finding solutions which work, but any help from us would rather depend on what Kleiner has in mind. The elimination of the Fiori kidnap gang pleased a lot of people, and gave the Italian Questura a lot of credit at no risk. Something like that might work with us. Perhaps there are a few undesirables meddling in the drug trade whom we could offer for Kleiner's attention. Certainly there are people we can't get at, people whom, for one reason or another, we cannot touch. Top people in society are certainly smuggling or distributing hard drugs at parties; diplomats are bringing in heroin via the diplomatic bags. We know who they are and what they are doing, but we can't touch them. Maybe Kleiner can. It's early days yet, but if the Medellín Cartel does come to Britain, we will need all the help we can get. So, whatever John here feels, I'm not shutting any doors at the moment."

Simon shook his head. "Kleiner doesn't give a damn about society, but hitting something big, like the Cartel, might interest him. But you've certainly changed your tune in the last couple of years, Alec. When I went after the Jihad three years ago, you shopped me to them and set me up for killing. I'm sorry to bring that up again, but it's true. Now, you are openly considering something on the same lines against this Cartel."

Yates dismissed that point with a wave of his hand. "You were before your time, Simon. Besides, you lack Kleiner's finesse. My brief is to stop the arrival in Britain of the Medellín Cartel, so I'm not rejecting any option. I am being frank with you," Yates continued, "because you have worked with Kleiner recently and know him better than we do. We need to know if—I repeat *if*—this business might interest him. We'd ask Philip Wintle, but he has been shot and is still seriously ill. Whatever happens, we don't propose to sit here and wait for the Cartel to set up shop here. John has been detached from the Special Branch and is now on assignment to the Home Office. He will expand on the information I already have, and he leaves for Miami in a couple of days. His brief is to meet Larry Teal and find out everything he can about the Cartel and the cocaine trade, how they operate in the U.S.A., and what we can do about it here. When we have all the information, I will present a number of options to the PM or the special Cabinet committee."

Simon switched his eyes to Catton. "How do you feel about this? About Kleiner . . . about me knowing all this?"

"My gut reaction is against it," Catton said. "Kleiner concerns me, but you worry me. As far as I know, what you do best is shoot people. Are you working for Kleiner now, and if so, doing what?"

Simon shook his head. "Kleiner and I do not get on, and the Medellín Cartel is your problem, not mine. If you'll take some advice, you'll solve it without Kleiner."

"I agree," Catton said.

"Well, we'd like to, but we're restricted," Yates said earnestly. "Look, a lot of crime is both international and political. There is a political element in this Cartel business which I'll come to later, and anyway, what we can do here is small beer. We need to strike at the roots of the traffic abroad, but we can't. Maybe Kleiner can."

"Well, hounding villains is Kleiner's hobby, not mine," Simon said. "If you want his help, go and see him and tell him what you want. Just leave me out of it."

"We don't *want* anything, or at least *I* don't," said Catton, leaning across the table toward Simon, "but Alec may be right. If all he tells me checks out, we may need all the help we can get to keep the Cartel out of Britain."

Simon shrugged. "Well, that's your concern. I've always thought that the police should do the dirty work. That's what you're paid for." Simon rubbed his eyes gently with thumb and forefinger and pushed his chair back from the table. "Gentlemen, thank you for the lunch and the chat, for the absence of threats, even for the advice. Now, let me tell you what I am going to do. I'm going to stay in England for a couple of weeks to entertain my lady and wait for Philip Wintle to get better. Then all three of us are going down to my house in Majorca, to soak up the sun and live happily ever after. So, if you will excuse me, I have an appointment for tea at Brown's Hotel. Alec . . . Mr. Catton . . ."

"Call me John, please."

"John, then. Alec, thank you for lunch, but this Cartel business is not my party."

"We haven't asked you to do anything yet," said Alec Yates, rising from the table, frowning.

"I know you haven't," said Simon, moving toward the door, "and I'm getting out of here before you do."

When he had gone, Yates and Catton sat on in the empty dining room for a while, saying little, gazing at the tablecloth or out of the window, each sipping another cup of coffee, thinking.

"It won't work, Alec," Catton said at last. "I've met Quarry now, and I can tell you that your little scheme won't work."

"What won't?"

"Your idea; to suck Quarry into this business and get him to do your dirty work for you. Whatever he used to do, he won't do this, not for you or anybody. He's not for hire."

Yates smiled briefly, then tapped his nose with his forefinger. "O ye of little faith," he said. "You'd be surprised what I can get people to do. Remember the old saying, 'When you have them by the balls, their hearts and minds will follow.' I haven't even started on Quarry yet."

Simon rolled over, switched on the light, and glanced at his wristwatch on the bedside table. Then he got out of bed and went in bare feet across the deep carpet to the bathroom, closing the door before switching on the light. When he came out a few minutes later, pulling on a robe, Lucia was propped on her elbows in bed, yawning.

"What time is it?" she asked.

"Just after six. We've only been out about an hour. Shall I ring down for tea? If we want to get to the opera, we'll have to leave in about half an hour."

"Please . . . What did they really want?"

Simon sat down on the bed and reached for the phone. "Who? Room Service, please."

"Yates and the policeman . . . what's his name?"

"Catton. Hello, could we have a pot of tea, lemon . . . maybe some biscuits, in suite one-thirty-one, as soon as possible . . . Quarry. Thank you." He put down the phone and turned to Lucia.

"You are looking quite remarkably sexy," he said. "Why don't we miss the opera and order dinner up here, later?"

"No," she said decisively. "Love in the afternoon is nice, but tickets for Placido Domingo are like gold dust. Besides, you still haven't answered my question. What did they want?"

"Nothing much. Information about Klaus. Where he is now, what he might do next, what our plans are."

"And what did you tell them?"

"The truth. I don't know anything. I said we were waiting for Philip to recover, and then we were all going to Majorca, and a happy life. Isn't that right?"

Lucia swung her legs out of bed, a flash of brown body, and began to wrap herself in a robe as she stalked over to the dressing table and began to brush her hair with long, vigorous strokes, staring hard into the mirror.

"What did they really want?"

Simon thought for a moment. "It's hard to say. Most of their interest was in Kleiner. Could he be useful with this drug business, and if so, could he be controlled? They know what he's like."

"And that's all?"

Simon laughed shortly. "With Yates? I doubt it. The Special Branch man would either lock me up or have me absent, but Yates sees people as things to be used. He was touching base to see if I might pull a trigger for him if the need arose. The drugs are Catton's problem. What's worrying Yates is something more . . . something political."

"And?"

"I told him—pardon the expression—to get fucked. We have our own lives to lead, and we'll stay well away from police and politicians and slimy Mr. Fixits like Alec Yates. Believe me."

Lucia turned to face him, swinging around on the stool. "Simon?"

"Mmm?"

"Is it possible?"

"Is what possible?"

"To get away. To live a happy life. With Philip and Klaus and Yates and this policeman and all these people you are connected with? If they need you, will they really leave you alone?"

"I'm not connected with them. And if we can't be left in peace in Majorca, we'll simply go somewhere else. I won't get involved in whatever they get up to. It's over."

"We're running out of places to run to, Simon. Italy for me, England for you, maybe Spain for both of us. I'd like to practice medicine again. People need doctors, and I'm a good doctor. I can't just wander the world, shopping, staying in big hotels, going to the opera."

He smiled at her, noting her anxious face. "Look, go and have your shower and don't worry. If trouble comes, even from Kleiner, I can handle it."

"How?"

"Simple. I'll just say no."

"You promise?"

"I promise."

Lucia walked over toward him, putting her arms around his neck and pressing her face into his body. Then the doorbell chimed, twice, and the handle rattled.

"Damn!" Lucia said.

"My sentiments exactly," Simon said.

=== 2 ===

John Catton opened the bottom drawer of his desk, put his hand in to grope about at the back, and found nothing. Sitting up in his chair again, he slid the drawer shut with his foot; that must be the lot. The contents of the drawer stood on the desktop before him, the filing cabinets had been checked and the files updated. All was ready for Catton's successor, so all he had to do was move to his smaller office along the corridor and create a new job. Catton still wasn't too sure how he felt about that. Life as head of the Special Branch had always been interesting.

There came a light tap at the door. Catton looked up to see Ted Bardsey standing there in shirtsleeves and braces, looking around at the empty shelves and then down toward the piled-up desktop, grinning. When he had taken it all in, Bardsey turned his little piggy eyes back to Catton, still smiling his gap-toothed smile.

"Well, well," he said. "So who's been a naughty boy then, eh? And when is little John going to tell his uncle Ted why he is getting the sideways heave-ho, eh?"

On the surface, Ted Bardsey, who ran Major Crimes just down the corridor, was a cheery, roly-poly little man, but around the Yard, the word was that if you had Ted Bardsey for a friend then you didn't need enemies. Ted was ambitious and prided himself on knowing all there was to know, but to rise from beat bobbie to head of an operational department at Scotland Yard indicated that he must have a brain in there somewhere. Even so, when he was around, wise men kept their backs to the wall, and Catton's glance was far from friendly.

"Look, Ted," he said wearily, "just to put your mind at rest, I am *not* being given the heave-ho. You saw the press release; I'm going to handle a special assignment for the Home Office with a view to creating a new department; and that's all. Got it?"

Bardsey tapped his nose. "That I know, old son, but you can't fool old Ted. I've had my eye on you since the day you came in here—how long ago was it? Five, six years? Under old Philip Wintle. You were marked out for the top even then. We all knew that. A lot of talk in the pub about you, I remember. And I told you then, didn't I, that you had to watch your step. The ladder to the top has slippery rungs."

"Now look, Ted . . ." Catton began. "For the first and last time . . ." Bardsey held up a beefy hand, three fingers of which wore rings, to interrupt him.

"No, you listen to me. You have to avoid specialization, John. Do your time on the beat, yes. Everyone has to do that. Then pick a department . . . Traffic, or go for the CID, into plainclothes, it doesn't matter. Go for your promotion exams if you like books, as you do. The trick is to move about, move up. Move in and out of the Uniformed Branch, get to be assistant commissioner on some provincial force. Do your stuff at Bramshill on the Staff Course—easy for you with your law degree and all. Not like old Ted here. I got my education in the School of Life, my son, at the University of Hard Knocks. What you need now is a stretch in Northern Ireland. You could make a name for yourself over there if you don't fuck it up, and then one day, tra-la, you'd be head of the Met and never off the telly."

"Very true," Catton said patiently. "But now, if you don't mind . . ."

It did no good. Ted Bardsey was in full flood. "That's what the future could have been for Philip Wintle's golden boy, but he has fucked it up. You went into the Branch too early, Johnny-lad, and you've peaked too young. Now,

Wintle is over there in Sister Agnes Hospital with bullet holes in his chest, and it is all over the Yard that not a week ago you were hobnobbing with that Simon Quarry, who, as all in the know, know, is a high-priced hit man. So now you are out. What did you expect? You have to stay away from the rough trade, John." Bardsey raised his finger in the air and intoned, " 'He who touches the shit shall get a smell about him. Here endeth the lesson.' "

John Catton shook his head and laughed, half-amused. "Well, Ted, all I can say is that if *that's* how you put your cases together over at Major Crimes, God help you when they get to court. Any judge would throw that lot out as sheer conjecture."

Ted waved that aside with another flash of jewelry. "Is that right?" he asked, eyebrows raised. "You mean Philip Wintle is *not* flat on his back? That you *weren't* waltzing Quarry around town in the Branch's flash limo, and even introducing him to young Harris, who came back here full of it? And, the final touch, aren't you now being shifted sideways and off the upward elevator? It's bloody logical. You've screwed up."

John Catton scratched the back of his neck and grinned up at his visitor. "Memo to self," he said aloud. "Twist Sergeant Harris's balls quite hard for yapping about Branch business in the canteen. On second thoughts, though, if I'd told him to keep it quiet, and it leaked anyway, as things do around here, that would have created a bigger stir. If this theory of yours gets around, I'll know where to look. As to the last bit, I don't think so. There is more than one 'up' elevator and, as you used to say—just loud enough for me to hear—the shit always floats to the top."

Bardsey chuckled, perching himself on the edge of Catton's desk. "Did I say that? Me? Well, maybe that was before I got to know you. Now we're colleagues, mates, commanders in the mighty Met, London's Finest. You with the Special Branch, and me holding the fort at Major Crimes. What a pair, eh? Listen, if they drop you down a rank or two and give you a second chance, I can find you a slot. I'll even put in for you. You can make my tea and fetch my sandwiches."

"Thanks a bunch," said John Catton, rising. "Look, I'm off abroad in a few days, and I still have to finish up here, hand over, and pack, but to shut you up, why don't we have a drink over at the Sherlock and I'll tell you what it's about. Bits of it, anyway. All right?"

"I thought you'd never ask," said Bardsey, turning. "I'll go and get my coat."

"Well, I'll believe you, though thousands wouldn't," said Ted, running the back of his hand across his lips. "But what I don't see is why they didn't hand this over to the Drug Squad. If the idea is to move you in there, Harry Bartlett won't like it."

"That's not the idea," said Catton, signaling up another round, "and I wouldn't go for it anyway. This is more of an assignment to check something out, make recommendations on what to do. I can't tell you more, partly because I'd better not, partly because I don't know any more. I expect it will come out at commanders' briefing in a few weeks' time, so you'll just have to wait. And Harry doesn't mind a bit, incidentally. He's tactics, I'm looking at strategy, at long-term plans for fresh problems. He hasn't got the time for that."

"Well, if they want some prick to write a report, I can see why they chose you, you being an academic and all. You were a lawyer, right? . . . Or could have been. That lovely girlfriend of yours, she's a brief, isn't she? Seen her at the Old Bailey. Very tasty, and brains too. Somehow, I've always seen you ending up head of Bramshill. Lecturing yuppie cops at the Police Staff College would be right up your alley. You brainy types ought to leave the operational stuff to old-time coppers like me." Bardsey's grin only just cut the acid from his tone.

"Should we now?" Catton said dryly. "Well, you might be right, though I don't agree with you. I did my beat time in Liverpool incidentally, not the leafy lanes of Cheltenham, like you. How many retired colonels tried to mug you up there in the Cotswolds? Don't come on the hard man with me, Ted, it won't wash."

"My, my, we are touchy tonight," said Bardsey, still grinning. "Listen, you'd be surprised what goes on in a spa town like Cheltenham. I was in hand-to-hand combat half the time with merry widows and Indian Army colonels."

"Piss off," Catton said cheerfully, "and get your money out."

"One pint of best, one large G and T," said the barmaid at his elbow.

"How much?" asked Catton and Bardsey together.

"Two pounds, fifteen pence."

"Christ!" Bardsey said. "And it's my shout."

"No, I'll get this," Catton said. "You got the first one."

"But it's my round." Ted produced a roll of money from his hip pocket and began to snap off some notes.

"Since when did someone else buying ever bother you?"

"Not often, but it's my shout. You can get the next one." Bardsey pushed Catton aside and handed the barmaid a ten-pound note.

"Don't you have anything smaller?" she asked, frowning. "These big notes use up my small change."

"Sorry, love, but that's it," Ted said. "Otherwise it'll have to be on the house."

"You'll be lucky."

"Could you split a fifty-pound note for me?" Catton interrupted. He turned toward Bardsey. "I told you I needed some change, so let me get it."

"I've never had a fifty-pound note," Bardsey said. "Going to do yourself nicely in America, I see."

"Give it here," the barmaid said. "Notes we can manage, it's silver we're out of. You coppers are all overpaid, if you ask me."

"I ordered some cash for this U.S. trip," Catton explained as she went away, "and they sent me up fifties, no U.S. currency, not even one dollar—fat chance of changing big notes outside the U.K.—or even here . . . people don't like them."

"There are a lot of counterfeit fifties about," Bardsey agreed, "but I like helping to spend your exes in the pub before you even start the trip. When are you off?"

"In a few days, maybe Friday—and the trip cash stays separate, in this envelope. So none of your funny stories about fiddling the exes behind my back, all right?"

"All right. And when do you get back from this holiday of yours?"

Catton shrugged, picking up his drink. "I couldn't say. When I have got enough information, I suppose. Say three or four weeks? Cheers!"

"Cheers! I hope it keeps fine for you."

"Here's the money, love," said the barmaid from across the counter. "Your change from the tenner, Ted, and five tenners for you, sir. The manager said he'll know where to come if that big note turns out to be a bummer."

"Fat chance," Bardsey said. "He'll be in America. But if you can't trust a London copper, love, you can't trust anyone."

An hour later, Ted Bardsey was feeding coins into a telephone at the Trafalgar Square exchange, dialing a long number from a well-worn slip of paper laid out on the top of the coin box.

"Hello?" The voice at the other end had a rough, East End, cockney accent.

"Who's that?" Ted asked.

"Who d'you want?"

"I want Freddie. Put him on."

"Who are you?"

"Never mind. Just put Fred on. Tell him it's London." The pause was short. "Ted?"

"Right. . . . Listen, I'm short of change. I've just had a jar with a copper here. He's off to Florida for talks about setting up a new unit here."

"Go on."

"It's the white stuff . . . you know? I thought your friend might want to know."

"He will, Ted, he will. Anything else?"

"No, not yet. I'll keep an eye open, see if I can find out more."

"You do that, Ted. Thanks for the tip. I'll see you right, my son."

The pips went. "See you, Ted."

"'Bye, Freddie."

Hands deep in his pockets, his chin sunk into the turned-up collar of his coat, Ted Bardsey shouldered his way out of the post office and turned down the street toward Charing Cross. It might be nothing, but it couldn't hurt to let Freddie know what was cooking at the Yard. That was what Freddie paid him for.

They flew to Palma, Majorca, in Kleiner's second-best jet, the silver Lear, the Pocket Rocket, the same aircraft that had carried them in from Milan a month ago. Kleiner had arrived in it from Italy, and was at the airport to see them off. Simon could see him, a dot on the grass before the control tower, as the aircraft turned back across the airfield and set course for the south. Then he unclipped his seat belt and, after squeezing Lucia's hand, made his way over to sit beside Philip Wintle.

"How are you?" he asked.

"I'm fine. It's good to be out again. Hospitals are all very well, but once you feel halfway better, it's nice to be up and about."

All things considered, Philip Wintle did look very well. He had been a little slow getting into the aircraft, perhaps not as sprightly as before the shooting, but in spite of his injuries, Philip Wintle looked several years younger than the sixty-plus he must be. His ever-neat clothes hung more loosely on him than they used to do, but a few weeks in the sun, a little rest, some good food and wine, and they would soon have him fully recovered. Simon said as much.

"Well, I hope so," Philip said. "Klaus has big plans afoot for KSI. I will have to get back in harness sooner or later. I think we will be hearing from him quite soon. Both of us."

Simon shook his head. "Not me. I'm not ungrateful for his help, and he seems to have tidied up the mess in Milan very nicely, but the game is over. I have definitely retired. Apart from anything else, I need to look after Lucia."

Wintle leaned forward to glance across at her. She was looking down out of the window, her chin cupped in one hand, her thoughts elsewhere.

"How is she?" he asked quietly.

"Subdued . . . unhappy."

"Well, she's young, she'll get over it," Wintle said, "and the pair of you can make a fresh start. You can go anywhere you want, do anything you want. What you need now is something worthwhile to occupy your time. You're too young to retire."

"All we want is to be left alone," Simon said. "The snag is that people think they can use me—certainly Yates and Kleiner, maybe your friend Commander Catton . . . maybe you too. Why didn't you tell me John Catton came to see you at the hospital?"

Wintle smiled slightly. "Come on, Simon. You know better than that. He came about Kleiner, and to see how I was. He hardly mentioned you, and asked me not to mention his visit, so I didn't. You saw him within hours, anyway. Look, I am truly sorry I got you involved with Kleiner in this Milan business, but I needed your help. Besides, you met Lucia; it's not all bad."

Simon took a look at Lucia, and when he turned back, he was smiling. "Well . . . look at her. It's crazy in a way. Klaus has tidied up everything, sold off Fiori's estate, buying the good bits himself, but at a fair price, I admit . . . paid back the money to the victims, some with compensation, and put the balance in a Swiss account for Lucia. There she sits, worth something over ten million dollars, yet looking as if she's lost the lot and found sixpence."

Philip shrugged. "Maybe she's not interested in money. Mind you, it's easy not to be interested in money when you have a lot of it. When you are poor, money becomes rather more significant. I think her worry is more about you and your lifestyle."

"Look, if it came to it, could we really get away?" Simon asked abruptly.

"Away? Where?" Wintle sounded surprised. "Away from what?"

"Away from people, from all this. From whatever is lurking in Yates's dirty mind. I know that everything I do gets noted down. Catton had me watched in London. He circulates my movements to all the intelligence services. He knew about what happened in Milan before we even got to London. Can Lucia and I get away and live free of you people? And if so, how?"

Wintle's shoulders lifted and fell. "I don't know. You could cut and run, I suppose. Leave everything behind, disappear, never return to your old haunts or touch your old money. That might work, but I don't know; it's a small world. Is it as bad as all that?"

"I'm not sure, but it's not good. Besides, like Yates, I like to keep my options open." Simon watched the clouds slipping past the window. "I take your point about a clean break though. That's the only way, but it's not easy."

"I wouldn't worry about it," Wintle said. "Why don't we all relax and have a little holiday? God knows we've earned it, and now, if you don't mind, I think I'll have a little snooze."

Simon shifted back into the seat beside Lucia. While Philip slept, and the little aircraft soared on across France, they put their heads together and talked very quietly, about the future.

3

Pete Sinker ran his thumb over the Drug Squad report, then tossed it heavily onto the top of his desk. Sinker was a tall man, running a little to fat, his stomach bulging heavily over his belt, his reddish hair turning gray and beginning to thin, thick freckles carpeting the peeling skin on his high forehead and among the hair on his arms below the turned-up shirt cuffs. He looked tired and a little harassed, but he was friendly.

"Yes," he said again, peering across at Catton. "Your guy in London has it about right. If what he says is anything to go by, you have one hell of a problem over there in England right now, and it's sure to get worse, especially if our Colombian friends get into the act. As Jolson said, 'You ain't seen nothin' yet.'" Sinker shook his head, lips pursed. "And I can't tell you what to do about it, Commander. Over here in the good old U.S. of A., we just about get by, that's all."

"That's depressing," Catton said. "Is it really as bad as all that, given all the resources and money you've poured into it?"

"It's a fact, Commander. Whatever the chemists say, cocaine is an addictive drug, and it's coming in all over. Here at the DEA, we do our best, and we can't do more. The only way to stop the cocaine trade is either to cut the supply or reduce the demand. If people didn't snort it and smoke it, there would be no market—but there's fat chance of that."

43

"If you can't win, why do you have seven separate agencies—federal, state, or local—right here in Florida, all fighting to defeat the drug trade?"

Sinker grinned and leaned forward to pick up his coffee cup. "Well, I'll tell you why. If one department can't hack it, you set up another one. That's the American Way. That way you can tell Joe Public that the administration is really concerned about the problem. It gives you somewhere to pass the buck; you can always blame it on the other guy. Not to be cynical, we are all trying to contain the problem. But, look, I could talk to you for a week. I want to thank you for sending over this report, and I'm sorry I didn't meet you at the airport. I can see the British picture now, and I've doped out a little program which will run you around all the agencies and show you what gives. You do that, then we'll meet back here and get right to it. What d'ya say?"

"Sounds fine," Catton said. "There's no point in talking until I know the situation. It's very kind of you."

Sinker snorted. "Kind? Shit! I had a directive from the Drug Enforcement Administration HQ, relayed to them direct from the Big House on Pennsylvania Avenue, Washington, D.C. It told them to tell me to cooperate with the British government's special representative from Scotland Yard. I'm mightily impressed, Commander, but I have to say that a phone call from you would have had the same effect. I've got nothing to hide, and I don't need the pressure. Drug enforcement is an international business. I help you today, you help me tomorrow. Right, or not right?"

Catton could almost feel the resentment. He wouldn't have liked it either.

"I'm sorry about the pressure," he said firmly. "I can assure you there has been no pressure from me. My visit was fixed up by our Home Office, following a meeting between your President and our PM. Maybe the request grew in the telling, I don't know. If you feel pressured, I'm sorry. I'm still grateful for whatever help and assistance you feel willing to give. I'm here to learn."

Sinker held up his hand. "Okay, okay, it's no real sweat

. . . desk directives just stick in my throat, that's all. Those people should come down on the street sometime. Look—what's your real name?"

"John."

"Okay, John, I'm Pete. Tell you what we'll do. You run around this course here, talk to all the guys, see how it is. That's better for you than a lot of talk from me. If you need any more help, ask them. If anyone says no or kind of drags their feet, ring me. Use this office as a base, take that desk over there. Mike's away on vacation, fishing down in the Keys, but he won't mind. That way we keep in touch day by day, and when you're done, we look at your problem in detail, and if I can help, I will. How's that? Anything else?"

"Just one thing. I need to meet a man called Larry Teal. Can you arrange that?"

Peter Sinker sniffed, his grin fading a little as he took more coffee and lit another cigar. "What do you know about Larry Teal?" he asked.

"Not a lot," Catton said. "I understand he has information on the Cartel's moves into the U.K., so I'd like to meet him."

"I know . . . it's right here on the request. I could fix it, but we have a problem." Sinker rubbed his nose between his fingers, and then took a long drag at his cigar. "Let me tell you how it is. Larry was a TWA pilot, and a good one, the youngest 747 pilot in the world. I know Larry, he's not a bad guy. Then he discovered dope. He started flying in marijuana from Mexico, then he switched to cocaine because it had less bulk and was more profitable. Then we nail him right here in Miami. How doesn't matter. And we turn him around. We fix a minimum bust, he tells us what gives with the Cartel. Larry is the best informant we have ever had. Even the President used information Larry got for him—camera film on the Nicaraguan Sandinistas, actually loading Larry's plane with coke for the good old U.S.A.—a gift to the administration. The President showed the film at a press conference, made a big thing of it. Anyway, that blows Larry's cover, so we pull him in. Thing is, we also have to deal with charges against Larry in Baton Rouge, Louisiana, and the judge down there wants to put him away for thirty years, which is not the deal we made."

"Difficult," said Catton, picking up his coffee cup.

"That it is. Larry has the IRS—the tax man—on his ass, he has this judge bringing charges, and it's fairly certain the Cartel has a contract on him. We need him helpful because we have Jorge Orchoa in the slammer in Madrid, Spain, and Larry is our only witness for the extradition hearing. Now, the Baton Rouge judge may go easy on Larry if Larry helps Uncle. Larry says he *has* helped Uncle, and he doesn't know any more—but he can help your Queen."

"Great!" Catton said. "So when do I see him?"

"When the Baton Rouge judge agrees that helping your Queen is enough to get Larry off the hook. Until then, Larry won't deal. Helping the British is his last card, and he has a lot of time sitting on it."

"Should I talk to the judge?" Catton asked. "If it might help, I'm willing to."

"Christ, no! We're working on him, and so are the prosecutors here. You're our lever on him, like the information Larry has is on us. You sit tight, leave it to me. I'll fix up a meeting with Larry for you, but it'll take a couple of weeks. Meantime, you can get to know the cocaine trade—okay?"

Catton smiled and shrugged. "That's fine, if that's what it takes. Where do I start?"

Sinker took two sheets of paper out of a drawer and slid one across the desk to Catton. "It will make more sense if you take it a step at a time. Lesson One: What is cocaine? In ten minutes, you are due over at the federal laboratory for a chat with our chief scientist. He'll tell you where it all starts . . . and I'll see you later."

When Ted Bardsey realized who was calling, he was less than pleased.

"Ted? 'allo? It's me . . . Freddie."

"I know who it is," Ted Bardsey said shortly. "I thought we agreed you wouldn't phone me at home, Freddie."

"Well, I can't very well phone you at the Yard, can I, old cock?" Freddie said. "Listen, your mate turned up in Miami yesterday."

"I told you that," Ted said. "What about it?"

"It makes my dago friend a bit uneasy, that's what's about it . . . being as he is setting up in Blighty to get away from the U.S. cops. Naturally, he wants to know what your bloke's game is."

"I've told you all I know, Fred. You'll have to wait a bit. Tell your mate that."

"He's not good at waiting, Ted. It's his Latin temperament. And he wants to meet you, so you'd better get your arse down here."

Ted hesitated. "I can't do that, Freddie . . . it's not wise—know what I mean? Better I keep my distance. Better for all of us."

"Sorry, old cock . . . just get yourself down to Gatwick soon as poss and jump a flight for Málaga. . . . I'll have one of the lads pick you up in the Roller . . . right?"

"But, Freddie . . ."

He could hear Freddie sighing. "Don't give me an argument, Ted. When Mr. Big here says jump, just say, 'How high?' Got it?"

"Well . . . I'll have to arrange it. I can't just walk off the job at a minute's notice."

"You arrange it then. In the next few days, tops, right? Give me a bell when you've got your flight booked."

Ted put down the phone slowly, and wiped the back of his hand across his sweaty brow. Nothing like this had ever happened before, and he was worried. Now, even his hands were shaking just a little, and that gave him the next idea. When the old nerves were jangling more than somewhat, nothing would calm them like a snort or two of snow.

"How much coke is coming in?" Catton asked. It was a week later, and they were back in Sinker's office, elbows on the desk, looking at ledgers.

"Jesus only knows," Sinker said. "I only see the busts,

because we have to check the consignments, estimate the quantity and the value. It's not all pure cocaine on the street, you know. The dopers cut it . . . add other ingredients."

"How?"

"Various ways. If you need the words, it's called 'stepping on it.' The exporter may ship in coke from Santa Marta that is ninety-five percent pure, but the dealers step it down at every stage, mixing it with borax or lactose. Some dealers use novocaine, the stuff the dentist shoots into your gums. The most popular cut at the moment is mannite, which is a laxative. Heavy users spend half their lives in the john. Most of the losers who buy it never meet real coke—they get stuff maybe thirty-five percent pure, and on that the high doesn't last long. Have you ever snorted cocaine?"

"No, never," said Catton, shaking his head. "It wouldn't be encouraged at the firm."

"Aw, now, don't get uptight—I have. Only in the interests of science, of course, but it's dangerous crap. Doping is a loser's game. Cocaine may not be physically addictive, but it's certainly psychologically addictive, and there is a growing body of opinion that says it fucks you up anyway. Cocaine-related deaths are way up and rising. Last week, over at Miami General, they brought a guy in with cocaine narcosis. His body temperature was a hundred and ten, and his heartbeat was nearly two hundred a minute. Having your blood boil, then having your heart explode, is not a nice way to go."

Catton frowned. "Poor bastard. But what about the money? Who makes the profit?"

"Not the poor Colombian peasant, you can bet on that," Sinker said. "In rough terms, and I'm quoting top dollar, the peasant gets a couple of bucks per kilo of leaves, although if he can sweat it, he'll get maybe five hundred dollars for a kilo of *basuko*, cocaine paste. You can move paste, so as it moves dealer to dealer, the price goes up. A Colombian refiner who wants to turn *basuko* into pure snow, *périca*, might pay what—two thousand a kilo? Then comes the big price hike—say, ten thousand for a kilo—we call them 'keys,' and a key of ninety-five percent pure currently comes into Miami at about twenty to twenty-three thousand bucks. That's where they refine it, right here in the city. We have coke labs exploding every week. That's another lead for you. To refine coke, you need ether, and it's a volatile gas. If you don't vent it and you catch a spark . . . whammo! So look for any lab using big quantities of ether—it may be for refining *périca*. Then the dealer steps on it, and the price goes up, see? He may sell a key for twenty-three or twenty-five thousand bucks, but it won't be pure. He's only invested thirty or maybe thirty-five percent of his pure in that, so he's making on one imported key around one hundred thousand dollars, maybe more. And that's serious money."

"I hear the price is falling."

"So do I. There is oversupply here, that's why the Cartel is moving into Europe. I'll give you one little figure to send you on your way—maybe three. Remember, most of the U.S. coke comes in through Florida. We've got coke in the federal warehouse right now which is worth more than all the gold in Fort Knox—and we don't seize more than twenty percent of what comes in. Second, the IRS, that's our tax service—Internal Revenue—estimates that drug trafficking in Florida clears nine *billion* dollars in a fiscal year. That's the amount in bank deposits they can't account for any other way. Finally, in this year alone, we have collected twenty-four thousand keys' worth, around six hundred twenty-four million dollars *before they step on it,* and that's maybe—*maybe,* remember—twenty percent of what has been arriving. Now, have you any more questions, or shall I get you a cab?"

Yates knew perfectly well that his presence made people uneasy, but his evident unpopularity bothered him not at all. If the truth were told, he rather liked it. He knew what he was doing, and precisely why he was needed. In simple terms, he was the government's Mr. Fixit. Not all policies could be executed by decree, let alone with the full knowledge and consent of Parliament; some were too delicate or politically suspect. When such situations arose, solutions had to be found, or actions taken, from which most politicians would recoil in alarm. Yet, as Yates would sometimes remark, somebody had to do it.

A nudge here, a wink there, a little pushing or armtwisting, the suggestion that a certain course of action, though forever unacknowledged, was valuable and would be greatly appreciated by the powers-that-be was usually all it took. No one was better than Yates at pushing reluctant functionaries up to and then over the brink of decision. Yates moved ministers, soldiers, civil servants, and sometimes more sinister people about the world like pawns on a chessboard. "Remember," he once remarked at the bar in White's, "a slope is much easier to descend than a brink, but no less inevitable. Unlike the late Mr. John Foster Dulles, I practice slopemanship." He conducted most of the secret business he was charged with in this fashion, and he did it very well. If that had been all, Yates would have been no more than useful, almost a fall guy should some scheme collapse, but he was much more than that. In his own way, Yates was lethal.

On this evening, he was entertaining Kleiner at his flat in the Albany, a rare honor had Kleiner been the type to care about things like that. Visitors to his flat were rarely allowed farther than the living room, but had the visitor entered the study lined with bookshelves where Yates spent most of his time, he might have been surprised, if not alarmed, at the thrust of Yates's political interests. His field was politics, but his masters were autocrats and dictators, generals and power brokers. On his shelves were works by Clausewitz and Machiavelli, books on Cesare Borgia, Napoleon, Franco, Frederick of Prussia, the Mafia, and the Spanish Inquisition. Yates rarely went to sleep without reading a page or two from *The Prince,* that guide to the grim world of realpolitik. There were works here on all the world's secret services, on Special Forces, Interpol, on various police units, and on all the agencies of the United Nations, plus yearbooks and gazetteers on all those nations with which Britain had dealings, friendly or otherwise. Yates believed that knowledge was power, and if pressure had to be applied anywhere and at any level, Yates could always be relied on to suggest a sensitive spot. In addition to all this, Yates had obtained access to a whole range of intelligence data at home and abroad. He rarely let a year go by without a visit to CIA Headquarters at Langley, and he had been in regular contact with J. Edgar Hoover of the FBI until the old man died. It was even rumored that they got on very well. Yates was in the study with Kleiner when the telephone rang, and Kleiner got up to roam the shelves while he answered it.

"Alec . . . it's John . . . John Catton."

"How are you getting on?" Catton's voice was as clear as a bell, straight into his ear across three thousand miles of ocean.

"I'm getting on fine, but I'm whacked," Catton said. "This is a huge business we are up against. I've been at it all week, and I've hardly scratched it. It's like a war here."

"That's what I told you." Catton heard Yates's voice fade out and come back again. "There is more useful information here for your report—official stuff, but you might want to include it. They took fifty kilos of coke off a Venezuelan freighter in Liverpool last week—a million dollars at least —and today the customs report a seizure in Southampton of over two hundred kilos, worth over fifty million pounds. That's more than they've seized in the last five years; it's already making the papers. You'll have to get a move on."

"I'm trying. Can you look up some information for me, and we can get ahead a little? There are some main areas we must take a look at."

Yates searched around his desk for a pen and a pad. "Fine . . . wait a minute. Right, go ahead."

"First, find out who are the major suppliers of ether in the U.K. and in Europe. Ether is used to refine cocaine. And find out who buys it. I want a list of suppliers, users, wholesalers of industrial gases, and consumers."

"Right, I'll check with all the major companies here. They will probably know. Anything else?"

"Yes. Tell CIB2 to run a check on any Met officer who has ever been accused or suspected of links with villains now living on the Costa del Sol. I'd prefer the request to come from you rather than me—CIB2 investigates corruption in the police force, and I have to work there. All right?"

"Fine, but why?"

"Because the head of the Cartel was talking to East End villains in Spain, remember? And I have just spent a day in the local courthouse hearing how the local cops, or some of them, are hand-in-glove with the Cartel. You said I should cover every angle, so what about our own doorstep—right?"

"All right. Anything else?"

"Not for the moment. Oh yes . . . the locals are very hot under the collar about the Bahama Islands and Cay Dorado being used for drug smuggling. I'm getting quite a lot of flak about it. Can you find out the limits of our jurisdiction?"

"Simple. We don't have any. They're both independent states within the Commonwealth. We may have aid and defense agreements, but that's all."

"Even so, can I have a rundown?"

"All right, but look, John, isn't this rather outside your brief? Leave the politics to me, will you?"

"I'd love to," Catton said, "but it's all the same business, and the Cartel are opening a U.K. branch. Think about it. That's all for now. I'll phone again in a couple of days . . . 'Bye."

"Catton?" Kleiner asked.

"Yes," Yates replied slowly. His eyes were still resting on his notes as his head lifted away from the telephone. "He seems to be getting to grips with the problem."

"He's a bright fellow."

"He is," Yates said absently. "He is. He's already picked up on the Americans' concern over Cay Dorado." He ran the pencil down the list in the notes in front of him, then picked up his brandy glass and joined Kleiner at the fireplace. It was nearly 11:00 P.M., and they had dined together in a restaurant before returning to Yates's flat at the Albany. It was a small, comfortable place, the perfect set of rooms, very discreet, ideal for clandestine meetings.

"So," said Yates, settling back in his armchair, "matters

are proceeding slowly but according to plan. I am rather enjoying this. It's nice to be legitimate for once."

"I don't suppose that will last," Kleiner said dryly, "so enjoy it while you can. The crunch will come when Catton files his report. Incidentally, since you are the top man and the one liaising with the Cabinet, why is he reporting to them and not you?"

"Reports have to be signed," Yates said smoothly, "and reports get filed and discussed and leaked to the press. If matters turn serious, or even worse, get out of hand, I'd rather it was the Catton Report that gets quoted and not the Yates Report."

"Whatever Catton recommends, I think you know what needs to be done," Kleiner said. "I mean about Cay Dorado."

"Catton is a policeman. They like numbers. To a policeman, three small arrests count three times as much as one major conviction. That won't work with the drug business. The little people are addicts themselves, and they traffic to pay for their habit. I've been reading myself in on this for months—some of it is high-level stuff from secret CIA and FBI reports, confidential memos from the bottom of the diplomatic bags. The Cartel would be trouble on their own, but we also have the problem of Cay Dorado. There is only one answer to that—hit the men at the top. My task is to clear up the entire mess, not just a little of it, so Catton may have to go along with some drastic action. That's why I wanted him appointed to the task force. With his Special Branch background, he's not just another Mr. Plod. When he sees what has to be done, he'll come round. We may need Quarry though, and I hope he'll be cooperative when the time comes."

"Catton may not go for it. He's not very different from Philip Wintle, and Philip is very strong on the correct procedures for law and order. I think Catton will shy away from using Quarry."

"Catton is a pragmatist," Yates said, "and his brief is to find a solution that works. I fancy he'll arrive at the same conclusion as I have. Indeed, that's one reason he is in Miami. He needs to know that this is a serious business. His American visit will give him invaluable experience at the sharp end of the drug trade, but then I need someone to handle the heavy end, someone expendable but reliable."

"Like Quarry?"

"Perhaps. How is he?"

"Fairly friendly. I spent the evening with Lucia and Simon the day I flew in. We took Philip out of hospital to a nearby restaurant—his first outing—and much to my relief, Simon has mellowed. When he left Milan, he was very hostile, but I think Lucia has been working on him. She and I are old friends."

Alec Yates went to refill their glasses, pacing back across the room with one in either hand, looking down at Kleiner. "There is one other point that rather bothers the minister, Mr. Kleiner. To be frank, it bothers most of Her Majesty's government. It also bothers me."

"Really?" Kleiner reached up and took his glass. "Tell me about it."

"Why are you doing this? What do you get out of it? We haven't even discussed a fee for the services of KSI. Even knowing how you feel about drugs, altruism is very rare these days. I'd like to know what's in this for you."

Kleiner swirled the brandy around his glass, waiting until Yates had moved back to stand in front of the fireplace before he spoke.

"What's in it for me? I think I can tell you that, Mr. Yates . . . Alec. Who is handling the security for the Channel Tunnel?"

"The Tunnel?" Yates's tone was surprised. "I've no idea. It's not even built yet. There will have to be consultations with the French, I suppose. I don't know."

"I see." Kleiner nodded. "Then what about the security for Sizewell 'B' and other nuclear-power stations your electricity boards will be building over the next decade or so?"

"I've no idea. But what . . . ?"

"What about the North Sea oil rigs? Who protects those?"

"That I do know," Yates said promptly. "The MOD—Ministry of Defense. The Royal Marines have a special force, Commachio Troop, which does little else. But may I ask . . . ?"

"Certainly. Security is big business, Alec. I want KSI, my security organization, to expand. The Channel Tunnel is, or will be, the world's top terrorist target. If the Iranians, or the PLO, or the IRA, get in there, you and the French don't really intend to sit on the bottom of the Channel arguing about who is responsible for security while one end or the other goes bang—or do you?"

"Well . . . we haven't thought about it."

"Then think about it; lease the Tunnel security to KSI. KSI can operate across frontiers, and not always according to the rules. Take your power stations—even those who don't want them built would almost welcome an accident or a terrorist attack. Chernobyl and Three Mile Island were meat and drink to the antinuclear lobby. As for Her Majesty's Royal Marines, surely in these days of defense cuts you can find something better for them to do than bobbing about the North Sea in rubber boats, unable to do anything until it is already too late."

"I don't really believe Her Majesty's government would welcome the drift of your thoughts, Mr. Kleiner."

Kleiner smiled and reached out to refill his glass. "Well, you asked what's in it for me. I want the British government to lease all the security contracts for sensitive areas to me; oil rigs, nuclear-power stations, coal stocks, certain airfields, and the Tunnel. KSI will move in with equipment, intelligence, manpower you cannot afford and could not politically maintain. If I hear of a threat, I won't simply double the guard or ask the army to come out of their barracks for half a day's exercise. I'll go after the terrorist group, track them down, eliminate them. I can do that, as you know. It will be forward defense, Alec, the only sort that works. And then, as you know, I have personal reasons. Apart from that, I enjoy it."

"Well . . ." Yates brooded. "I begin to see the idea. I could propose it . . . see what people say. But this is not mere altruism? Could I have some idea of costs?"

"I haven't worked it out fully," said Kleiner, sipping from his glass, "but something up to five percent of turnover, perhaps?"

"What!" Yates was aghast. "You want five percent of our oil revenues, our landing fees, Channel Tunnel revenue, even electricity? Is that what you mean? That's ridiculous—crazy!"

"Well, not quite that much, perhaps," Kleiner said smoothly. "Something between one and five percent, depending on the turnover and, of course, only for the particular KSI protection provided. Add it to the standing charge, Alec, and no one will notice."

"It could mean millions."

"Tens of millions, I hope," said Kleiner, rising and reaching for his coat. "But when you think about it, giving me a piece of the action is not only equitable, it ensures my best efforts. I have personal reasons for attacking the Cartel, so hitting them comes free, as a sample of what I can do, but I am not mad, Alec. I know what people say about me, but at the end of the day it's a business."

"Why would a percentage ensure your best efforts?" asked Yates, puzzled.

Kleiner struggled into his overcoat and moved toward the door. "Doesn't every man have a special interest in protecting his investments? Think about it, Alec . . . good night."

4

John Catton handed up the bullhorn to the police lieutenant and lay down again, peering around the front wheel at the crack house. The green-and-white police car was still slewed up on the sidewalk, where it had stopped when they leapt out to make their first wild rush at the house. That was when they discovered that the doors were locked and steel-plated and the grimy windows covered with thick wire mesh. Then the shooting started. The Miami cops had now been bickering with the people inside for nearly twenty minutes, trading shots across the gap with no visible results to the dopers, but there was one officer hit full in the chest to put on the debit side. Meanwhile, more cop cars had come rumbling up, and the growing crowd of onlookers had been pushed back to a safe distance, where they stood drinking beer and cheering at every shot from inside the house. Now, Lieutenant Stu Clayton, of the Miami P.D. Narcotics Squad, had clearly had enough.

"Okay," he said, sliding down off the wing of the green-and-white. "They've had their chance. John, stay down. We'll give 'em one more warning, then hit them with the gas and go in." The horn clicked. "Okay, motherfuckers . . . the jig's up . . . you've got just fifteen seconds to throw out those weapons and crawl . . . you hear me . . . crawl out of there. I'm not messing with you. One . . . two . . . get ready, you jerks . . . three . . . Time's running out in there."

"Can I go in?" asked Catton, looking up and tugging at Clayton's trouser leg. Clayton looked down and shook his head impatiently.

"Hell no, John. You stay here—got it? One nick on your pinky and I'm ass-deep in paper for the next month. Where was I? Eleven . . . twelve . . . to hell with it . . . Go!!"

The police poured fire at the house from all around the perimeter, bullets and buckshot kicking out the remaining glass, splinters flying from the wooden walls, ricochets howling back from the armor-plated door. Three officers carrying sledgehammers and shotguns were up and running for the door now. . . . *Stonk!!* Gas canisters curved lazily through the air, smashing in through the one unprotected window. They were still shooting from inside, and Catton ducked as a bullet smashed into the side-view mirror just above his head, showering him with sharp splinters.

"Jesus!" he exclaimed, burrowing down into the gravel. "This is bloody dangerous."

Other cops were away now, running hard for the house. The three men in the lead hit the door hard, one blasting the lock and hinges off it with solid rounds from a pump shotgun, the others beating it in with sledgehammers. The noise was deafening, the crowd yelling, the cops shouting above a steady rattle of gunfire. Catton felt the first prickle in his eyes as the gas swept back, and reached up to pull the mask down over his forehead. Then a scream cut through the general din. He saw one of the cops reeling back out of the house, hands pressed to his face, saw the paramedics running forward, heard two heavy shots thudding somewhere inside—and then, suddenly, it was all over.

The tension had gone. Catton could feel it seeping out of the air as he levered himself up from behind the car, dusted the gravel and glass splinters from his borrowed dark blue SWAT-team overalls, and began to walk across the rubbish-littered grass toward the house. The medics had the injured man down on the grass by the sidewalk, and were swabbing at his face with cottonballs steeped in some solution.

"What happened to him?" he asked, crouching down at their sides.

"The fuckers threw acid in his face," one of the medics said. "Nice, huh? Sulfuric, at a guess. They were going for his eyes."

"Christ!"

"He'll be okay; he had his mask on . . . it's just his forehead and neck here—this time."

Shaking his head, Catton got up and walked on. The cops were hustling a host of people out of the house now—a surprising number of people—black, white, Hispanic, all kicking and yelling. Not all of them were young. One by one, they were wrestled to the ground, relieved of wallets, money, knives, read their rights—"Miranda-Escobedo" muttered on every side like a prayer—their hands trussed behind them with thin strips of masking tape. The crowd was thinning out now that the excitement was over, wandering off, flinging the odd obscenity back at the cops. Stu Clayton stood watching all this from the doorstep, the gas mask pushed up on his sweating forehead, shoving fresh loads into his .38 pistol. He looked up, grinning, as Catton approached.

"Well, we finally got a live one for you, John. After a week on the job, I was beginning to think we'd never show you any excitement at all."

"What got into them?" asked Catton, pulling off his mask. The gas was almost gone now. "Are they always this aggressive?"

"Hell, no. Mostly, they're too zonked out to stand. But these were heavy users—they get less spaced out but more demented. Come on, I'll show you."

He led the way back into the house. It stank of teargas, dope, and dirty lavatories, a rank mixture spiked with cordite fumes. There was blood on the floor and a dead, draped body in one of the rooms, while another man, cursing, bleeding from a bruising cut across his head, lay chained by the wrist to a waterpipe, talking to a kneeling cop. Clayton led on into the kitchen and picked out a dented beer can from the pile in the grimy sink.

"See here. They've been freebasing . . . smoking coke. They brew it up, like I showed you, here in the can, and suck in the smoke. It gives the dope a better hit. Also, see here, they were on bazookas. That's crack and marijuana mixed in a pipe. Smoke that for a couple of days, and it fries your brain. They were already out of their skulls when we hit them, so they went for it. Also, they were dealing, hence the guns."

"Did you find much stuff?"

"Naw . . . fat chance of that. They had plenty of time to flush it down the john. We'll go for doping busts, which we won't get . . . but resisting arrest, possession of firearms, assault on an officer—you saw they used the acid—malicious wounding . . . whatever else we can dream up, might hold one or two, but I doubt it. Some smart-ass lawyer will be down at the precinct in half an hour, some liberal judge will hear them out this evening, one or two will cop a plea, and since we can't prove who did what, they'll be back on the street by tonight. Aw, what the hell, is it worth it? Come on, the guys will clean up. Let's get out of here and get some coffee, and then I'll run you back to Sinker's office. He'll be glad to get you back in one piece."

"Okay," Stu said. "So here's where it's at. Let's look around and spot the pushers."

They had stripped off their SWAT overalls and left them in the trunk of the locked cruiser down in the basement carpark. Now, they were sitting in their shirtsleeves in a mall coffee shop near the airport, their sweat chilling nicely under the air-conditioning, sipping black coffee and looking around.

"Okay," said Stu, his eyes on the counter. "I make it three in here, and that clutch of guys by the pay phones. See the guy in the booth? He's dealing. Note the little bleeper on his belt and the little cloth tote bag—that's full of quarters and dimes for the phone. Likewise he paid for his coffee and pie when it arrived, so he's wired to go. How it works is that when his customers need a line or two, they call their connection. They bleep young Alberto over there—he can't be more than nineteen—and he calls in . . . hence the bag of quarters. They tell him the drop—probably to a guy

60

down in the parking lot or just cruising by, and Alberto nips out, delivers the shit, gets the cash, and is back here for the next call. Apart from him, there's the guy three booths back and the one by the door, all waiting for a bleep."

"Why don't you bust them?"

"It's not worth it. They top up from their suppliers only as they need it, and never too much. They don't carry much dope on them—enough to deal but not enough for us to nail them for more than possession—and a small amount only counts as a misdemeanor. They'd be out inside the day."

"They're not daft, are they?" Catton said, thoughtfully.

"Let no one ever tell you the bastards are stupid. Also, never forget they are vicious, especially the Colombians. That's how the Colombians control the trade, with guns. When the Cartel decided to move in on the Cubans here, three . . . four years ago, we had the Cocaine Wars right here in the city. They would walk in and blast the Cuban pushers at the pay phones with Mac-10 machine guns. Inside six months, we had nearly six hundred drug-related deaths, right here in Miami. How many troops did you lose in the Falklands War, John, in ships and planes and on the ground and all?"

"I don't know for sure," Catton said. "About two hundred."

"Well, there you have the scale of it. Most of the killings here are drug-related. Even the Mob is afraid of the Colombians. See, your Mafia hit man takes pride in a clean kill, no civilians, but the Colombians clean out the block . . . you, your *esposa*, the kids, the guy in the den repairing your TV set . . . whoever's around. Lately, they've taken to dismembering the opposition pushers with chain saws—real nice—and rank doesn't faze them. Down in Colombia, they've killed around sixty judges for hearing cases against the Cartel. I hear in Medellín, where the Cartel *jefes* hang out, they have a murder every three hours . . . about three thousand last year alone. They killed one minister of justice in Bogotá, and when the next one heard of their contract on him and skipped to Budapest—Budapest, Hungary—they sent gunmen after him and shot him four times in the head.

They have long arms, John. So, when the Colombian Cartel comes to London, forget your famous British fair play. Pack a gun and order up plenty of body bags. Come on, I'll run you back to the DEA."

Simon and Lucia Fiori settled in quickly in Majorca. On arrival they put Philip to bed, pale and drawn after the flight. Then Simon took Lucia for a tour of the house and garden, wandering after her while she took it all in. He introduced her to Lito Lopez and his wife, Magdalena, watched her exchanging small smiles and taking quiet note of the little feminine touches that Simon's previous lady had put about the house a year before.

"Well," he said at last, as they settled into chairs out on the terrace, "let's break the uneasy silence. Do we keep it, or shall I sell it, or pull it down, or what? Speak!"

Lucia sipped her drink slowly, her eyes on the valley and the olive groves climbing the distant sides of the mountains, and shook her head, putting the glass back on the table. "No. I think we'll keep it—with certain changes. What's-her-name—Clio?—had very good taste, but even so . . ." She shrugged, once, giving him one of her half-smiles. "I really don't want to live in another woman's house, Simon. I'd feel uncomfortable."

"It's really my house," he said. "Our house, I mean. I hope."

"It's not our house yet," she said, rising, "but it will be. Give me a few days, and you won't know the place. Then we can meet the neighbors and start to live like normal people."

She kept them all busy for the next week. Philip took over the garden, getting browner and stronger every day, ordering Simon about over the heavy work. Lito was dispatched to Palma and returned with pots of paint, and the house colors were changed from Clio's cool blue and white to Lucia's warmer, softer yellows and browns. Lucia spent hours with Magdalena, running up fresh covers and curtains, moving the furniture about, dragging Simon and Philip off to the art galleries in Pollensa, returning with

Villalonga paintings to brighten the walls, a sculpture by Bob Brotherton for the corner of the terrace, big ceramic pots, which she painted and filled with flowers. After ten days, the whole house had been transformed.

"She's a real whirlwind," Simon remarked to Philip, straightening up from a flower bed to watch Lucia's car disappear down the driveway on another mission. "I hope she doesn't wear herself out, dashing about the island like this." He put a hand onto the middle of his back and groaned. "She's certainly killing me. I ache all over."

"Don't worry about Lucia," Philip said. "All this is doing her good, keeping her mind off the past. Now, she's creating a home for you both and loving it."

Philip was sitting on a wall, dabbing his neck with a handkerchief. "Whew! It's getting hot. In another half an hour, or when you have finished that, whichever is the sooner, I suggest a beer—before our slave-mistress returns. By the way, did you know that she's planning a party? No? I thought not. It's a surprise for you, when all this work is done. You are going to meet all the neighbors, hundreds of them. However, it's supposed to be a surprise, so don't let on I told you."

Simon groaned. "Oh no . . . I hate parties."

"Well, you'll have to enjoy this one, and you don't have to do anything else. I've been put in charge of the barbecue. Lucia, Lito, Magdalena, and I have been plotting it for days, and we're all rather looking forward to it."

"I'll try," Simon said. "And that reminds me . . . Damn!" He put the spade on the edge of the trench and straightened up. "Blast . . . now look what you've made me do."

"What is it?" Philip got up and came over to peer into the trench. "What's that?"

"That one's the power cable for the surveillance cameras —and that one runs current out to the Claymore mines. I've just rammed the spade right through them."

"And a good job too," Philip said. "Claymore mines are damned dangerous things to put in the garden. Where are they exactly?"

Simon pointed about the garden. "Over there, and over there. I built them in when we first came here, in case the Jihad had another go at me. Picked them up from an arms dealer in Barcelona with the cameras and the barbed wire. It took a little sweat, but I turned the place into a regular fortress, just so I could sleep at night with both eyes shut."

"Ancient history, Simon," Philip said shortly. "Dig the damned things up and get rid of them. If Lucia knows about them . . . well, they don't go with homemaking."

"Maybe you're right," said Simon, kneeling in the trench. "We'll keep the cameras though, so I'll replace this wire, and that reminds me . . . you like it here, don't you?"

"Very much . . . thank you for having me."

"We like having you. Now look up there. The house is unbalanced. It has the garage and Lito's flat there at one end, but nothing at the other. So why don't you buy that piece of land at the side for a small sum and build on a flat? You'd be our favorite neighbor."

"Oh no!" Philip shook his head firmly. "Thanks for the suggestion, but two's company."

Simon got up, and sat on the edge of the trench. "It's as much for our sakes as yours," he said. "I want you where I can keep an eye on you. I don't want you getting into any more trouble . . . and I need someone to talk to. So does Lucia. We're putting on a brave front, but it's difficult. Too many ghosts, too many people in the shadows. Say you'll think about it, anyway."

"I've got things to do as well," Philip pointed out. "I still have my job with Klaus Kleiner—at least, I'm still on his payroll. I've spoken to him on the phone . . . he sends his regards."

"He's one of the people in the shadows," grunted Simon, picking up the spade and hacking at the stony ground again. "The last place you spoke to him was at Yates's office. You jotted it down on the desk blotter, and I recognized the number from the old days. They are up to something, Philip, so why don't you quit while you can? Kleiner can always get someone else to run KSI. If he likes ex-Special Branch people, then he can hire John Catton. A young, capable chap like that would be perfect for KSI."

"John's busy," said Philip, moving the plant box forward to Simon's feet. "Besides, I don't think he'd work for Kleiner. He's got his hands full with this drugs business and his new department."

"Have you heard from him?" Simon asked.

"Only yesterday," said Philip, feeling in his pocket. "He sent me this postcard from Miami. He's having the time of his life."

A week after the crack-house raid, Catton took Pete Sinker out to dinner. They drove down Miami Beach to dine on Chinese at Christine's on Collins, had a couple of bottles of wine there, and then went back to Sinker's apartment at Bal Harbor for more coffee and what Sinker described as a snootful or two of Ciento y Tres—Spanish brandy. Sinker's apartment was almost empty of furniture. He had an army cot in one corner, covered with a blanket, a couple of sagging armchairs, a pair of tables, one littered with bottles. Shirts and jackets hung from wire coat hangers hooked on the picture rail. Dark Haitian masks adorned the walls, but lighter squares showed where pictures had once brightened the room. When Pete's wife walked out, she had taken more than the children.

Sinker swirled the brandy around his balloon glass. "I got into this stuff when I spent a year in Salamanca, over in Europe," he said. "I took languages at college, Spanish and French. I can't speak a word of French anymore, and my old professor would curl up and die at my *Cubano* accent, but it still comes in handy. Write it in your little book, John . . . must learn Spanish. It's the lingua franca of the cocaine trade."

Catton smiled, put his glass back on the table, and stretched out, arms above his head, bones cracking.

"Tired?" Sinker asked. "You've been busy these last few weeks."

"Not tired. Confused."

"That's not surprising. You've done a one-month course on the cocaine trade, and you've done good. Everyone here loves you, and that could be useful later on. All the trade routes run through here, John. Here or at Cay Dorado or in the Bahamas. So, a few guys you know and who know you hereabouts could be useful."

"Everyone has been more than helpful. I have you to thank for that, and I don't know how to thank you."

"You bought me dinner at Christine's," Sinker said, "so let's call it quits. What happens now? Have you got enough to pad out your report? Do you really know what you are up against?"

Catton rubbed his chin, brooding. "I don't know. I do know that I can't take in any more. I've spent time with the Miami PD, the Narcotics squads in both Dade and Broward counties, the Coast Guard, the Customs, the Vice President's task force, the SWAT boys, the OCB, and, of course, the DEA. I'm drenched in the Cocaine Wars. Now, I need to sort out my ideas and get them down on paper. The big snag is to relate your solutions to our problems."

"So it's all helped? It's different here, but it's the same war, right?"

"Heavens, yes. We in Britain are about to face an attack, and that's what it is. It's a war. No ships or aircraft, but it's a war. If we let the *narco-traficantes* into Britain, they will take over the town. The snag is that your solutions don't work, even here. We will have to think of something more . . . well, effective."

"Well, it sounds like you've got the picture. At least you're in at the beginning, moving on the bastards before the bastards move in on you. Is there anything else we can do here?"

"I still need to see Larry Teal. He has leads I could use on the Cartel."

"That's why I suggested we come back here. I'm still trying to get the okay for you to talk to Teal. His lawyers say he can, if the Louisiana court in Baton Rouge will go easy on his probation. Larry isn't happy in that Salvation Army hostel they stuck him in. He thinks it's not safe. Now, if he talks to you, we ask the judge to go easy on him. The snag is that the judge still won't buy it. So I had a man go down there and talk to him. He'll phone tonight and tell me what gives. You can't hang about here forever, and I don't have much more for you to see, except maybe one thing, and I have that right here."

"What's that?" Catton asked.

"Coupla things. Did you know the bad guys know you're here?"

"No!" Catton's tone was surprised. "How on earth . . . ?"

"Don't sweat it. The Cartel moves in a mysterious way, and you've been all over the place, poking around, asking about them. Naturally, they take an interest in you too. They have people everywhere, passing the word."

"How do you know this?"

Sinker smiled. "Friend of mine, *Cubano* down in Calle Ocho, gave me the word. 'Tell your Anglo friend to watch his back.' That's good advice, John."

"I'll take it," Catton said thoughtfully.

Sinker got up, picked up the bottle, and poured another round of Ciento y Tres into the glasses. Then he stood over Catton, a large man in that shabby, empty room, brooding over his guest.

"Next thing, John, you may not like. Everyone keeps telling me what a nice guy you are, and that bothers me. I think I ought to show you something, so that you're not so nice when it matters. Nice can get you killed, or worse. You don't even carry a gun. It's crazy. Stay there while I find that something."

That something was a video film. Sinker took the cassette from a drawer, slipped it into the recorder, turned on the TV set, and sank back in his chair.

"Sit tight and hold on to your drink," he said, taking a pull at his glass. "This isn't a movie."

On the screen, four men were torturing another. He had already been severely beaten when the film began, for the camera focused on his bloody, swollen face. From then on, the level of violence and the sadism rose steadily. Ordered to strip, the man was beaten with clubs and an iron bar as he reeled about, one foot stuck in the leg of his trousers. In the next scene, he was chained to a wall, drenched with water, and an electric cattle prod applied to his nipples, his eyeballs, his penis. There was no sound, but the torment was clear.

"Jesus Christ!" Catton whispered to Sinker. "What the hell is this? Why?"

"Shut up," Sinker said shortly. "They took days filming this. Give it time."

It went on. Mercifully, they couldn't hear the screaming as the torturers carved bloody lumps with razors from their victim's chest. Catton watched as boiling water was poured in the wounds, on and on. . . . Finally, Catton leapt up and switched off the machine, turning angrily to Sinker, who was watching him quietly from his chair, his eyes steady behind blue swirls of cigar smoke.

"That was just disgusting!" Catton said. "Why show me that? What the hell's the point?"

"That guy," said Sinker, his eyes back on the empty screen, "the one with the cattle prod up his ass, was a friend of mine. He was a DEA investigator down in Guadalajara, Mexico, and last year he vanished. Two days after his body and that of his driver were found in a ditch near Guadalajara, that tape turned up by mail at the DEA office in El Paso, compliments of the *narco-traficantes*. When our boys saw it, they friggin' near retook Juárez. Now, I make sure that all our recruits see it and know what they're up against, what can happen even to them. This isn't 'Miami Vice,' my friend." Pete's voice was harsh and edgy. "This is the cocaine trade. Smart society people stuff snow-candy up their noses; people like you and me can get an electric enema. You'd better realize that. Your 'oh-so-nice, let's-be-fair, with-justice-and-freedom-for-all' crap won't work against the Cartel . . . got it?"

Catton discovered he was shaking. Knees weak, he sat down in his chair and needed two hands to hold the brandy glass steady while he drained it.

"Oh . . . and there's a little sweetener," Sinker went on

remorselessly. "The four boys on the video, and the guy giving the commentary—which I had cut out—we know them. Three of the guys have been identified as Mexican cops. The guy talking offscreen, supervising the torture, telling the cops what to do next, is a senior official in the judicial police in Guadalajara. We know that from voice-prints. The state judge let the local cops destroy all the other evidence before our guys got down there. The locals couldn't even remember where they found the bodies." Pete Sinker heaved himself out of his chair and was halfway toward the drinks table when the phone rang, breaking the tension.

"That'll be Baton Rouge," he said over his shoulder. "Maybe you'll have beginner's luck. Keep your fingers crossed that Teal is on the go and has good things to tell you."

Catton sat on in his chair, clutching the brandy glass to his shirtfront, hardly listening to the murmur of Sinker's voice, only looking up as the receiver clicked and Sinker put down the phone, then plodded over to the drinks table, returning to refill both glasses from a fresh bottle. He picked up his own glass and drank deeply before flopping heavily back into his chair, his eyes resting on Catton.

"Well?" John asked at last. "Can I talk to Larry Teal or not?"

"Nope," Sinker said. "You sure as hell can't."

"The judge won't go for it? That's ridiculous. Why not?"

"The judge no longer gives a damn, one way or another. Remember that Larry Teal was restricted to a halfway house in a Salvation Army hostel? Nice and secure for a federal witness, huh? Well, he got back there tonight around seven-thirty, and two gentlemen of Colombian extraction blew his head off with Mac-10 machine guns. Your big lead has gone down the tube, my friend. Welcome to Shit City!"

Much later that night, just as the dawn came up across the harbor far below, John Catton sat on his bed and put in a call to London. When she answered, she sounded drowsy, half-asleep.

"Hello," he said. "Christine? Chris? It's me."

"Hello . . . who? John? Darling, where are you?"

"I'm still in Miami—at the hotel. It's late . . . or early . . . dawn's just breaking."

"What time is it?"

"Here? About five-thirty in the morning."

"You sound tired. Have you been out on the town?"

"Not really, though it's been a long night. I am tired, but it's not that. Fact is, one way or another I've had one hell of a day—bloody awful."

Christine Hitchcock's voice was anxious. "What's happened? Are you all right? John?"

"I'm fine. Don't worry. How are you? Listen . . . it's too complicated to tell you all about it on the phone, but I've finished here. I still have to write the report, but now there's a chance for a break, so could you fly out and join me? We could go to the Everglades, or to Disney World, or see Flipper. I'd like to see some part of Florida away from the drug trade."

There was a long silent pause, with just clicks on the line. "I'd love to see Flipper," Christine said wistfully. "And I'd love to see you, but I'm right in the middle of preparing a case. I think we'll go to trial soon—the Williams business— so I can't. I have to keep in touch. . . . John?"

"I know . . . well . . . I remember how it is. But you could read your papers here while I draft my report. If I come back, it will be all go, we'll never see each other. I need time to think, and I need some advice."

"Well. No, I can't . . . really. But I could use some sun. Can't we meet midway? Maybe somewhere not so far?"

"But where? Midway is in the Atlantic Ocean—or Bermuda?"

"Still too far. Why not Portugal, or Spain? I could easily pick up a charter to Majorca, and meet you there. That's only an hour or so's flight, and there's no real time difference. I can phone in to my chambers every day. Let's go there . . . yes, I can do that . . . John?"

"Majorca," Catton said slowly. "That's not a bad idea.

Philip's there, staying with a friend of his. I don't have the phone number, but you could get it from Tom at the Yard. Give Philip a ring and ask him if we can come, and if he can find us somewhere to stay close by. It's somewhere in the north of the island, near a place called Puerto Pollensa."

"Spell it," Christine said.

5

Simon Quarry's party was a great success; Lucia saw to that. Everyone she invited came, and practically everyone brought someone else. A large, chattering crowd flowed across the terrace and down around the edge of the pool, sitting in long rows along the garden walls, grouped in the shade of the pine trees, eating, arguing, discussing local life and times and summer gossip. Most of all, they discussed their host. When a resident has emerged from his house after three years' seclusion, throwing it open to the world at large, that is something worth talking about. To everyone's surprise, their host turned out to be rather nice, his lady was beautiful, and his houseguests interesting. The party became the event of the season.

"How's it going?" asked Simon, grabbing Lucia's arm and steering her away from her throng of admirers into a quieter corner of the terrace. "Who are all these people? Do you really like this sort of thing?"

"I like it fine, and don't knock it. We're a social success. Can't you tell from the din? Half the women are after your body, and half the men are after mine. I've already had my bottom pinched twice."

"Well, when I saw you undulate past in that tight little cocktail number, I had half a mind to pinch it myself. Instead, I decided to wait until everyone had gone and bite it. I shall nibble your ear for the moment." He did so.

"Mmmm . . . nice . . . maybe I'll stop the party now. By the way, that woman over there is a reporter from the local paper, and a stringer, whatever that is, for the London press. I didn't invite her, but we can hardly throw her out. She wants to do a feature on the house for her British paper and the Palma rag. I smiled sweetly and said she'd have to talk to you. She has a camera with her, but don't you dare agree."

Simon let his eyes rest on the woman. She was standing at the edge of the terrace, a notebook in one hand, a camera over her shoulder, scanning the crowd.

"I won't," he said. "Good for you. What are the rest of our people up to?"

"Working, I hope. Philip is running the barbecue, assisted by John, while Chris says she is fulfilling a lifetime's ambition by acting as a cocktail waitress down by the pool. She has already stripped down to a bikini and asked me to find her some rabbit ears and a fluffy tail—her bottom is under fairly serious attack."

"Well, it's a very nice bottom," Simon said, "but then, she's a very nice girl."

"She certainly is," Lucia said, "and very, very bright. I like John too . . . they make a nice couple. Anyway, we can't stand here nattering all night. Get out there and mingle with your guests. I think I had better ask Lito to dig out some more *rosado*. 'Bye for now . . . but if people start going, don't urge them to stay."

It was Simon who first noticed the difference, the low murmur that spread among his guests, the turning of heads, the shifting of positions for a better view. He was standing by the pool with the RAF people, half listening to their talk, when he noticed that some of them were losing interest, turning their attention toward the terrace.

"Excuse me," he said, and turned to walk up the steps, but he had not gone more than a stride when the crowd swirled open and Lucia appeared, hanging on to the arm of a tall, slim man in a beautifully cut white suit. The sight stopped Simon in his tracks, and as they stood there facing each other, a small hush fell on the crowd.

"Good Lord!" said one of the ladies softly. "Isn't that . . . ?"

"Hello, Simon. I hope you will excuse me just turning up like this. I saw the gate was open, so I walked right in. I think there are some people I know here."

"You're very welcome," said Simon slowly, glancing at Lucia's face and nodding slightly. "Let me get you a glass of wine."

"Yes, it is," the lady from the press said. "I'm positive it is . . . that's Klaus Kleiner. I must get his picture."

"I thought they'd never go," Lucia said. "Now, I suggest we all sit here for an hour or so, and stay very, very quiet."

"It was a good party though," Catton said. "Everyone enjoyed it. Well done, Lucia . . . Simon."

"Lito and Magdalena did all the work," Simon said, "plus you two slaving away at the barbecue and the bar."

"I shall never eat another hamburger as long as I live," Philip declared. "Or a sausage, for that matter."

"You may never have to," Simon said. "How many people asked you to dinner?"

"Five," Philip said. "All of them merry widows. I gather I'm the catch of the season."

"I only picked up two," John said. "Both from cryptofascists who want to press the merits of hanging and flogging."

"I'm tops with seven," Christine said. "All from men with four hands. Lucia would have scored higher, but the men are afraid of Simon."

"I rather think it's because of that bikini," Simon said. "Anyway, it serves you right. What about you, Klaus? You were almost killed in the rush. What were they after—share tips?"

"I rather lost count after I ran out of excuses. Say six—I can't possibly do as well as Chris, not having a bikini. . . ."

"If you chauvinist pigs don't stop droning on about my bikini, I shall scream," Chris said. "Why are you all picking on me?"

They were making conversation, trying to keep the atmosphere light. It was late in the evening now, and a soft, balmy night was coming on as they sat on the terrace, their feet up on the low wall, watching the sun ease down behind the mountains. From the house behind came the murmur of voices and the clink of glasses as Lito and Magdalena cleared away the last of the plates and glassware and stacked empty wine bottles back into crates.

"So," said Simon, tilting his chair back, "what brings you to this part of the world, Klaus? I know you get about a bit, but the thought that you just happened to be passing and felt like gate-crashing is a little hard to swallow. Why are you here?"

"Business," Kleiner said briefly. "Philip runs KSI for me, and we need to talk about new business. I am staying up in Formentor, but since I was coming over anyway, I've brought some stuff that Alec Yates has been collecting for John. It's here in this file, John, with a letter. He thought you might need it for this famous report of yours."

"I hate to sound ungrateful, but Yates has no business discussing this business with you," said Catton, ripping open the envelope, "let alone using you to send me files, even if you offered. Incidentally, it's supposed to be a *confidential* report."

"May we know what your conclusions are?" asked Kleiner, quite unfazed.

"No, you may not," said Catton, his eyes scanning the letter. "You'll need to find out from Yates. Anyway, I can't guarantee that my solution will be tried, but if it is, you will probably be the first to know."

"Really!" Kleiner said. "I find that interesting. Why should I be the first to know?"

"Come on, Klaus, I don't know what you two are up to, but we all know you're up to something," Catton said. "Well, here's something else . . . too good to keep to myself, I think, and you know the situation anyway. This letter you brought—it's a gold mine. Listen. . . ."

"Baton Rouge, Louisiana
May 6, '89

"Dear Mr. Catton,

"If you ever get this letter, I will be dead. However, I do not want to go out a total loser, or have you think I am holding out on you because I don't like the British or something. I often flew to London when I was with TWA, and everyone was always great to me there. It's a pity about the weather though. No sir, it was because you are my last chance to get back to the deal I had in Miami. Here they want me to serve time, so you are—sorry, *were*—my last card. Well sir, it is over for me. I have paid a con in this halfway house fifty bucks to mail this if anything happens to me, like it now has. I told him that Pete Sinker, to whom this will go because I do not know where you are except Miami, will pay another fifty if he gets it, so it should be O.K. (Do it, Pete, and I'll owe you.)

"This is what I know, and it isn't much. The man who will handle the U.K. end for the Cartel is Emiliano Vargas—a real mean mother. Do not mess with him. He lives in Cay Dorado, and they will operate from there through Spain. They intended to run their own airline, Air Dorado, to Colombia, the U.S., and Madrid. I would have been chief pilot—imagine that!! I was advising them on it when I got picked up by the DEA. Anyway sir, that's it. You have time because the runway at Cay Dorado is no good for long-range jets, they are going to extend it. That will thrill Uncle Sam, you bet. And that's about it, sir. My best wishes to you and your country, and when you fix them, as I hope you will, give them one for . . .

"Yours sincerely,
Larry Teal (Deceased)"

Catton stopped reading and passed the letter to Wintle, who read it over and passed it to Kleiner, while the others sat there in silence for a moment.

"You may not know this, Klaus, but Mr. Teal was one of

the people I had to see in Miami," Catton said. "The Cartel got to him before I could."

"Mr. Teal must have been quite a guy," said Simon at last, nodding to himself. "Yes, quite a guy. He went down kicking."

"I imagine you will want to include that in your confidential report," Kleiner said. "It's final confirmation of what we all suspected. The bit about Cay Dorado will drive Yates mad."

"It means more typing to get it in," Chris said, "but it will be worth it. Your Mr. Teal had guts."

"What do you know of this Cay Dorado place?" asked Wintle, looking up from the letter.

"I know *about* it," Catton said. "The people at the DEA talk of little else. It's a dopers' haven. I didn't know about this Vargas fellow. I'll get Sinker to fill me in on him. He's stuck a note in . . . let's see. 'Dear John . . . This is a little bonus, you owe me fifty bucks.' If you don't mind, Simon, perhaps I could use the phone and give him a ring."

"Maybe we ought to discuss this later, in private," Wintle suggested. "Especially since the matter is confidential for the moment. It's your affair, John, but if you'd like a word . . ."

"If what you really mean is, let's all talk when the two featherheaded ladies are in bed, you can forget it," Chris said. "I've been typing John's precious report every afternoon, and Lucia has been collating the documentation. We probably know what John has in mind much better than you do, and we are quite capable of keeping our mouths shut."

"I meant when Alec Yates is present. He will have to present John's report to the Cabinet committee."

"I am sure we can discuss it if we wish," Kleiner said. "I've already put up a proposal to Yates on behalf of KSI, and I understand that we will be handling the overseas end of the Cartel problem. Yates should have official approval by the time the report goes in."

"If you two have already decided what is going to be done, I can't see why I have spent six weeks researching the problem and writing the report," Catton said. "Yates has no business discussing this business with you without consulting me. You have no official standing, you know."

"I think Yates is rather more interested in my unofficial standing," Kleiner said. "I am not trying to steal your thunder, I am just letting you know that matters are in hand, so that you can take them into account when writing your report. . . ."

When the others had gone to bed, Klaus Kleiner and Simon Quarry sat together in the darkness. The silence between them dragged on for a while, until Simon broke it.

"How's business?" he asked.

"Fine," Kleiner said. "Business is always fine."

"Making plenty of money?"

"Yes . . . why do you ask?"

"Because with plenty of business to do, and plenty of money to spend, I'd have thought you'd have enough on your plate without roaming the world messing in affairs which don't concern you. Why are you here? Why are you dragging Philip into this? Why don't you leave Catton and the Drug Squad to do their business, and mind your own? Catton is no fool, but you and Yates have gone behind his back and left him with little choice but to fall in with what you have already decided, none of which is really your concern."

"Drugs do concern me . . . drugs killed my daughter."

"That's a reason," Simon conceded, "but it's not the only one, is it? You like playing dangerous games, Klaus. You were very charming here today, but I've seen the other side of your face. It wasn't pretty."

Even thinking about it brought the shock back, made the sweat seep into the palms of Simon's hands. He remembered it, all too well, Kleiner and Fiori, Lucia's father, for godsake, the hatred pulsing between them in that dark, smoke-ridden room, so deep that you could almost see it. Then the sudden gunfire, but more than that—Quarry knew about gunfire—the way Kleiner kept on his feet, firing again and again at Fiori, stepping around the desk like a cat to gun down the man behind. . . . Simon shook his head and looked again at Kleiner, cool and elegant now, tilted back in the chair, his feet propped up on the poolside wall.

"You're a real bastard," he said. "D'you know that? I watched them tonight, all those people trying to have a word with the great Klaus Kleiner; if only they knew what I know."

"I knew I wouldn't be welcome, which is why I didn't ask for an invitation," Kleiner said. "I know there is still dirt between us. I saw it in your face when I arrived here. Look, I was wrong in Milan . . . it won't happen again, I promise."

Simon continued to look out over the dark bulk of the hills and said nothing, sipping quietly at his drink.

"You can't help yourself, Klaus," he said at last. "It's the way you are."

"Does Lucia know about her father . . . and about me?" Kleiner said. "I'd hate to cause her more pain."

"Then what are you doing here?" Simon asked. "We are trying to build a life together and live like real people; hence the party. We want to get back to the real world, have friends, go out to dinner, go sailing, do dull, boring, everyday things like that. You'd hate it. People like you and Yates are made for each other, plotting, scheming, treating people like pawns. I know that, but what I don't know—yet —is why both of you persist in hanging around my life."

"Then I'm sorry I intruded."

"It depends on what you want. As a friend, you are welcome here . . . anytime." Simon took his feet off the wall and swung his chair around, close to Kleiner. "Look, Klaus, I know how you are. I've seen it. You *like* whacking people. You are dealing yourself into this drug business because you have this . . . this obsession to hit out at people. I can tell you from my own experience that nothing you can do will bring your daughter back, and you will destroy yourself unless you stop now."

"I can't stop," Kleiner said. "It's not that I don't want to. It's that I can't."

"Then God help you."

"More to the point, will *you* help me?"

"Ah, now we're getting to it," Simon said. "It's lonely out there, isn't it? When push comes to shove, and you have to go through with whatever you've set up? Well, count me out. My gunning days are over, and anyway, you don't need me for that."

"There could be other things," Kleiner urged. "Look, if KSI gets to handle it, this Cartel business will be big, exciting, important . . . it may even be fun. I am talking a total security business with Yates and the British government. If I can pull off the Cartel thing, there will be other problems, and other governments will be interested in what we can do. Anyway, as I say, it could be fun . . . working together."

"I like your idea of fun," Simon said. "I think it will be dangerous. See Larry Teal (Deceased)."

"Yes . . . but isn't that part of it? You'll get bored here. Look at those people at the party . . . all bored. If we are all in it—Philip, Catton, me—can you stay out? Would Lucia even want you to?"

"Yes," Simon said firmly. "I think she would. Personally, I might come along for Philip's sake, but we—Lucia and I—have our own lives to lead. So let's just wait and see what happens. We'll still be here when you get tired of all this, and you might need somewhere to run. You heard what John said about the Cartel. They play rough."

"I'm not worried about that," Kleiner said. "That's part of the fun. We can play rough too."

"You're crazy," Simon said, "quite crazy. See a doctor, that's my advice. And sell KSI . . . it's only a front for your fantasies."

Kleiner smiled, unruffled. "I don't think so . . . and by the way, Alec Yates sent his regards. He often talks about you."

"Does he now," Simon said. "I wonder why."

About the same time, a few hundred miles to the west, in Freddie Bright's villa on the Costa del Sol, Ted Bardsey was having a bad time. He was crouched well forward on the yellow silk sofa, sweating, watching the ice slowly melt in his gin. Matters he had to control were now getting seriously out of hand.

"Look, Freddie, be reasonable," he said. "I can't go poking my nose too deep into Special Branch business, not without somebody noticing. It's not bloody possible. Even coming down here is risky. I'm sticking my neck out as it is."

"That's your problem though, isn't it, my son?" Freddie Bright said. "I've been paying you fifty big ones every year since I don't know when to help me out and keep me in the picture. That's worth a little extra effort now and again. You've got this much information, now get some more."

"I can't. Bloody hell, Freddie!" Ted shook his head. "How did I ever get into this?"

"By being greedy, Ted. And you're in too deep to get out now. My associate, Mr. Vargas, will want to know who these coves are, and what they're up to. This is a very heavy investment we are making down here, and Mr. Vargas won't like it if we fuck it up. He's not what you might call tolerant. In fact, just between us, the last person who crossed with Mr. Vargas ended up without any arms or legs. Some of Mr. Vargas's boys cut them off with a chain saw—and left him alive. That's a new one, eh?"

"Piss off, Fred," Ted Bardsey said weakly. "This is England we're talking about."

"This is *cocaine,* my son. If you can't find out more about this special unit at the Yard, Mr. Vargas won't like it."

"Look"—Ted put his drink down on the glass-topped table and wiped his hands on a napkin—"one more time, this is how it goes. I just had this chat with Catton before he went over to the States. He said he had to write a report about a new drug ring that was about to set up shop in Blighty, and how it might be stopped. I told you about it on the phone that same night, right?"

"You did, Ted, and Catton turned up in Miami . . . we know that. So, since controlling the U.K. market is Mr. Vargas's intention, I told you to find out more."

"And I *have,* Fred, for Christ's sake! Look, John Catton

used to be assistant to Philip Wintle, who retired a couple of years back. Wintle now works for a bloke called Klaus Kleiner, some rich bloody Nazi. You must have read about him. Anyway, a month or so back, Wintle gets shot in Italy, where, or so I gather, he had the help of a bloke called Simon Quarry. With me so far? Now this Quarry has been in London having meetings with John Catton. It was all over the Yard. People say that's why Catton got the heave-ho from the Branch . . . for mixing with undesirables. Just like I would, if it leaked out I was down here, boozing with you."

"Who's this Quarry when he's at home?"

"He's a killer. Look, all Yard records are in the central computer, right? If I want some info from outside Major Crimes, which is my own manor, I have to make a request to the head of that branch—Drugs, Fraud, whatever, and then get at least an AC—an assistant commissioner—to endorse it. We can't just have every Tom, Dick, or Harry getting at the confidential files, can we?"

"So?"

"Well, to get at Quarry's file, you have to get permission from the Home Secretary. Not even the head of the Met has access to Quarry's file. He's a hit man for the bloody Government—or that's the buzz I hear."

"So how do you know about him, if it's all so secret?"

"Ah well . . ." Bardsey tapped his nose. "I have my little ways. I punched it up and got a no-no, so I had a think, see. Right now, no one is heading up the Special Branch. They have a new boss, but he's still reading himself in and handing over his old job in Northern Ireland. Meanwhile, a Super is keeping the chair warm. I waltzed in, came on a bit strong, got him to give me access, and punched up Wintle's name. It says on a note that Wintle left the Yard on early retirement after someone shopped Quarry to a bunch of wog terrorists . . . who Quarry was killing. It was all there cross-referenced in Wintle's file. Of course, you need to know the connection or you wouldn't look, but the fact is that Catton, Wintle, Quarry, and maybe this Kleiner are all involved somehow and—that is another point—Kleiner is *insane* about drugs. Harry Bartlett in the Drug Squad told me that half the flak he gets about pushers comes from Kleiner. Kleiner's daughter died in London from an overdose of heroin, see? So, do you see where it's at? How they are all connected?"

Freddie chewed his lower lip. "Yes . . . well . . . maybe. Where is this Quarry now?"

"I dunno."

"Where is Wintle?"

"I dunno."

"Kleiner? Catton?"

"I dunno. Catton was due back at the Yard a week ago, but I haven't seen him around."

"You don't know much, do you, Ted?"

"I've done all I can, Freddie."

"No, you haven't, Ted, but this'll do for now. Now, I want you to go back to London and keep your eyes and ears open. I want to know about this report of Catton's. I want to see it."

"Blimey! How can I do that? It won't come round on the tea trolley."

"That's your problem. I want you to find Wintle and this gunfighter Quarry. If Catton gets nosy, let me know, and I'll deal with him."

"Fred, Catton's a policeman. You can't touch a copper. Leave that idea right out."

"Ted, Ted!" Freddie Bright shook his head. "You've got to give up these old-fashioned ideas, or Mr. Vargas will have to have a word with you. Back home, Mr. Vargas *owns* coppers, judges, politicians, countries. Back home, Mr. Vargas has his own private *army*. They have ground-to-air missiles, Ted. So think big. Mr. Vargas isn't going to be put off his big deal by a band of nosy-parking, flat-footed busies and a contract killer, so don't kid yourself."

"I don't want any part of this, Fred."

"Hard luck then, Ted, because you *are* part of it." Freddie Bright turned to call over to one of two men sitting on another sofa close by the door. "Billy . . . I want you to take our guest back to Málaga. Take him to a nice hotel and round a couple of clubs. Find him a nice fat *señorita* if he wants one, but don't make no fuss. Don't get even a little pissed or out of order. Stay with him and pop him on a plane in the morning."

"Right, boss." Billy got up and reached for his jacket. "I'll go get the motor."

Freddie Bright turned back to his guest. "Ted, you are just starting to earn your keep, but I'll slip you an extra five next month, on account of more on this report. You'll have to take it in cocaine, but I'll let you have half a kilo. You get me the juice on this new squad and this Quarry bloke, and there might even be a bonus. But Ted . . ."

"Yes, Fred," Ted said wearily.

"Don't fuck it up now, will you? Mr. Vargas wouldn't like that at all."

Yates put down the magnifying glass and pushed his chair back from the desk, tapping the sheet of film with one finger. "Well done," he said. "That's a beautiful set of contacts, and you have them all in."

"That was the hard part," the woman said. "They were all moving about, and Kleiner didn't arrive until quite late. I was worried there might not be enough light left, but they came out all right."

"You did well," Yates said, "and I'll see you get your fee. Now, I have one other task for you, which pays a bonus."

"That's nice," the woman said cautiously.

Yates opened a drawer in his desk and took out a thin sheaf of papers. "Here is a press release," he said. "Several copies, all slightly different, but they cover the same ground. I want you to print up some seven-by-five glossies of these two shots and send them with a release to the main newspapers and one or two magazines, addressed by name to whoever writes the gossip column. I've put their names and papers at the head of each release. Don't put your name on or do anything else, is that quite clear?"

"Yes . . . but . . ."

"No buts. Just do it, and I'll see you get your money."

When the woman had gone, Yates poured himself a stiff whisky and walked over to the window, stopping to look out at the night, smiling at his image in the glass.

"That should stir things up for Mr. Quarry and his chums," he said, raising the glass to his reflection. "Cheers!"

Ted never had a chance to earn his bonus. Three days later, leafing through an English paper, Freddie Bright saw an entry in the gossip column.

Heads turned at reclusive publisher Simon Quarry's poolside party when international tycoon Klaus Kleiner turned up uninvited to join the throng. Majorcan summer chit-chat would have got a further boost had the sunshine funsters realized that among Quarry's other guests were John Catton, erstwhile Head of Scotland Yard's Special Branch, Catton's old boss, Philip Wintle, another top cop, now retired, and among the ladies, leading barrister Christine Hitchcock, and the daughter of a murdered Milan industrialist, Lucia Fiori, with whom Quarry (whose wife, readers may recall, was killed by terrorists some years ago) is said to be playing house. The plot thickens, but remember you first heard about it here.

Freddie read this item over a couple of times, studying the photographs that went with it, then got up from his deck chair, folded the paper carefully to display the report, and padded back into his house, up the stairs to the guest wing, and tapped on a bedroom door.

"Mr. Vargas, it's Freddie. I've got something to show you. Something interesting."

"Momentito."

Freddie stood there, feeling chilly from the air-conditioning. The chain rattled, the door opened, and Vargas's bodyguard stood on the threshold, blocking his path. Whose bloody home is this anyway? thought Freddie.

"Sí?" the guard asked. *"¿Qué es?"*

"I don't want to see *you*, Sunny Jim," Freddie said. "My business is with the *Jefe*, so get out of the bloody way."

"Come in, Freddie," came Vargas's voice from inside the room. "Don't mind Carlosito, he is just doing his job. What is it?"

Vargas was out on the terrace, lying stark naked on a towel-draped lounger. He made no attempt to cover himself as Freddie came through the open door, just held up his hand for the paper.

"Read that," Freddie said. "Five thousand quid down the drain, and I could have got it from the paper for a hundred pesetas. I oughta sue that bloody Bardsey, 'stead of paying him."

Vargas read the item through, his lips moving softly, then he motioned Freddie into a chair, tapping the paper with one long, polished fingernail.

"Freddie, you know England . . . is this usual? Gunmen and police mixing like this? I hear your police and your judges can't be bought. Is that correct . . . true?"

"Fairly true," Freddie said. "I've never heard of anyone buying a judge. You can get at juries though, if you're careful, and while most coppers are straight, I've always owned a few . . . look at Ted."

"*Si* . . . but this group here—two senior policemen, a woman lawyer, a very rich man—I wish I were as rich as Klaus Kleiner . . . and this Quarry, the hit man? Is that usual, to have them all together like this?"

"Hell, no! Well, I wouldn't think so. Mind you, from what Ted told me, not everyone knows about this Quarry. It might mean nothing, at least have nothing to do with us."

"Then why are they all in Spain? This Catton man—him here in the photograph—is investigating me. He was in Miami, and now he is in Spain. That is not coincidence."

"We don't know if Catton knows about you. Majorca's a very long way from here, Mr. Vargas, and lots of English people go there. They like the sun."

"*Si, pero turistas.* These people are not tourists, Freddie. It says this Quarry has a house there."

"Yes, that's right. So, what do you want me to do, Mr. Vargas?"

"Do nothing. I will send a man to Majorca to find out where this Quarry lives and what he does. No . . . wait! Tell your man in London to find out all he can about the report. Put pressure on him."

"Right, Mr. Vargas. I'll get onto that again."

"And Freddie . . ." Vargas held out a glass. "On your way out, can you fetch me a glass of white wine? No ice, remember."

He treats me like a bloody servant, Freddie thought, in my own house too. But he took the glass.

Everyone was leaving. Kleiner was going to take Catton and Christine back to London in his jet, Philip was restless and eager to start work. Suddenly, it seemed the holiday was over. Over a last lunch at the Montellin in Puerto, tucked away at Jochem's best table on the far side of the pool, Catton placed the report before them, a slim, neatly bound file, which he tapped lightly with one finger.

"Well, there it is, and by tonight it will be on Yates's desk. Then it's up to him to sell it to the Boss and get the go-ahead. Until then, we wait."

"It's a bit thin," said Simon, looking down at the file. "Or is that an extract?"

"No, that's it. I could have written a couple of books on the subject; getting it down to just this has been half the battle. Chris must have typed this twenty times, trying to keep it short."

"Plus honing your arguments and making them follow to build up the case," Christine put in. "Considering I had my own briefs to prepare, I think you should be grateful for the help."

"Very true," said Catton, looking around the table. "I can't let you see this, but you know the gist of it. Thanks to Chris, what we have here is a cogently argued case for a special unit to deal with the Cartel, a one-off team for a one-off situation. Specifically, I am proposing that we commission KSI, Klaus's security company, to 'investigate'

Vargas's activities in Europe. That's not unusual, they'll buy that concept. Philip Wintle runs KSI for Klaus, and I once worked for Philip. That's Logic Link Number One. I deal with Yates, Yates deals with the Cabinet, or whomever the Cabinet nominate to carry the can, and Klaus uses his influence to oil the wheels and keep the politicians happy, and off our backs. Just for the record, I had come to that conclusion anyway, before I discovered that Yates and Klaus were intending to stitch me up."

"And what do you think will happen?" Lucia asked. "Do you think the British government will go for it? Isn't it a bit . . . well, a bit radical . . . hiring outside help on something like this?"

"On the contrary, I think they'll leap at it," Catton said. "After all, something has to be done, and who else can do it? According to Klaus, it won't cost them a penny, and if anything should go wrong, they won't be blamed. They will love that part."

"Well, in that case," said Kleiner, raising his glass, "let us drink to the success of your report."

"I can drink to that," Simon agreed, "and if any of you want a little rest, or a spot of sunshine, you will find Lucia and me down here with the door wide open and 'Welcome' on the mat. Hurry back down whenever you feel like it."

"And that's it?" asked Catton, flashing a glance around the table. "You're not . . . er . . . going to help Philip again? I thought Klaus said . . ."

"No . . . definitely not," Philip said firmly. "Simon is staying here, and this is not his concern."

"Is that right, Simon?"

"Philip's the boss," Simon said, "and what he says goes. Just one word before you go though. The people you are tackling are mean and dangerous. Just remember Larry Teal (Deceased). . . ."

6

Yates had learned one thing well during his years of government service. He had learned how to wait. He had been waiting for a week, for seven long days since the Catton Report had gone through to the Cabinet Office, and he was still waiting. He was sitting in an upright chair in the minister's office, his long legs stuck out before him, studying the well-polished toe caps of his shoes. If he moved his shoes a little, turning them from side to side on his heels, the reflection changed, winking under the pool of light from the desk lamp. Yates leaned against the desk on one elbow, allowing his fingers to drum on the top, but otherwise he was just waiting. It couldn't be long now.

The minister was worried. He had waved Yates in and returned to a study of the report, turning the pages, running a pencil line down certain sections, frowning. Clearly, the buck had been passed around the Cabinet table a time or two, and now lay on the minister's desk. The final decision was his, and he didn't like it. They never did, Yates thought.

"Well, Alec," said the minister, looking up at last. "I don't like this."

"No, Minister."

"It looks highly irregular. I'm surprised an officer of Catton's experience should propose it."

"Well, Minister, hardly irregular, just novel." Christ! The

minister had been worrying at Catton's Report for a week, and he *still* hadn't got the point.

"So you think we should go for this suggestion?"

Now, he wants me to make up his mind for him. Well, that was what civil servants were paid for. That "we" was interesting, but a word to avoid.

"You really have no choice, Minister," said Yates, stressing the pronoun. "You can hardly sit back and let what is happening in America happen here, and unless we do something drastic, you have no reason to suppose that it will be any different. Catton has proposed setting up a monitoring unit, and hiring out the real work to Kleiner's company, KSI. I will liaise between them and you as required. That gives two cutouts, so there is no real need for you to get involved on a day-to-day basis, but Catton and I are both servants of the government, and we do need your approval."

That nudge, a reminder of what they paid him for, should get the go-ahead.

"Yes . . . well, I suppose I must approve it then," the minister said grudgingly, "but what worries me is the possibility of trouble in Spain or Cay Dorado. I want no linkage with this office."

"There will be no linkage, Minister. It will be Kleiner's problem."

The minister got up and went over to his drinks tray, returning after a moment with two glasses of pale sherry, passing one across to Yates before sipping his own thoughtfully and then placing it carefully on his blotter and sitting down.

"Yes, you say that, Alec, but can I be sure? Take Spain . . . I accept that the Medellín Cartel will come into Europe via Spain, but if we ask for official Spanish help, they inevitably link it to concessions on Gibraltar. They *always* do. Dammit, only last week they torpedoed an EEC airspace deal in Brussels over the Rock. I won't go cap in hand to the Spaniards if Catton gets in over his head, capering about in their country."

"He knows that, Minister. It's in the report." Keep nudging.

"Then there is Cay Dorado. You and I both know, and Catton must strongly suspect, that the Cartel will use Cay Dorado to transship the cocaine paste to Europe. I know it. You know it. That corrupt creature who runs Cay Dorado knows we know it, but we can do nothing, at least officially. And if we do anything unofficially . . . well, just don't get caught, that's all. Catton's suggestions say nothing about Cay Dorado, but I cannot, and will not, get involved there. Enough is enough."

We'll see about that, Yates thought.

"Can I take it that the loan for the Dorado runway extension will not be approved?" Yates asked. "According to this Teal person's letter, they only want it to operate big jets directly in from South America and so avoid interdiction by the Americans. Later on, they will use Doradan planes to fly cocaine in bulk direct to Europe. That will save them a lot of fiddling about."

"I know that, man," the minister snapped. "But Cay Dorado has access to overseas aid, just like anyone else. I can't block it directly, and God knows, that poor benighted country needs it. Of course, the Yanks will be livid, but what can I do? For the present, I'm stalling."

"There are problems with air-traffic control in the Cay Dorado area, Minister. It might take months for IATA to approve the flight plans."

"Not if Cay Dorado and Colombia reach a bilateral agreement," the minister said. "That can be ratified in weeks—but that's for later. Right now we have this proposal of Catton's . . . and that brings me to another matter. Catton proposes leasing the overseas side of this work to KSI, Kleiner's company, run by Philip Wintle. I can accept that. What I cannot accept is that Kleiner and Catton work with Simon Quarry. I remember him very well, too well. The man is dangerous."

"I only wish that were so, Minister. In fact, Quarry has no links with KSI. We could use him."

"For what?" the minister asked shortly. "Or should I ask?"

Yates held the minister's eyes steadily. "Well," he said at

last, "let us say that there are situations where he might be useful. There is, however, a point beyond which I might not go . . . for your sake, Minister."

"Indeed?"

"Yes, Minister. I think the Americans call it 'deniability.' What you don't know can't hurt you."

The minister put down the pen. "What, exactly, are you up to, Yates?"

"I am executing my brief in the best way I know how, Minister. At the moment, I am attempting to muster suitable forces to contain this threat. It calls for a certain deftness. I'd rather not go into details . . . and I don't think I need to, Minister." Yates put his sherry glass down carefully on the desk. "It's like this. We have a little time, but not much, so if I could just have your note ordering the execution of the report . . ." He paused and let it hang there, waiting.

"Oh, very well." A stroke or two of the pen, and it was done. Yates put the note in his pocket and went off, whistling, to talk to his Admiralty contact in the Ministry of Defense. What he needed now was a warship.

Two days later, Klaus Kleiner flew to Majorca, hired a car at the Palma airport, and drove north across the island to Pollensa, driving directly through the open gates of Quarry's house to find him by the pool enjoying a pre-lunch drink with Lucia and Philip Wintle. This time the welcome was warmer.

"Klaus!" exclaimed Simon, looking up without rising. "You are welcome at any time, but does it ever occur to you that we might not be here?"

"No," replied Kleiner, bending down to kiss Lucia, smiling at Wintle. "The thought never entered my head. May I have a drink?"

"The bar's over there, help yourself. If you insist on making yourself at home, I'm damned if I'll wait on you—and you could even freshen up this gin while you are at it . . . just a touch of Mahon."

They waited until Klaus had returned with the drinks,

taken off his jacket and tie, arranged himself on a lounger, and propped his feet up easily on the wall. Then they shifted in their seats, turning to face him.

"Well, this is nice," he said cheerfully. "What a beautiful day."

"Don't be irritating," Lucia said.

"Just get on with it," Simon said shortly. "Did they buy it?"

"Hook, line, and sinker," said Klaus, his voice heavy with satisfaction. "Yates got the signature the day before yesterday, and he gave the nod to John. I saw John yesterday, and here I am, with the contract in my pocket, signed and sealed."

"You and your contracts," Simon said.

"And what do you want now?" Philip Wintle asked carefully.

"I want you, specifically," Kleiner said. "Our brief is to give the Medellín Cartel a clout they will never forget, but how we do it is up to you. I want you to come back to London, open up a KSI office, and get to work."

"He has work here," Simon said. "Philip is remodeling my garden. I need him."

"You'll cope," Klaus said. "This is more important. We have to locate and identify the Cartel's connection, and I need Philip in London to do it. I don't think that will take too long. Then we might come back to Spain. We're pretty sure their European base will be down here. But it's not your concern . . . and we won't bother you. Leave this to us."

"I shall," Simon said blandly. "Lucia and I will go sailing. In my spare time, I may even play the money market . . . remind me to phone my broker, Lucia. Just for the record though, I am willing to offer advice, if you need it, and I insist you take good care of Philip. If you get him into trouble, I might get cross."

"I know that," Kleiner said. "I'll take care of Philip, and if we need help, we won't be too proud to ask for it."

"Good," said Lucia, rising. "In that case, I'll go and see about lunch."

* * *

That night, after Wintle and Kleiner had gone, Simon and Lucia went to bed early.

"I love them all dearly," said Simon, holding Lucia close, "but it is rather nice to be on our own again. It gives us a chance to think, and things."

"Especially things," Lucia said.

"Mmm . . . naturally. Did I ever tell you, you have a beautiful back?"

"Tell me again."

"Later . . . first tell me something. Have you heard any more of that woman . . . the reporter?"

"The reporter?"

"The one from the local rag who crashed the party."

"No . . . not a word. Why?"

"She isn't from the Palma paper. They never sent her . . . don't know anything about her."

"How do you know?"

"Simple. I rang them up and asked." Simon leaned out of bed and opened the drawer of a side table. "Seen this?"

Lucia read the article carefully, tilting the paper to throw the bedside light onto the photograph. "Did she take that?"

"Who else? She got the lot of us in there . . . must have waited awhile for the shot—and that's an intriguing bit of copy to go with it. That paper had never heard of her either. The copy and photo just arrived. The editor was a mite peeved because he thought he had an exclusive, but that article, or one very like it, plus the photo, was in three other tabloids and in *¡Hola!,* the largest-circulation magazine in Spain. That could be a bit of a nuisance."

"Does it matter?"

"I don't know. I do know that I'm trying, really trying, to keep out of this Cartel business. I also know that whoever planted that article did it deliberately, to put us together. So who? Incidentally, Kleiner is keen to get me in and, please note, Kleiner owns two of the papers which ran the story."

"Klaus didn't do it."

"How do you know?"

"He promised me he'd not put any pressure on you. I know he wants you in, but it's your decision."

"And you believed him?"

"Yes . . . Klaus has never lied to me."

Simon sighed and stared up at the ceiling. "I think you'd better be careful which questions you ask him. He might tell you something you'd rather not know."

"Fancy a beer?" Ted Bardsey asked from the doorway. "A pie and a pint at the Sherlock?"

"Sorry, Ted," said Catton, looking up. "Got a lunch—and a lot to do here. Maybe next week."

Bardsey came into the room, looking around curiously, letting his fingers wander across the thick files resting in the "In" basket. Catton's new office was small, with space for just one desk, two chairs, and against the partition wall, three filing cabinets equipped with combination locks. It was a start.

"Take your nose out of there, Ted," Catton said. "That's all hush-hush stuff."

"Is it now," Ted said. "I guess you got the go-ahead to raise your private army?"

"Privatization, they call it," said Catton, tilting his chair back and swinging his feet up onto the desk. " 'Costs can be reduced and efficiency increased by contracting out government tasks to private enterprise.' . . . I quote. Traffic have privatized wheel-clamping, Fraud are privatizing art thefts, credit-card scams, finance fiddles . . . it's the coming thing. You ought to start thinking of it for Major Crimes; it might get your arrest rate up."

"Piss off," Ted said. "Come on, tell me what you're up to. What's this new unit for? You can tell old Ted."

"No," Catton said. "So don't ask. Those files go under lock and key, so stop glooming over them. I've said all I'm going to say, so push off."

"There will be rumors," Bardsey warned. "There will be talk. Do you still rank as commander with a department of one?"

"Yes," Catton said, "but I may expand."

"And you still get commander's pay?"

"Yes, thanks."

"You crafty bastard. There's no bloody justice in this world, is there?"

"What do you care?" Catton asked. "Ah . . . Philip! Come on in."

He swung his feet off the desk, got up, and walked around to welcome Philip Wintle, who had suddenly appeared in the open doorway. That pause gave Bardsey just a second to glance down at the top file in the basket.

"Did you find your way up all right?"

"Well, considering I worked in this building for quite a number of years, I didn't find it too difficult," Wintle said, smiling. "Though having to get a pass at the front desk seemed very odd. How are you, Ted? It's nice to see you again."

"I'm fine, Mr. Wintle. How are you? You look well."

"I am well. How is Crime?"

"Flourishing, same as always."

"Ted never lacks for employment," said Catton, reaching back to pick up the top file, "but we have to get on. . . . Philip, this copy is for you. You can read it over in the car, but you know what's in it. Where are we going?"

"Klaus has booked a table at the Connaught, and Yates will join us there. Simon is still in Spain . . . he sends his best. How is Christine?"

"She's fine."

"Good. Listen . . . one thing, Ted," Wintle said, turning to Bardsey. "I wonder if you could help me? I'm staying at a hotel. It's nice enough, but I don't really like it. You know all the stations, Ted—do you know of a flat I could rent for a few weeks, somewhere fairly central?"

Bardsey nodded. "No problem, Mr. Wintle. Always have people coming and going, and we keep a place or two for the provincials or a witness. I'll see what's going spare and let you know. Just give me a day or two."

"That's very good of you. I hate hotels or imposing on friends, don't you?"

"Leave it to me, Mr. Wintle. It'll be my pleasure."

"Right, then, that's settled. Everybody outside." Catton ushered them both into the corridor, double-locked the door of his office, and slapping Bardsey on the shoulder in farewell, led his guest over to the elevator.

Fifteen minutes later, from the post-office telephone exchange just off Trafalgar Square, Ted Bardsey got through to Freddie Bright.

"Fred . . . it's me."

"Who? Who is it?"

"Me, for Christ's sake! I've ducked out of the office to give you a bell, so listen carefully. Can you hear me now?"

"Right, my son . . . talk on."

"I think—no, I'm *sure*—what I told you about is coming off. I've seen the report."

"Great! What's in it?"

"No, listen . . . I can't get at it, I only saw the cover, but the copy I saw had a ministerial slip on it marked 'Approved.' Catton has a new office at the Yard. Wintle is already here, and they've gone off to meet Kleiner, the rich kraut."

"Mr. Vargas still wants a squint at that report, my son."

"No chance. Catton's copy is under lock and key. He gave a copy to Wintle though. You might try and nick that. I'm going to fix him up with somewhere to stay. Nice, eh? Don't forget to mention that to Vargas. I could use a bit of credit in that quarter."

"Mr. Vargas to you and me, my son. Where is this Wintle staying?"

"Blimey, give me a chance. I haven't started ringing round, but one of the stations will know somewhere that's going spare. I'll let you know as soon as I know."

"You do that."

"So there you are, Mr. Vargas. We are definitely getting there." Freddie Bright was sitting on the terrace, with the big Colombian guard looming behind him. Vargas was looking less than pleased.

"I want that report, Freddie. I want to know what they are planning. If you say they can't be bought, you must steal it, and don't let anything stop you. Get on with it."

"That's what I intend to do, Mr. Vargas," Freddie said. "We could try and nick it in the street or have a go at getting into his hotel, but if he moves out to a flat—an apartment on his own—that will be simpler and safer. He can't sleep with the bloody thing."

"You have people in London? Good people?"

"Of course. Why else are we dealing? You want my firm because it's a good one, right?"

"Then tell your firm to get that report . . . and tell them to kill this Wintle. If he is in charge, removing him will scare off the rest. In Bogotá we had to execute a minister once. After that, we had no problems."

Freddie was aghast. "Mr. Vargas, Wintle is a *copper!* You can't . . ."

"Just get it done, Freddie," Vargas said, "and soon. And he is no longer a policeman. He works for this man Kleiner's security company. So do it."

"But why? Why look for trouble, Mr. Vargas? Killing a copper, even a retired one, will cause big trouble. I'm not even sure my lads will tackle that, but why do it anyway?"

"Because these people are messing in my affairs. They have to be taught not to do that. In my country, we spent years learning that you cannot work with honest officials. You either buy them or remove them."

"But, Mr. Vargas . . . see, coppers look after each other. I'm not sure if Ted Bardsey will keep quiet if we top a copper."

Vargas shrugged. "Bardsey is bought and paid for. Anyway, why tell him? Just do it, or I will find someone who will. But if I have to do it myself, what do I need you for? Will you arrange this thing for me, Freddie? I would regard it as a test of your loyalty."

"Yes, Mr. Vargas," Freddie said wearily, heaving himself out of the chair. How had he ever got into all this?

7

The Kleiner Building stands in a small Italianate square just off St. James's Street, a tall, modern structure in steel and stone and reflecting glass, every floor occupied by one or other of the company offices controlling Kleiner's ever-spreading empire. His newest venture, Kleiner Security, occupied merely a desk in a small office on the top floor, but there was a direct-access elevator that made no stops at other floors, so that people dealing directly with Kleiner, or those who—like Wintle—worked with him in an associate capacity, could come and go unobserved. A week after Wintle's arrival from Majorca, four of the leading participants in the Cartel affair assembled at the Kleiner Building to implement the Catton Report. It was Catton himself who opened the discussion.

"I think we can see the picture. We know what is happening, and can more or less guess where—and I'll come back to that. We know some of the Cartel people involved, like Vargas, but we don't yet know his U.K. connection. However, we can narrow it down to one or more of the British villains who are currently soaking up the sun on the Costa del Crime. So, how shall we set about finding the right one?"

Philip Wintle was sitting birdlike behind the desk, half-rim glasses perched on the end of his nose, his head bent over an open, well-thumbed copy of the Catton Report.

"I've been over this a lot in the last few days," he said, removing his glasses and tapping the report with the edge of the frame, "and let me say that I think it's excellent. Why don't we begin by concentrating our enquiries on two areas, both in Spain. John, you believe, and I agree, that Vargas will import cocaine base into Spain and refine it there. Now, to refine it, he will need a laboratory and commercial quantities of ether, unless he tries to refine the base with kerosene, which, since the result is an inferior end product, I would rather doubt. So, first let us look for someone importing ether, and constructing a well-ventilated warehouse or lab. Once we find that, we can be sure that Vargas won't be far away. Anyway, we can narrow the area of search to southern Spain."

"That's fine as an idea," Yates said, "but even the Costa del Sol is a big place, and we can't ask the Spanish to open up import and customs records without risking a song and dance about cooperation over Gibraltar."

"It's not quite as bad as that," Catton said. "I've already had a chat with the DEA man at the U.S. embassy here in London. They keep a record of ether shipments to Spain, because the U.S. have big military bases there, and they don't want anyone peddling dope to their servicemen. They also have a DEA operative working on the Costa del Sol. He is going to snoop around and report back. It's a smaller task than it might look, because there are only two major ports in the area, Málaga and Cartagena. He will see if any ships from South America have docked there recently, or do so on a regular basis."

"So far, so good," Yates said, "but what about the second part? Vargas's U.K. connection? How do we winkle out that one?"

Catton produced another file from his briefcase, and began to unfold a long computer printout across the desk, pushing their coffee cups aside and using Wintle's ashtray to stop the paper from slipping over the far end.

"Impressive, isn't it?" he said, looking around at the others. "Straight out of the Yard's central computer—a list of villains, large and small, living in the south of Spain.

There are nearly a hundred, and the list grows all the time. Pull off a major haul here, and it's heigh-ho for the villa 'n' pool in sunny Spain, and the company of other expats in like condition."

"God knows why we let this go on," Wintle said. "Surely there must be a way to extradite these people, Yates?"

"Well . . . yes and no. We had an extradition treaty with Spain from the middle of the last century, but the Spanish government ended it in 1978 because they said we were not being cooperative in arresting and extraditing ETA suspects hiding here. The fact is that our courts require better prima facie evidence than the Spanish seemed able to provide; although, to be fair, that is often the case with terrorist charges. However, there is some good news. Firstly, extradition treaties do not usually cover conspiracy charges, except, fortunately, when the conspiracy concerns drugs. Secondly, we do now have a new extradition treaty with Spain, but it is not back-dated. Those already there are safe unless they leave Spain and have to reapply for a resident's permit or they have a criminal record carrying a sentence here of more than one year. Or—and here I quote—'engage in any activity which is contrary to Spanish interests or might adversely affect Spain's relationship with other countries.'"

"You've been looking that up," Catton said admiringly.

"Well, I thought the question of extradition might occur," Yates said placidly, "and the diplomatic area is my forte. I like to feel I am contributing to this affair. The snag with invoking that useful clause, though, is the inevitable linkage with Gibraltar."

"Where do these U.K. villains live now?" Wintle asked.

"According to this printout, largely in Marbella." Catton produced a map and placed it across the printout. "Jorge Orchoa, the Cartel boss, was arrested while dining in a restaurant farther up the coast and a bit inland, here, at San Pedro de Alcantara. However, I don't think location is the necessary lead-in. I think we need to look at these people's records. Most of them are wanted for armed robbery, like the Brinks Mat or the Security Express raid from 1983—

someone got away with six million quid from that one. Some are just swindlers . . . here is a couple wanted for a three-million fraud . . . here's a jewel thief . . . he got yet another three million. These men are not exactly hurting."

"Even so, some of them must be getting a bit strapped for cash," Wintle said. "It goes out very fast once it stops coming in. Vargas will have had no trouble making his connection. In fact, I bet they'd queue up to get into the gravy."

"Funnily enough, not all of them would," Catton said. "A lot of dyed-in-the-wool East End villains are very old-fashioned about drugs. And not all of them are strapped for cash. Quite a number still keep their firms operating here in London. They haven't retired, they've just moved their main office a bit farther south. They have people going to and fro, and they still mastermind the jobs."

"Then there's another link to look for," Kleiner said. "If I were Vargas—and I'm more like him than any of you are because I'm a businessman, and I bet that's how he sees himself—so, if I were Vargas, I'd want a man with a distribution network here in the U.K. It's pointless to go into the distribution business with someone who can't provide the relevant facilities, whatever the product. Also, I'd need someone who sees the problem my way."

"Well, if that's right," Wintle said, "we can narrow down our U.K. connection to someone who is not too fussy where the bread comes from, and who is still operating a gang here in London. Can you pick those out from the list?"

"Probably," Catton said. "Ted Bardsey is heading up Major Crimes, and he knows most of these people personally. He claims he grew up with half of them. I'll have a discreet word with him and get him to tick off the most likely contenders."

"We could also ask Quarry to take a prowl along the coast," Yates said. "He speaks Spanish, he has good cover, and he's used to nosing out his targets. If we give him these leads, he might be able to pinpoint our man with surprising speed. I think he'd do that for us."

"No." Wintle shook his head decisively. "Leave him alone. We don't need him, and it's time he and Lucia had some time to themselves."

"I agree with Philip," Catton said. "I can run this very nicely during the investigative phase. It's when we move against the Cartel that we may need to get . . . well, aggressive. But we still have a lot to do before we hand this over to KSI completely."

"Well, in that case, you'd better all get on with it," said Yates, rising. "I will get back to my office and carry on with my appointed round—very dull stuff, but it has to be done."

"I'll come with you," Catton said, "if you fancy a walk across the park. We'll see you tonight, Philip. How's the flat?"

"Fine . . . thank Ted for me, will you? No . . . on second thought, I'll walk back with you and thank him myself—more polite. It's ideal and right on the Victoria line, only twenty minutes door-to-door."

"I can't see why you don't stay at my suite here," Kleiner said, "or in some other hotel, if you didn't like the first one."

"Because we'd talk about this business all the time, and I need time to think," Wintle said. "Also, hotel rooms are not at all secure. Maids are always popping in and out. Even as it is, I have to keep some of this stuff with me all the time. As to dinner this evening, John, I'll expect you around seven, shall I? And bring your young lady."

"She'll insist on it," Catton said. "Chris has developed this strange passion for older men."

"That girl has taste as well as brains and beauty," Philip said. "Come on, let's get over to the Yard."

Freddie Bright's men let themselves into the flat in the late afternoon. The front door of the block gave in easily enough; just a simple Yale lock, so it was in with the credit card and a little twist. Then they were in the entrance hall, easing the door shut behind them, breathing heavily. The flat lay on the second floor, and they took the stairs up to it, moving softly, flattening back against the wall as the elevator suddenly sprang to life on some floor far above and sank past them softly, a brief circle of light descending with it down the walls.

The apartment door took longer. There were two locks, one morticed, which had to be levered off its bolts by pure force, the wood rending loudly as the metal plate came away from the doorframe. The bolts should have been sunk deeper into the brick, or better still, into a steel-and-concrete socket; but they were in, the door damage minimal. The tall black one set to work to screw the locks back into place and rebolt the door. The white one, big and burly, was already in the bedroom, jerking an empty suitcase up onto the bed and flinging it open. Then he went about the room, pulling open drawers, sifting through the contents, discarding clothing, ties, handkerchiefs, but throwing any paper or notes he could find into the suitcase, removing everything that might be useful. Then he snapped the lid of the suitcase shut, picked it up, and headed for the living room, meeting the other man in the doorway.

"I've done in here. I'll do the living room, you do the kitchen. See if there's a noticeboard, one of those cork jobs—or phone numbers on a pad by the blower, anything you can find—they said all the paper—right? All of it."

"Got it," the black man said.

They half filled the suitcase, throwing in all the paper they could find. They didn't look at it. They weren't interested in what they were taking, only in doing what they had been paid to do. When they had finished, they checked the flat over one more time; then, on an afterthought, the white man stepped outside to remove the bulb from the landing light. Back inside, he removed the bulb from the socket in the hall as well. Then they pulled chairs over to the window and sat down to wait. They waited, saying nothing, shifting quietly in their chairs, for nearly an hour, until the black one fumbled in his pockets, and the scrape of a match sounded loudly in the room.

"Don't!" the white man hissed sharply. "Put it out."

"One cigarette, man . . . a little *ganja* helps pass the time."

"No. Put it out."

Silence. Another fifteen minutes passed.

"When they phone? You sure we get a tip?"

"They'll phone when he leaves. Just relax."

"I can relax more with a little *ganja.*"

"You heard. No *ganja.* You don't need dope, not now."

They both jumped when the phone rang shrilly, shattering the silence, until the white man got up and answered it, listening briefly, putting it down and picking his way carefully to his chair.

"He's coming," he said. "In a taxi. He'll be here in fifteen, maybe twenty minutes and he definitely has the stuff we want. It's a file on the Boss, and he's been trying to flog it at the Yard."

"He's the grass?" the black man asked. "He's the one shopping Mr. Bright to the piggies?"

The white man grunted again, settling again into the chair by the window.

"So they say. He's just an old snitch who needs sorting out. What's it to you, anyway? You already got paid for the job."

"It's nothin' to me. I jus' don't like grassers . . . one got me three years in the Scrubs. Still, I fixed him good the night I got out."

The white man said nothing. They continued to wait.

From the window, hidden by the curtain, they saw him arrive and get out of the taxi, walking up the steps to the house. They heard him on the far side of the front door, listening as he snapped at the light switch and muttered— then there was a rattle of keys and a scratching at the lock. The door swung open, and they stayed back in the shadows, letting him get well inside the hall, a hand groping for the inner switch, before they struck.

Shoulders slamming into the door, knocking the bolt plate loose, they were on him in a rush, iron bar and hammer swinging, striking for the glint of silver hair, hitting hard, driving the man down. He fought back, briefly, until a blow broke his forearm and another crushed in his skull above one eye. They had been told to make sure, very sure, so they kept on hitting until the man's head was soft and pulpy, and their shoes began to stick on the bloody carpet. Only then did they stop, their breath coming quick and heavy, chests heaving and hands unsteady.

"Jesus!" said the black one, panting. "Let's go. Let's get out of here." He had the door open before the other man caught his arm and hauled him back, the door swinging loose behind him.

"No! Wait! Not yet. Get the suitcase. Get it, you prick! Hurry!"

In the pause, he turned the body over, flipped open the blood-soaked jacket, and began to go through the pockets, tossing wallet, diary, checkbook, notebook, and keys into the open case, picking up the briefcase to add that to their haul, squashing the lid down to force the locks home.

"Come on, man," the black one said softly, urgently. "Come on. Let's get out of here."

"I'm coming. Keep calm. Move slow."

They left as they had come, running quickly but quietly down the stairs. Then they were gone, disappearing into the night, amid the turmoil of the London rush hour.

It was nearly seven before the lady across the hall began to worry about the open door. It had been open, if only just ajar, when she arrived home at six, but after she had replaced the light bulb in the hall, she noticed the deep grooves on the lock plate and the hanging bolt. Finally, she pushed the door open and went in timidly, knocking gently on the hall table, calling out "Hello" several times, softly, in the dark. She had just begun to realize that her shoes were sticking in something when she fell over the body.

From the kitchen right through to the bedroom, the flat was a shambles. Every drawer had been removed, emptied, and then thrown in a heap in the middle of the room. The body was lying just outside the living-room door, the head oozing onto the bright green pile of the hall carpet, but the slaughter had clearly taken place in the darkness of the hall.

Once they had replaced the light bulb, they could see the long, sweeping lines of blood flecks up the walls and ceiling, even the scores and dents in the plaster where some heavy implement had struck again and again at the start of its swing.

"Well, whoever he is, they really did a job on him, didn't they?" Inspector Fitzwater said thoughtfully, looking down at the body. "Any ideas, Stan?"

"Not yet," said his sergeant, scribbling in his notebook. "Give us a chance. Obviously, more than one did this, but I don't think it's just one of your run-of-the-mill burglaries. They left the radio in there, a nice one, and his watch, and a brand-new telly, see? They really hammered the old boy . . . well, he's not young anyway, though you can't really tell . . . but there's bits of white hair under all that blood. They must have been looking for something—the place has been well rummaged. His wallet, diary if he had one, pocket contents, all gone. Once the lab boys have finished, we'll have a proper go-round, but it looks like a setup. The lady who found him said he had only moved in there days ago. Once we find out who he is, that may give us the answer. I'll get onto the letting agents and see if they have a name."

They didn't have to wait that long. Catton saw the blue lights flashing far ahead as he drove up Highgate Hill and felt the first, somehow half-expected nudge of alarm. Sure enough, checking the house numbers, he found the police cars were parked outside Wintle's flat. He pulled in behind and stopped, switching off the windshield wipers and killing the engine, his heart pounding loudly in his chest.

"What do you think is going on?" Christine asked anxiously.

"God knows," replied Catton, winding down the window. "But I'll find out."

"You can't stop here," said a policeman, moving toward the car, one hand held up. "Move on now, and quickly. There's nothing for you to see here. Come on, move it!"

"Take it easy, Constable," said Catton, producing his warrant card. "What's going on here? What's the trouble?"

"Sorry, sir," said the constable, saluting. "I can't say exactly. Pretty nasty though. The lab boys have gone in . . . you know? The inspector is inside, if you want to ask him."

"I see," Catton said slowly. "Chris, you'd better wait here while I find out what's happened. It might not be too nice."

"Let me come with you." She unclipped the seat belt and reached for the door handle.

"I'd rather you didn't," he said. "This is a police matter."

"If it concerns Philip, it's also a personal matter, and anyway, I'm coming. I've seen unpleasant things before."

"Come on then."

There were plenty of policemen in the entrance hall, but they slowly parted as Catton led Christine up to the second floor, his identity card held before him like Aaron's rod. On the second landing, a photographer was blasting away, his flashgun sending stark white bursts of light over the stairwell as he took shots of the hall from a doorway. What Catton glimpsed inside made him stop in midstride.

"Jesus Christ!" he exclaimed softly, pushing Chris behind him. "You stay out here . . . don't look. And don't argue."

A uniformed inspector, frowning, came edging down the hall toward them, stepping carefully but quickly into the hall, his voice edged with anger.

"Who the hell are you? Who let you in here?"

Catton held out his card again. "I'm John Catton, Inspector. Commander Catton from the Yard. What's going on? This lady is all right, she's with me." The inspector studied the card for a moment before looking up.

"Looks like there's been a murder, Commander. The Murder Squad are already on their way. Can you help on this? Do you know who he is in there?"

"I'm afraid so," Catton said. "Where's the body?"

"In there. But you'd better stay out here, miss."

Minutes later, the phone calls started. Catton to Kleiner: "Klaus? It's John Catton. Shut up and listen. They've hit Philip. He's dead. In his flat. Yes, I'm quite certain. I'm there now. Get onto Yates and Quarry. No, I don't know who did it, but the place has been ransacked, every bit of paper gone. Think about that. No, I can't, I've got other things to do. You get on with it, and I'll call you later. Oh, and Klaus—ring Quarry."

Catton again: "Heathrow? Give me Airport Security. I don't *care* if the line is busy, this is a Red Alert call. Well, cut in. My name is Catton. I'm on the list, but hurry. Hello! Who am I talking to? My name is Catton. This is a Red Alert. I want you to get someone over to Terminal Two and hold any flights for Spain, especially the Málaga flight, and Gibraltar too . . . hold them until I get back to you. Hello . . . Gatwick? Give me Airport Security. This is a Red Alert call. I want a hold on any charter flights to Spain . . ."

Kleiner to Yates: "Ten minutes ago. Yes, I'm quite certain. Catton wouldn't make a mistake like that. Shocked, stunned, what do you think? Right now I hardly give a damn about your bloody minister. Philip Wintle was a friend of mine."

Yates: "I'm afraid so, Minister . . . really, there is no need to shout. I have no idea. I did not conceal from you that matters might become delicate. Well, in that case, the less you know, the better, Minister. Quite so. I will keep you informed. And good night to you too, Minister."

Ted Bardsey to Freddie Bright: "They killed him . . . those fucking apes of yours *killed* him. Don't you dare hang up on me, Fred. It was supposed to be a simple mugging to nick the stuff. Of course I'm sure. It's all over the Yard. He was a *copper,* Freddie. I'm not panicking, I'm bloody terrified. I'm getting out of here right now and keeping my head down, and I don't ever want to hear from you again. What? Go screw yourself, Freddie."

The news hit Simon Quarry like a blow, driving the breath from his body in a groan. He swayed a little on his feet, and put out one hand to steady himself against the wall, clutching the telephone tightly.

"What is it?" Lucia hissed anxiously from her seat at the dinner table. "Tell me what's the matter."

He held out his hand, shushing her, still listening. "Yes, I understand . . . yes. I'll be over tomorrow. I'll catch the first flight. I don't care what you think . . . I'm coming. No, she'll stay here. I'll make her. Yes, yes . . . I agree. It might be safer. Thank you for calling, Klaus. Good night."

He put the receiver down and stood there for a moment, his face set, looking across the room and out of the terrace doorway into the soft Spanish night, rubbing the back of his hand slowly across his lips, his face working. Lucia had never seen anyone look like that.

"It's something terrible, isn't it?" she asked, rising from the table and moving toward him, one hand outstretched. "What's happened? Simon! Who was it on the phone?"

"That was Kleiner. They've killed Philip, that's what's happened. Those bloody bastards have killed him. I'll . . . I'll . . . Philip never did any harm to anyone, and they killed him . . . Jesus! What in the name . . . get me a drink, will you . . . I think I'm going to choke."

"What . . . who? Oh my God . . . No!"

Her hands shaking, it took Lucia some time to fill the brandy glasses, and it was actually Lito, shocked and quiet, who placed the drinks on a tray and carried them into the study, while Magdalena came out and watched them from the kitchen door, wiping her hands nervously on a towel. Simon was standing in front of his desk, his face still working, clasping and unclasping his fists. Lucia found her legs unsteady, and collapsed suddenly onto the sofa.

"Simon, please. Don't look like that," she said unsteadily. "Come and sit down here . . . please. Tell me what has happened."

"I'm very sorry, Señor Simon," Lito said softly. "He was a very nice man, Señor Philip. Magdalena and I . . . we are both very sorry. You should drink this, Señor Simon, *por favor.*"

"Find one yourself, Lito," said Simon, handing one of the glasses to Lucia, "and then get back in here." His voice was thick, as if the words would not come out past the lump in his throat, but when Lito returned with another glass, Simon had more control of himself.

He sat down, took Lucia by the hand. "This was not a

coincidence. They broke into his flat—someone set him up, and when I find out who . . . Meanwhile, we are going to fort up. I don't know what has happened back there yet, but we are not taking any chances down here. There's no bloody peace, is there? You can try to find it, but there's no bloody peace. I never wanted this, Lucia, you know that."

"Simon . . . please," Lucia said. "Let's talk this over."

He ignored her. "Lito, get out the twelve-gauge pump and keep it by you. Get buckshot in the four-ten and stash it in the kitchen. Activate the wire alarms and the fence cameras. Find the *señorita* here a pistol, and if anyone pokes his nose in here uninvited, cut loose. Right? *¿Claro?*"

"Sí, Señor Simon."

"Good . . . what else?"

"Simon," said Lucia, pleading, sinking her fingers into his arm. "You are upset . . . we all are, but don't do anything rash. We need time to think this through."

Simon broke away from her, striding away across the room to throw open the door of the gun cabinet, returning with his old black squat shotgun held in his hands, placing it before them on his desk, opening the drawer to pull out a box of cartridges.

"I've thought it through," he said. "All I can think of now is who would willfully beat an old friend of mine to death. I can't think of anything else. I'm sorry about that, but I can't help it." He picked up his glass and peered into it before raising it to them. "If that's the way it is, then that's the way it is. *¡Salud!*"

"¡Salud!" Lito and Lucia said quietly.

Much later that night, Freddie Bright and Vargas were sitting round a table on Freddie's terrace, examining the material taken from Philip Wintle's flat. Freddie was far from happy. There had been that phone call from Ted; his two lads, just arrived from London, were curious about the fuss; and here he sat, with ten of Vargas's crew lounging about the room, earwigging every word, while his own boys were kept outside.

"They have been busy, your English policemen," said

Vargas, looking up from the Catton Report. "We should have killed Larry Teal before we did. He started all this. If you have any doubts about someone, Freddie, then it is best to eliminate them. It is by far the best way. Believe me, I know."

This was not the sort of talk that Freddie cared for. Quite apart from anything else, there was the thin edge of a threat in there somewhere.

"Maybe," he grunted, "but it's not our way. Over the years, I've had to put a few people out of the way, but this is very messy, Mr. Vargas. Ted was shitting himself tonight, and we need Ted for protection, for tip-offs. I don't want him upset, see? My boys aren't too happy either. They've already rumbled that this wasn't just some old narc they knocked over. When they find out who he really was, they might get in a panic. Whacking a copper is serious stuff in England, Mr. Vargas."

Vargas shrugged. "So, pay them a little more, and keep them here until things are quieter. Since your people are so sensitive about killing, you can leave the next one to me." He leaned forward and tapped Freddie on the knee with one sharp, manicured fingernail. "But I'll have no opposition. You understand me?"

"The next one?" Freddie's voice was almost a squeak. "Haven't you done enough? Who now, for godsake? Mr. Vargas, be reasonable. Things just aren't done this way."

Vargas slapped Freddie's knee with the Catton Report. "Don't you see what they are doing, eh? It's all here. They have done like the Americans, and set up a team to hunt us down. Who do they think they are dealing with, eh? Well . . . they will have to be taught a lesson. In the background, they keep this man Quarry, their enforcer . . . now, he has to be hit. He lives here, in Spain, on my ground. Listen, Freddie . . . to get this concession, I have had to buy whole countries. I have given a fortune—a fortune—to the Cartel, to get a free hand here in Europe. I will not have these little English people in my way. Is that clear, Freddie? Do you understand that?"

"But I can't have any trouble in Spain," Freddie said

desperately. "I've got no place to run if they kick me out of here. I'll handle the London end like we agreed, but trouble here in Spain is just not on. I'm not shitting on my own doorstep."

Freddie was not just a cipher. He had run a manor in London, and he didn't scare easily, or hardly at all. Vargas felt that and eased back a little.

"You will have no trouble. I have my own people here," he said. "But your people need to learn how my people operate. I have heard from Majorca that Quarry has only two people living in his house, as well as his woman. So, I shall send six of my people to deal with them. But I shall need your boat. . . ."

"My boat?" Freddie gasped. The idea took his breath away. The sixty-foot Riva at Puerto Banus was the apple of his eye. "Why my boat, for Christ's sake? Look, Mr. Vargas, I—"

"Majorca is an island," Vargas went on smoothly. "Six Latinos might be noticed arriving at the airport, and then there is the hardware they must take in. Quarry's house is just a few miles from the sea. . . . So? Anyway, this is not your concern. You want to stay out of it, yes? So stay out of it. Just give me the keys to the boat."

"I don't want nothing to happen to my boat," Freddie said desperately. "That's an expensive machine. It cost me a right packet, Mr. Vargas."

"Just give me the keys," said Vargas, holding out his hand, "and I will deal with Quarry. The keys . . ."

= 8 =

From his post at the window of the Customs Office, Catton spotted Simon coming across the arrivals' hall, his face set. He ran down the stairs, pushed through the crowd of people awaiting the arrivals on the concourse, and took up his position in the front rank, leaning on the rail among the chauffeurs. Simon saw him as he came through the door.

"Thanks for meeting me. You must be busy."

"No problem," Catton said. "I was coming to the airport anyway. Look, do you feel like a coffee? We need to talk."

They went up to the mezzanine floor, took cups from the counter, and made their way over to a small table in the corner where their talk could be submerged in the babble from the other tables.

"So, what happened?" asked Simon, hunched over his cup.

"We were hit," Catton said briefly. "I'll tell you all I know. . . ."

"And that's it?" Simon asked when Catton had finished. "No leads, no ideas, nothing?"

"I have plenty of ideas," Catton said. "When I realized that this couldn't just be two muggers robbing an old man who disturbed them in his flat, I tried to block anyone getting the hell out of here with all Philip's stuff, *and* a copy of my report. I'm certain that's what they were after. They left the valuables but took every scrap of paper. I think they would go to Spain, because that's where Vargas is. Anyway, no villain would willingly stay in England after killing a policeman, even a retired one. The Met is seething ... every copper on the force is out there working—even those on leave reported back to help. Anyway, I was too late to stop whoever it was getting away. The Málaga and Madrid flights had left, and were already outside our airspace. I phoned Madrid, pulled a little wire, but got no joy. The Spanish customs kindly rummaged the passengers at Madrid but found nothing, and the Málaga flight passengers had already cleared the airport. We stopped two charters at Gatwick and another at Luton, but they were just holiday-makers, booked up months ahead."

"So, zilch?"

"Well, not quite. That's partly why I'm here—to collect the passenger lists from Iberia. I have them here. I also had a natter with a girl at the late check-in desk. She said two Anglos arrived late, with a heavy suitcase. She remembers them because one was black and one was white, and they were so late they had to check in the suitcase at the gate. The snag is that she can't remember the names—and the printout is alphabetical, so it's not the last two names on the list. However, we can run all the names through the Records computer at the Yard and see if any match. If the young lady's Anglos are in there, that helps. Otherwise, we still have a problem, because half the people on this list could be Colombians. There must be twenty called García."

"So, if the killers don't have records, you are back at square one."

"Not at all. Anyone into heavy work will have made his way there from petty crime, so we'll have him somewhere. Also, I'm now going to phone Ted Bardsey, the commander at Major Crimes, and ask him to run his eye down this list. He knows every villain in London, and if anyone here works for a major firm, especially one controlled out of Spain, Ted will know. This is straight police work, Simon. I'll go and ring Ted now, and get him to meet us. Do you want another coffee?"

Simon shook his head. "This'll do me. You go ahead, I'll wait here."

Catton was back inside five minutes, frowning. "It never rains but it pours," he said. "Ted isn't in today. He reported sick last night, and they don't know when he'll be back. Anyway, I've got his home address, so we can nip round and see him on the way back to town. He lives in Sunbury, down by the river. He can't be *that* sick, because I saw him at four yesterday afternoon, and he looked fine then. Coming?"

Inside the car, reaching for the ignition, Catton nodded toward the glove compartment. "The times they are a-changing," he said. "So look in there and you'll find a pistol permit. You will also find a .38. I didn't know if you were carrying, so I brought one for you."

"Are you? Carrying?"

"Bloody right I am. So is Kleiner." Catton switched off the engine and hitched himself around in his seat toward Simon. "We'd better get something clear," he said. "I worked for Philip Wintle for six years. He got me my job at the Branch, trained me, groomed me. He was also my friend. I take what happened as hard as you do."

"It's still different for me," said Simon, staring ahead through the windshield. "He went out on a limb for me, not once but several times. He put his reputation and his career, even his life, on the line for me, not once but several times. I should have been here, I should have looked after him. Instead, I sat down there in Majorca, playing house, while somebody beat him to death. I got Philip into these danger-ous games. Besides, I can't stay out of this even if I wanted to. Someone set Philip up, and that same someone—probably Señor Vargas—will know, or at least think, that I am involved in this business. I expect you saw that article in the paper? Well, I think that puts me in. I'd rather it didn't, but I don't have a choice. I have to think of Lucia."

Catton thought this over for a minute. "Well . . . I think I'm glad to hear that," he said. "As for Philip, I should have been more careful, because I know, better than anyone, what these people are like. Dammit, I did a full month in Miami, having it all set out before me. Almost the first question the DEA asked was, 'Are you carrying a gun?' but I thought them melodramatic. They told me all about the risks, the contracts, the killings, the bribes, the corruption, the leaks of information, but I only half listened because, like a typical smug Englishman, I thought it couldn't happen here. Whatever they do in the USA, whacking a policeman is unheard of here, except—had I but checked—where drugs are concerned. There have been three drug-related murders of police or Customs staff in the last year alone. The Cartel don't care who they hit or where. Sinker told me they followed one Colombian minister into Eastern Europe and shot him in Budapest. I should have listened."

"So you agree there is a leak?" Simon asked.

"Maybe. I'm not sure. But how did they know where he was? He'd only just moved there. Still, that newspaper clipping . . . that gossip piece certainly put us all together. That might have caused it, but I'm not dismissing the possibility of a leak. It's just that I have other things in my mind at the moment. Look out a map, will you, and steer me to Sunbury-on-Thames? You can wait in the car while I talk to Ted."

Freddie Bright and his minders were playing golf. Or rather, Freddie was playing golf, putting and chipping his way around the smooth greens of the *campo de golf* while his men trudged after him carrying the clubs, their shirts sticking to their backs, their mouths gritty after a long night on the whisky. On the fourteenth green, Freddie got down in one over par, shot the putter into his bag, and headed at a good pace toward the clubhouse.

"Come on," he called over his shoulder. "Bring the bag and I'll buy you a beer. Anyone asks, say you came here to play golf. Scores of people have seen you here this morning, so what could be more innocent?"

He said nothing more until the three of them were seated in front of three large glasses in a shady corner of the golf-club terrace, looking down toward the billiard-smooth greens where brightly clad golfers moved in and out between the sun and shadow.

117

"The beer down here is piss," said Freddie, wiping his mouth. "I'd give quite a lot for a pint of draught from any pub down the Mile End Road . . . but you can't have everything. At least down here we can have a natter without Señor Bleedin' Vargas earholing every word."

"He looks like a ponce," Errol said. "A poncy pimp. Last night he had on more jewelry than my bird wears down at the disco."

"He's a Colombian," said Freddie, shrugging. "They all look like that. Don't let it fool you. He's a mean one, and he's got a big crew with him."

"Where's the rest of his crew gone to?" Eddie asked. "I'd just got my head down when I heard them go roaring off, the bastards."

Freddie looked moody. "Half a dozen of 'em are buggering off tonight in my beautiful *Mariposa Acero,* that's what," he said. "My beautiful Riva in the hands of those berks! Breaks yer bleedin' 'eart."

"Your what?"

"My Riva. My boat, you stupid idiot. The *Steel Butterfly* . . . nice eh? Sounds even better in Spanish. She does twenty knots, flies like a bird. If they put a scratch on her, just one scratch, I'll do my bleedin' nut. Cost me the best part of three 'undred grand. The rest of Vargas's mob are over at the lab . . . behind the hill at the back of the house. I'll show you later."

"Where are they off to then?" Errol asked.

"Better you don't know," said Freddie, waving to a waiter. "I'll get three more pints of this piss, and put you in the picture."

"Thing is," he said, handing round the glasses, "our Mr. Vargas has been getting a bit out of order. He's our link to the coke trade, but he's a fucking animal, and now we're all in the shit."

"You mean *we* are," Eddie said. "That's what you really mean, ain't it?"

"Well, yes, you in particular. Brace yourselves for the bad news about that bloke you topped. He wasn't just any old narc—he was Philip Wintle. Heard of him? No? Well, he used to head the Special Branch at the Yard. Steady! I thought you ought to know, 'cos it'll be in the papers by this afternoon anyway. So you see, lads, we're in it deep."

The men changed color. Eddie's face went white, then mottled over slowly to a deep, rage-powered patchy red. Errol Washington went a tinge of green. The sick color spread up from his mouth, and when it reached his eyes, Freddie thought he was going to vomit his pint back up over the table.

"I thought I'd better tell you," Freddie said. "You don't want no nasty surprises. And keep it down, I don't need no scenes in here. No more do you. You've got to act natural, see?"

"You set us up, you . . ." Eddie said angrily. "We never took on to murder no copper. Every busy in Britain will be looking for who done it, and someone will talk for sure. Bloody hell . . . Jesus!" Eddie's voice faded away in obscenities.

"Man, that's heavy," said Errol, turning slowly toward Eddie. "There ain't no place for us to run from that kind of heat."

"Wait a minute," Freddie said soothingly. "Stay calm and have a think. He isn't a cop now, he's been retired for years and works for some rich Hun, so who gives a damn? Besides, you're my boys. I'll look after you. You're down here with me, playing golf, so who can touch you? You can stay here, help me keep an eye on Vargas, drink a little of this piss, work up a nice tan. In a week or two, when we see what's happening, you can go back to the Smoke and carry on as normal. Right?"

They thought it over for a while, exchanging glances, brooding over their glasses, getting used to the idea, getting over the shock.

"Haven't I always looked out for you?" Freddie asked, "and you've hammered people before this, right? I would've told you before, but . . . well . . . better you didn't know. What's the difference?"

"He's different, that's what's different," Eddie said. Eddie was the brighter one. "Dealing with the odd nosy, kicking

119

some prick who was getting seriously out of order, that's one thing—but this! Bloody hell, Fred! We could go down forever. Killing a copper is not on, Freddie."

"Well, it's done now, my son, and I'll slip you a little extra for the difference. Like a bonus."

They thought about that too, for a moment.

"How much extra?" Errol asked at last. Errol wasn't so dumb either.

Catton's car came bumping gently down the private road, rolling over the deep potholes in the surface, and across the high ridges of the "sleeping policemen," the tires crunching through the deep gravel that lay like a white carpet over the tarmac.

"That must be it," Simon said. "The Millstone . . . very funny. Is that it? Surely not?"

"It must be," said Catton, braking gently. They sat there for a moment, looking at the house through the screen of trees. It stood at the back of a long lawn, the smooth emerald grass broken here and there by flower beds and the graceful sweeping branches of weeping willow trees. Beyond that, at the edge of another gravel sweep before the house, a fountain sent sprays of water dancing in the morning sunshine, while beyond that again, on the red-tiled forecourt before the double garage, stood the sleek outline of a Jaguar XJ6. The house, long, mellow, and draped with red-leaved Virginia creeper, just failed to block a view of more lawn sweeping down to the river Thames behind.

"Nice," Simon said thoughtfully. "Very nice indeed. Very, very nice."

"Just what I was thinking," Catton said. "Very nice, very elegant. I didn't think that Ted had that much taste."

"Mmm . . . he's the same rank as you, isn't he? Tell me, how much do you earn? Or is that flash motor an issue vehicle? Perhaps your colleague is an eccentric millionaire, serving in the police force for a hobby?"

"Stop it, Simon. I know what you're thinking, but you're getting ahead of yourself."

"Well, could you afford a house like this on what you

earn? I'm not hard up for a quid or two, but that place would strain my resources."

"It might depend on when I bought it. Property prices have soared around here in the last ten years."

"It smells," Simon said flatly, "and you know it. Any leak must have come from your end. I wouldn't do it, you wouldn't do it. Kleiner wouldn't do it. Yates would do anything, but he needed Philip . . . that leaves your friend Bardsey, who knows every villain in the business . . . you said so yourself."

"You're jumping to conclusions. You don't even know the man."

"I'm using my head. He went sick rather suddenly, just after Philip got hit, didn't you say?"

"Yes, he did," Catton said slowly.

"It's something," said Simon, his eyes still on the house. "Is there anything else?"

"Maybe. Ted's been on my back ever since this thing started," Catton said. "At first I thought it might just be jealousy. He and I get on well enough professionally, but we aren't friends. He thinks I've raced up the promotion ladder on the strength of my degree, plus a bit of crawling. But he was more than keen to find out about the new setup. Also, he found the flat for Philip. So he could have fingered Philip— and then he suddenly goes sick. He was as right as rain yesterday afternoon. Philip went in to see him, to thank him for finding the flat, just before he left the Yard. So he knew where and when Philip could be attacked. But even so . . . hitting a fellow officer, even a retired one . . . no, I can't see Ted doing that . . . and it's still all conjecture, and Ted won't cough, ever. He's one of the old school, as hard as nails. I think we'll put off this visit for the moment." Catton put his car in reverse, rolled back down the road away from Bardsey's house, and began to turn.

"If he was responsible for what happened to Philip, he's in serious trouble anyway," Simon said. "Kleiner will hit him . . . or have it done."

"If you or Klaus have any respect for Philip's memory, you will remember his first rule—no gunplay on his patch," said Catton, accelerating away over the bumps. "If Ted is dirty, and it's still a big 'if,' I can nail him. You might consider what fun a former commander of the Major Crimes Squad will have if we send him to prison. A lot of old mates will be waiting for him in the showers. Shooting him might even be a kindness. Ah . . . here's a phone box. Wait here."

When Catton returned, nothing much was said until they were back on the motorway and speeding toward Central London. Catton kept his eyes on the road, but his face looked worried and his mouth was tense.

"Who did you call?" Simon asked. "Someone at the top?"

"CIB2—that's like . . . what? . . . Internal Affairs, the squad that checks on allegations of corruption. I gave them what little I had, and they didn't like it. I'll have to go in this afternoon and lay it out for them in detail. Allegations made against a senior officer, especially one with Ted's background, are a serious business. If it doesn't hold up, I'm in real trouble. I've already asked CIB2 to check on coppers who might have been overfriendly with villains now living on the Costa del Crime, but Ted's name didn't come up. It's all a bit thin, Simon."

"What will they do now?"

"Depends . . . sniff around a bit, then if they find anything, or think that mansion excessive, suspend him on full pay, for openers. Then they will open up his bank account, tax position, all his assets, and ask him to account for them. They'll keep digging. If they can prove nothing, but he is involved, then at least it will put a kink in his plans. It's pretty sad, really. He gets his pension in four years—and now this."

"It's funny though," Simon said, after a while. "It's all so stupid. Even if he is on the take, why flaunt it? You earn enough to live decently, and so must he. So why go over the top and live like a prince in a riverside house, with a flash car in the drive for everyone to see? It must stick out like a sore thumb."

"Not really," said Catton, still concentrating on the traffic. "Coppers don't mix much socially, and if we do, it's only in the pub or canteen, so who's to know? Besides, for people like Ted, if you have it and don't spend it, somehow you haven't really got it. Sticking it in the bank isn't the same thing. My only surprise—and this sounds snobbish, but I can't help it—my big surprise is that the house was so, well, *posh*. Very upper class. Ted has always struck me as a bit flash, as if the lifestyle of the villains he chases has rubbed off on him. Anyway, I hope he's clean. If not, the sky's going to fall in on him, one way or another."

A day later, twelve hours out from Puerto Banus, Freddie's big Riva was soaring over the waves, pounding heavily on the swell, crashing from crest to crest, as the big rollers came swooping in from the northeast. The southern coast of Spain was just in sight of the port beam, with lights beginning to show on shore, as the sun went down behind the mountains.

"I shall have to slow down," Ernesto said from the wheel. "The sea is really getting up, and anyway we don't have enough fuel to reach the island in one hop. It's just a summer storm and it won't last long, but we will have to put in somewhere and wait it out."

"We can go into Cartagena," said Carlosito, who sat in one corner of the wheelhouse, his back braced against the bulkhead. "We can wait out the storm there and refuel. Any way we do it, it's a two-day trip. I want us to get to this Puerto after dark tomorrow night, so throttle down to fifteen knots. Steer zero-ten degrees. We can go ashore for a few hours in Cartagena, and I will phone the *Jefe*. He will understand the delay."

"Cartagena, hey?" said Ernesto, spinning the wheel through his fingers and turning the Riva onto the new heading. "Just like home."

When the group gathered in Kleiner's office, the atmosphere was subdued. The directors' chef had done his best, and produced a great array of snacks to go with the wine, but nobody felt like eating, and the bottles remained unopened.

"The minister is, to say the least, shocked," Yates said.

"Fortunately, the news of Wintle's death won't appear until the later editions, so if there are no leaks, he can avoid Question Time in the House till Thursday. Even so, the killing of someone of Wintle's professional standing, with his links to you, Klaus, is bound to invite comment. There may be some back-pedaling on our proposals. We shall have to see."

Kleiner shrugged. "We already know all we need to know. As far as I am concerned, killing Philip has made this a personal matter, and we will proceed with or without official backing. You can tell the minister to sit tight and keep his nose out of this business. Unless you prefer that I tell him myself?"

Yates smiled thinly at the suggestion. "If it comes to it, you may have to," he said. "I still have my career to think about."

"This is interesting," said Simon, looking up from the printout on the boardroom table. The list trailed out, across to the far side of the table and down onto the floor, and Simon had been studying it for some time, pulling it steadily through his fingers.

"What is?" Catton asked. "Have you found something useful?"

"Maybe. This man here, on the list of Costa del Crime villains. Terry Cockerill—I know him."

"Really? How?" Catton sounded more surprised than interested. "When?"

"Years ago. He was in the Marines with me. He was in my troop. In fact, when I was a lot younger and a little poorer, I used to stay with him and his wife, Renée, quite a lot. He was an explosives expert in the assault engineer platoon of my commando. Terry was very good at blowing things up."

Catton had taken a buff folder from the stack on a nearby table and was studying the contents. "It looks like he carried on blowing things up after he left the Marines," he said. "Like bank vaults and security vans. Nice friends you have, Simon. Just look at this. Cockerill has a sheet as long as your arm . . . petty crime, probation, Borstal, two years, one suspended . . . running prostitutes . . . very diverse occupations, plenty of form."

"Well, Terry liked the girls, but when he got married, Renée told him to get rid of them—she's very proper."

"Mmm, no particular record of violence . . . I'll give him that. Well, yes, indeed, here you are, Simon . . . a letter from you at the Quarry Press, offering Cockerill a job on early release from the Scrubs."

"He needed a job to get parole," Simon said mildly. "Anyway, what else are friends for? Before he got put away, he used to baby-sit for us after my second daughter was born. Besides, Renée asked me to help him, and she's a hard lady to refuse."

"Even though you knew he was a villain?"

Simon laughed shortly. "Terry was a villain long before he joined the Corps," he said. "His family have been villains since the eighteenth century, and so have Renée's. I did think he'd gone straight after he got out of the Corps, but then he turned up at one reunion in a pink Rolls-Royce and mentioned over a drink that he always kept ten grand in the glove compartment, and a shotgun under the front seat. That did make me wonder a bit."

"You are impossible," said Kleiner, smiling, "but could this friend of yours be useful?"

"Probably, if I put it to him the right way," Simon said. "Terry is a mate of mine, and you know what they say— 'Once a Marine, always a Marine.' My point is that if anything is going on along the Costa del Sol, Terry will probably know about it. Maybe I should fly down and see him? I'll chat him up for old times' sake, and see what he knows."

"Cockerill skipped the U.K. after taking three million in gold from the Heathrow Bullion Store," said Catton, still leafing through the file, "but his firm is still operating here. If he is the Cartel's connection, you could be walking right into their hands. I've seen what they do to people they catch, and you wouldn't like it."

Simon shook his head. "Terry wouldn't deal in drugs.

He's not the type. Even if he was, Renée wouldn't let him. If you think any different, you simply don't know Renée. Terry may run a firm, but Renée runs Terry."

"Maybe you should go down and see him," Kleiner said. "It's well worth it, and we need some lead to Vargas's U.K. connection."

"Then maybe I will," Simon said. "We can't sit here in the dark, waiting for what happens next, so I'll go down there after Philip's funeral. When is it?"

"The day after tomorrow," Catton said briefly. "The inquest is this afternoon, and after that the coroner will release the body. I've spoken to his daughter, and she wants the funeral as soon as possible. He'll be buried in the family plot, at Sixpenny Handley in Dorset. I suppose we will all go?"

"Of course we will," Kleiner said. "Sixpenny Handley— that's so British, but that somehow makes it right for Philip."

"Nothing will ever make it right for Philip," Simon said. "Nothing."

9

Lucia was sound asleep and dreaming when a hand gripped her bare shoulder, and a voice, Lito's voice, began whispering urgently in her ear, a hand shaking her awake roughly, urgently.

"Señorita . . . there are men in the garden."

Lucia came awake suddenly, in a flush of alarm, rolled over, and sat up, braced on her elbows, the sheet falling away from her breasts. Neither of them noticed nor cared, their heads close together, their eyes glinting at each other in the darkness of the room, speaking in whispers.

"What's the time? Are you sure?"

"Two? Three? *Pero sí.* Listen to the alarm."

Lucia could hear it now, the steady sharp bleeping from the repeater in the bedroom. There was another bleeper in the study, and another, the one that had roused him, in Lito's flat above the garage across the way. Lucia bit her lip, thought for a moment, then pushed him back and swung her legs out of bed.

"Cut it off," she said quietly, "and then check all the doors." As he moved away, silent on his bare feet, she reached under the bed and pulled out the shotgun, tossing it onto the pillow while she hurriedly pulled on her shorts and took her T-shirt from the chair. Then she picked up the weapon and padded out after Lito into the study. The bleeping stopped just as she passed through the door.

Out in the big cool room that occupied the whole front of the house, Lito had cut the bleeper and was crouched now over the radar screen, the green light turning his features ghastly. Lucia went over and crouched beside him, her eyes on the picture, watching the maze of dark and changing shadows on the screen.

"Mira," said Lito. He tapped the surface with his finger. "Three men . . . there were four."

There were men in the garden down by the fence, casting long shadows in the moonlight. The screen showed three of them, picked up and held by the gate camera. Lito fiddled with the focus and zoomed in on the group. Two of them carried small machine guns. Lucia felt a cold rush of fear sweep over her—then, like a counterwave, a hot flush that suddenly had her T-shirt sticking to her back.

"Hay otro," Lito said. "There is another one somewhere." He spun the control, rapidly switching from one camera to another, scanning the garden but finding nothing. When he switched the screen back to the gate camera, the three men there had gone.

"They are coming in," he whispered urgently. "What shall we do, Señorita?"

Simon said it was always like this, and better when the action started. She wished he were here. "We're going to get the hell out of here," she said quietly. "Where is Magdalena?"

"In our *casita,* down on the floor. I locked her in before I came here . . . she is safe enough."

"Get her out—take the twelve-gauge from the kitchen and go back along the roofwalk and over the wall. I'll meet you on the hill at the back. Hurry!"

When he had gone, the swing door to the kitchen slapping softly behind him, Lucia thought for a minute, then snapped off the screen, and putting the shotgun into the crook of one arm, she closed the cupboard doors and began to pad back toward the bedroom. She needed shoes. She was halfway across the room when the shooting started.

The killers began by machine-gunning the front of the house, pumping half a magazine each through all the

128

windows. With luck, that might kill the Anglos, directly or by ricochet. If not, then it would frighten them, and the surprise would bring them out of bed to their feet, putting them in position for the second phase. Then the grenades came in, three of them. Two made it, arcing silently through the shattered glass, one bouncing into the bedroom, one into the study, clattering as they rolled across the tiled floor. The third hit the shuttered window frame, came back off the closed slats of the venetian blind, and rattled down the steps, forcing the men below to scatter, before it rolled into the pool and exploded.

When the shooting started, Lucia flung herself down and huddled close to the outer wall, and when the grenade sailed in over her head and went off, it was not being up on her feet that saved her. The metal fragments lacerated the room, shredding the furniture, shattering the window glass, licking the walls with a fireball of flame, but missed her. She crawled away along the floor, cutting her hands and knees on the broken glass, and got up fighting mad.

"Right," she said aloud. "Right! That bloody does it." She stood before the bookcase, where the glass was still miraculously intact, and with no time for keys, drove the butt of the shotgun through the glass. Simon kept a pistol in there, behind the books. She just had her hands on it when the shooting started again outside, the heavy boom of a 12-gauge coming from the roof above her head.

Lito had come back. Although he was halfway out when the gunfire started, they were killing the *señorita* in there, and so he came back, crouching below the parapet of the walkway between his flat and the main house, coming out onto the roof just as the spout of water from the grenade in the pool fell with a mighty slap across the tiles. As he reached the parapet and peered over, one of the killers was rushing up the steps just below. When the gunman reached the terrace, Lito fired both barrels full into his chest. He would have done more and was kneeling below the wall to reload, the ejected cartridges flying out over his shoulder, but the fourth man came onto the roof behind and put a long burst into Lito's back. The impact lifted Lito off the roof, and sent him out and over, curling through the air. He was dead before he hit the terrace. The man turned and ran off along the walkway, raking the door of Lito's flat with the remains of the magazine, then lobbed a grenade down through the open garage doors. There were two cars in there, cans of kerosene for the mowers, drums of gasoline for those days when the filling stations were shut. Seconds after the grenade exploded, the garage erupted, wrapping the flat above in a great gushing tulip of flame.

Lucia killed the second man. The gunman had rushed the steps, leaping over his partner, over Lito's sprawled body, firing as he came, bouncing his shoulder off the locked door, then coming to the window and flinging his leg over the sill, clawing for the pistol on his belt, yelling to his friend behind to come on. Standing just to the side of the window, her back flat against the wall, Lucia put the pistol muzzle against his knee and fired. Until they invented the Magnum, the Colt Python she had in her fist had been the most powerful handgun in the world. Most of the man's leg came off. Lucia put the pistol on the table, picked up the shotgun, and, stepping fully into the window, looked out to where the man was rolling and screaming, back across the tiles. Trembling, she fired into him twice before he lay still. It was then, in the light of the flames from the garage, that she saw Lito's body and thought with a rush of Magdalena.

"Magdalena!" Lucia rushed across the room, cutting her feet to ribbons on the shards of glass, through the swing doors into the kitchen, as more bullets thrashed the walls behind, then through the back door and up the outer stairwell, taking the steps three at a time. The man on the roof leapt off the walkway as she burst through the outer door, and they exchanged fire, but his hasty burst missed, rattling across the roof into the night. Lucia pumped the action and fired again, seeing the buckshot whipping at his shirt. Ten strides across the roof she skidded to a stop, halted by the heat from the flames ahead, and leaned over the wall to fire at the man again as he crawled painfully away into the bushes. Up ahead, the garage and the flat were hidden in a roaring wall of flame. Even as she stood out there, shielding her face from the searing heat, a gasoline tank went up, the explosion rocking the building, blowing out the walls. There was nothing she could do now for Magdalena.

There was more shooting now, a crash of glass, the thump of another grenade from somewhere below. The last man was taking his time, clearing his way through the house toward her, room by room, first putting in a burst of gunfire, then a grenade, then leaping in after it. Meanwhile, the wounded man below, down but not out, began to chip at her, firing single shots from somewhere in the trees, trying to pin her in the firelight until his friend could come up behind and box her in. Lucia dropped below the parapet and crawled back across the terrace, waiting until she heard the crash of a grenade in the kitchen, more firing, and the thud of the lower door. Then she emptied the shotgun down the stairwell, pumping the action, firing again and again, long tongues of flame pouring from the muzzle before the hammer clicked. Then she dropped the gun and vaulted over the rear wall, falling heavily onto the rocky ground, and fled away up the hillside into the sheltering darkness of the trees.

It was raining, softly, gently, persistently. The grass was soaking it up, the turned earth exhaling a soft, distinctive smell, evocative of England in the rain. Simon Quarry stood at the back of the small gathering, letting the rain patter down onto his shoulders, the sound of drops on the umbrellas almost drowning out the soft murmur of the vicar's voice ". . . has but a short time to live and is full of sorrow. He riseth up and is cut down like a flower . . ."

Simon was glad the vicar had kept to the old version of the service; Philip would have preferred that. The coffin rested on muddy planks stretched across the open grave, the raindrops gathering on the brass plate: PHILIP JOHN WINTLE 1923–1989. So Philip had been sixty-six when he had been cut down, like a flower, ". . . in sure and certain hope . . . our dear brother here departed . . . ashes to ashes . . ."

Simon knew when these words came, it was nearly over.

Soon the mourners would go away, and the grave would be closed, and slowly but with gathering speed, life would go on again. He caught Kleiner's eye as the party around the grave broke up, and saw the vicar speaking to Wintle's daughter, who stood by the path, holding her small son firmly by one hand. Simon joined the line of people waiting to say a few words, glancing down at the wet sprays of flowers and wreaths and hearing the heavy thuds as thick clods of Dorset earth began to fall on Wintle's coffin.

Up ahead, Catton had already broken away from the line and was hurrying toward the gate, throwing an apologetic glance over his shoulder. Curious, Simon watched him, then looked beyond to where Kleiner's chauffeur was beckoning frantically from the gate. What now? Simon wondered. Then Kleiner too was heading after Catton, shaking the girl's hand briefly before turning hurriedly away and breaking into a trot. Then it was Simon's turn.

"I'm very sorry," he said inadequately. "Your father was a fine man . . . we will all miss him." She was a pleasant young woman, her face set but coping well with this sudden tragedy. A naval officer's wife, Simon remembered, her husband away at sea.

"You are Simon Quarry, aren't you?" she said. "My father said you were to have all his books. He was very fond of reading."

They stood there in the rain for a moment, clasping hands. There were no tears in her eyes, no blame, no reproach, just friendship. Simon tried to think of something to say, but nothing came.

"I'll pack them up for you," she said, pushing him away gently. "I think your friends want you. But when you are free, I would like to talk to you about my father."

Simon turned away and walked quickly past the other mourners toward the lych-gate where the chauffeur was still sheltering and through which Kleiner and Catton had already disappeared.

"What's going on?" he asked, pushing the gate open. "What's all the fuss about?"

"I don't know, sir," the chauffeur said. "There was a phone call from London, and I was told to get you all on the line, urgent."

Kleiner was coming back toward him, running down the footpath past the parked cars, his face set, the persistent rain plastering his fair hair across his forehead.

"What's up?" Simon asked again. "Not more trouble?"

"Now listen," said Kleiner, taking him by the arms, holding him tightly above the elbows. "It's bad news. They hit your house last night—and Lucia is missing."

Lucia knew the mountains. She and Simon walked there every day. Up there, in a little rocky hollow in the hillside, he had taught her to shoot—pistol, rifle, shotgun. She didn't like it much, but she did it, learning how to keep both eyes open, to swing the barrel onto the target, to squeeze the trigger gently. Then she started to hit things, and before long, she was hitting the targets often. There was even pleasure in that, of a kind.

Lucia ran away from the flames, on up the bare hillside, hopping from one sharp-edged rock to another, slashing her feet to pieces, up to the little cave where, so Simon had told her, the rock doves came to nest in the spring. From there, she saw the fire blaze up and fade away, guttering down to a dim red glow. Even up here, half a mile from the house, she could smell the burning and feel the gentle rain of ash drifting across the hillside. When it began to get light, a gray chill dawn, she stayed on in the cave, shivering with cold and shock. It was not until the sun was well up and she saw the green figures of the Guardia Civil sweeping up the mountain toward her that she crawled out of her hole and found that she was unable to stand. It was by following her blood-stained footprints that they eventually found her.

A police escort can be useful. Siren on, blue lights flashing, the car ahead touched 120 miles an hour on its way to the airport near Southampton, forcing Kleiner's chauffeur to the limits of his skill just to keep up. Kleiner's jet was already on the tarmac, engines still running after the brief flight from London, and after a few words with Catton, they ran up the steps, and were hardly in their seats before the little aircraft was racing down the runway and soaring out over the sea.

When the aircraft leveled off, Kleiner got up and went to the bar, returning with two large brandies.

"I don't want it," said Simon, pushing the glass away.

"No, but you need it," Kleiner said, "and so do I. Take it and drink up."

They sat together for a moment or two, brooding, Simon's eyes on the sea far below, watching the approaching coast of France.

"This is almost like old times," Kleiner said. "We should have learned the lesson back in Milan. Do it to them before they do it to you."

"They aren't doing it to us, they are doing it to Philip and Lito and Magdalena and Lucia. I hope to God they don't have Lucia. Can't this plane of yours go any faster?"

"We'll be there in less than ninety minutes . . . the Guardia say they will meet us at the airport. You had better decide what we are going to say when they start asking questions."

"What about?"

"About why a gang should murder your people and burn your house down. About what is going on."

"I'll tell them the truth, and the truth is, I don't know why."

"Whatever you do, don't tell them the truth!" Kleiner said. "Tell them anything, but not that. Vargas and his people, the people who did this, and probably killed Philip, are somewhere in Spain. If you let the Spanish police know what we are doing, it will get complicated, and they will certainly tie our hands. Besides, we can have no linkage with the British government. Remember what Yates said."

"I don't give a damn what Yates said."

"Well, neither do I, but the rest still holds. I suggest you act shocked and stay silent. You certainly look ghastly enough. Leave the talking to me, and don't let on why we were in London. Two killings in a week is too much of a coincidence for even the Spanish police to swallow."

"So what do I tell them?"

Klaus shook his head and got up to pour himself another brandy. "I don't know yet, but I'm working on it—just leave it to me."

Kleiner lied very well. The big green Guardia car was hardly out of the airport, speeding down the Via Cintura toward Inca, when the *capitán* began the inevitable questions.

"I think I can answer that, *Capitán*. I think these men, whoever they are, were after me. Have you seen this?" From his wallet, Kleiner produced the gossip clipping and the photograph from *¡Hola!* "That also appeared in several foreign newspapers. Some time ago, I became the target for a group of kidnappers in Italy. Mr. Quarry was very helpful to me there. I can only think that this photograph revealed my present whereabouts to another gang, or it may even be the same gang, and they made another attempt to seize me, or even to kill me. We industrialists lead dangerous lives, *Capitán*. I can give you the telephone number of a Captain Cirillo, with the Squadra Anti-Terrorismo in Milan. He will confirm this."

I bet he will, Simon thought, half-admiringly. This is the way to tell lies, stringing them like pearls along a thin thread of truth.

"Unfortunately, or fortunately," Kleiner continued, "Mr. Quarry and I were absent. This is still a tragedy . . . but thank you for the good news about Señorita Fiori. What is your name, *Capitán?* I shall mention your swift action to the minister next time I am in Madrid. . . ."

Lucia was with the Sisters of Charity in Puerto, lying in a narrow bed in a small whitewashed room, her feet cleaned of glass but still swollen and wrapped in bandages, her face pale and drawn. Klaus stayed only a moment, to kiss her on the cheek and press her hand. Then, shaking his head warningly at Simon, he slipped out and left them alone, closing the door quietly behind him.

Simon sat on the edge of the bed and watched the tears well up slowly out of her eyes and run down onto the pillow, her throat working as she tried to speak.

"They killed Lito," she said at last, thickly. "He came back to help me, and they killed him."

"I know . . . the police told me."

"They killed Magdalena. Lito locked her in to stop them getting her, and she couldn't get out. They burned her alive. They burned your house down."

"I know," Simon said. "I should have been there. I wish I had been there."

She lifted her head from the pillow and looked at him, searching his face with her eyes.

"What are you going to do?" she asked.

Simon's shoulders lifted slightly. "I don't know yet. We're working on it," he said. "I want you to rest here. I have to go up to the house and see about Lito and Magdalena. Then we will decide what to do. I'll be back soon, I promise."

She clutched at his hand, grasping it hard. "I don't want you to go," she said desperately. "I need you here. I need you. . . ."

"I have to go," he said, taking his hand away, "but I will be back very soon. I promise. And then we can talk. And, Lucia, there will be an end to all this, believe me."

"No, there won't," she said wearily, letting her head fall back on the pillow. "Death follows you around, Simon, wherever you go. It will always be like this."

He rose from the chair and looked down at her for a moment, letting his eyes stray from her face down to the bandaged feet. "I'll be back soon," he said again. "I promise. And it won't always be like this. I'll find a way to escape."

The man who met them at the house was in plainclothes, a tall officer with a grim face and hard eyes, nobody's fool. He stood at the top of the steps, his back to the gutted house, and watched them come slowly toward him, his eyes flicking curiously from one to the other.

"Buenas tardes, Señor Kleiner. Señor Quarry? I am sorry to meet you for the first time like this. I hope the *señorita* is feeling better." His English was perfect. "Señor Quarry, I do not like to ask you, but can you . . . please . . ." He gestured to the shrouded bodies laid out on the heat-cracked tiles of the terrace. At his nod, the young Guardia pulled back the sheets, turning his head away from the sight and the buzzing cloud of flies.

"That man is Lito Lopez. He lived here and worked for me. I don't know the other one. I have never seen him before."

The plainclothes man nodded, and the Guardia replaced the sheets. "There is another body in the fire, but I think we can assume it is that of Señora Magdalena Lopez. Well, the autopsy will show. I will not ask you to look."

"I don't mind looking," Simon said briefly, "if it will help find the bastards who did all this." He waved his hand around, indicating the bodies and the house. His home was a wreck. The garage was just a jumble of blackened bricks and burned beams surrounded by a ring of flame-scorched trees, the cracked pool had bled water down the garden, washing out the flower beds, while the main house, half-burned, was pocked from end-to-end with bullet holes, the walls cracked and plaster-flaked by the grenades, every window shattered. But worst of all, there were the bodies. Lito and Magdalena had been Simon's friends, and they had been happy here.

Simon stood in the sunshine, the air reeking with the smell of wet ash and burning, taking it all in while the police gleaned cartridge cases from the bushes, and the firemen damped down the last of the embers. After a few moments, the plainclothes man led them over to sit on the wall, taking a notebook from his pocket. When he had found a clean page, he looked up at them and began.

"Have you any idea who can have done this?" he asked Simon. "This has been a most serious attack. There must be some explanation."

Given the practice, Kleiner did even better this time, but

the man didn't buy it. He listened carefully enough, nodding sometimes, jotting notes in his book, but his manner remained unconvinced.

"Well, that may well be the reason, Señor Kleiner," he said when Klaus had finished. "But I still need some explanation from Señor Quarry. The people who came here had grenades and Mac-10 machine guns. We found one in the bushes. These are serious weapons. Your man, Lito Lopez, had only a shotgun, and he was a brave man to fight with that against machine guns and grenades. But this house has a very sophisticated alarm system, and up there I see Israeli razor wire. Also, there are four American Claymore mines built into the walls—my men found the circuits. The *señorita's* shotgun we found up on the roof was a twelve-gauge Winchester pump, another serious weapon. We have also found a Ruger rifle with a telescopic sight, and a .357 Colt Python revolver. Apart from that man there, another body was found this morning in the sea off Formentor—the wounds on it are consistent with damage from a heavy-caliber pistol. Mr. Quarry, will you tell me why your home is a *castillo?* Were you expecting something like this? What is going on here?"

Simon looked at him squarely. "I have no idea," he said. "I suffer from insecurity, as does my . . . that is to say, as does Señorita Fiori, who lives with me. Her father was murdered in Milan some little time ago, during that business Señor Kleiner was referring to. She is a woman, and women are easily frightened."

The man smiled but shook his head. "Not *this* woman, Señor Quarry. She is a *chica brava.* She fought off at least four armed men who came at her out of the night with machine guns and grenades. A woman like that is very rare, Señor Quarry, and not to be talked of as if she were a child."

There was silence for a moment until Klaus said, *"Capitán,* if Señor Quarry has built his house for defense, maybe, in view of this"—Klaus gestured at the ruins—"maybe he had good reason. He is the victim here, his friends have been killed. Could we not address ourselves to the question of who did this, rather than why Señor Quarry protects himself?"

The man didn't back down. "The two are linked, Señor Kleiner, and we all know that. If I have the *why,* I will soon find the *who.*"

"What about the *how?*" Simon said.

"Well, there I can help. Last night four men were seen rowing ashore by the Club Nautico. The *marinero* saw them. Since they had not brought whatever boat they came in to his dock, he paid no real attention, but that is our first clue. This morning we found a car by the Hotel Diana, just behind the beach. There were blood and empty cartridge cases inside. It had been stolen about midnight from outside the Marcha Fresca disco—the owner did not discover it missing until he came out at four, and it was not reported to the Guardia Civil until after five. We did not find it until nearly noon. Shortly after that, a yacht picked up a body off Cabo Formentor. We have it down in the *puerto.*"

"So?" Kleiner asked.

"So I think these men came by sea. I think they already knew where you live, Señor Quarry. They asked no questions, simply stole a car, drove here, and broke in. When they had done all they could, they fled, taking an injured man with them. Why they left the other one here, I do not know. It is a pity the *marinero* did not get a sight of their boat, but at this time of the year there are hundreds of yachts cruising in the Balearics, to Ibiza and Minorca, even over to the peninsula. I have put out an alert, but unless you tell me who your enemies are, Señor Quarry, or unless they give themselves away, I do not think we will have a lot of luck in finding these people."

They went over it again and again for nearly two hours, until the firemen had rolled up their hoses, the ambulances had taken the bodies away, and all three had finally run out of words.

"Well," said the *capitán* at last, snapping his notebook shut, "I am not satisfied you are telling me all you know. I shall report this affair to the Departamento del Imigración,

Señor Quarry. We do not like armed men roaming Spain, fighting private wars in our country. I expect you will hear from them, and you will certainly hear from me."

"I expect I shall," Simon said wearily, "but may I go now? I want to get back to Señorita Fiori."

The man dismissed them with a wave of his hand. "Please give the lady my compliments, and say I would like to see her as soon as she feels able to see me. Perhaps tomorrow? *Adiós, señores.*"

"That is one more piece we can fit into our puzzle," Klaus said thoughtfully, as they walked down to the gate.

"Really? What is that?"

"I'll tell Catton to look for a bastard with a boat."

══ 10 ══

Freddie Bright's day usually began with a big English breakfast that he cooked for himself in the kitchen and ate out on the back terrace by the pool, with the English papers propped up on the teapot. For this big moment, Freddie liked the whole thing, sausages, a couple of eggs, bacon, a mushroom or two, fried bread, tomato ketchup . . . none of your foreign rubbish, and a decent cup of tea. All this was wonderful, but when his eye fell on a long column on page two, he could hardly believe his luck. He read it through, twice, riffled through the *Sun* and the *Mail,* which carried the same news with rather more gory details, and then, folding the papers to show the story, he wiped his mouth, pushed back his chair, and went in search of his houseguest. This was one in the eye for Mr. Bleedin' Vargas, and Freddie wanted to deliver the news in person.

Vargas, inevitably, was still in bed, with one of his Colombian bodyguards pouring him out a cup of thick coffee, but he waved Freddie in and asked him what he wanted.

"Thought you might like to see this," Freddie said genially. "Little item in the paper . . ." He passed the newspapers over.

If Freddie hoped for an outburst—and he did—he was to be disappointed. Vargas read all the articles and then fired

141

off a burst of Spanish to his bodyguard, sending him scurrying from the room. Then he looked at Freddie with one raised eyebrow.

"So . . . ?"

A little gloat won't hurt, Freddie thought. "It looks like your boys fucked up, Mr. Vargas. Right house, wrong bloke. This report here says they killed a couple of birds . . . one of them Simon Quarry's ladylove."

"So? This is of no consequence. We have shown this Quarry and his friends that we have long arms. He will prefer to leave us alone now."

Freddie laughed. Maybe it wasn't a good idea to laugh at Vargas, but you really couldn't help yourself sometimes.

"Come on, Mr. Vargas . . . don't kid old Freddie. It's a fucking disaster—got two of your blokes killed an' all. Thing is, I was talking to Ted about this Quarry. Seems that a few years back, a gang of Arabs killed his family. Quarry tracked 'em down, set 'em up, and killed the fucking lot. I reckon he'll be pretty pissed off with you for killing his bird."

That changed Vargas. He glared at Freddie for a moment, then flung the sheets aside and leapt out of bed and marched to the door, bare-assed, balls swinging, to shriek more Spanish down the stairs, setting off a gaggle of *"Sí, Jefe"*'s from the bodyguards down below, before turning to stare again into Freddie's grinning face.

"He may come after you, Freddie. Have you thought of that? They can only track me through you, and we used your boat."

"Er . . . that's another thing . . . where's the *Mariposa?*"

"In Cartegena. She'll be back at her moorings in Banus by tonight. Not a scratch, as I promised."

"Thank Gawd for that," Freddie breathed. "I'll send Errol and Eddie down to keep an eye on her."

Vargas nodded. "One of my men was wounded in the attack, Freddie. He will have to stay on board . . . your people can look after him. Now, you may be right about this Quarry. Anyway, we shall have to deal with him and Kleiner, and this policeman, Catton—all of them. I shall send more people, give instructions. Your friend Bardsey can put the finger on them as with the man Wintle, and my men will do the rest."

Cocky bastard, Freddie thought. "Ah well, I'm afraid not, Mr. Vargas. Ted is shitting himself about the Wintle job, and the Yard—Catton, in fact—has already sussed out that Ted isn't quite kosher."

"What do you mean, Freddie? 'Sussed'? What is 'sussed'? Why don't you speak English?"

Bleedin' liberty, Freddie thought. "I mean the police know that Ted has been on the take . . . I mean, works for me, you know."

"Has he been arrested?" Vargas asked. "You did not tell me this."

"Didn't know until last night. The bastard won't speak to me . . . tells me to fuck off and slams the phone down. I read in the papers he'd been suspended—it's on page three. He's not been arrested yet."

"If he talks, it could be bad for us," Vargas said.

"It'd be even worse for Ted," Freddie said. "Besides, he's a tough nut, is Ted. He won't talk."

"No," Vargas said. "He won't."

Four days after the funeral, Catton flew in from England. In the interval, Kleiner, Lucia, and Simon had moved into the Illa d'Or Hotel, half a mile up the beach from the Sisters' little hospital, and they walked Lucia down there every evening to have her dressings changed. Every day she walked a little easier, spending long hours soaking her feet in the sea from the end of the hotel jetty. Her feet were healing fast, but she didn't smile much, avoided their eyes, spoke only briefly and when spoken to. When Simon touched her, she shuddered.

Kleiner and Simon spent a lot of their time with the police, answering or avoiding questions, making statements, dodging a swarm of reporters, or picking over the ruins of Simon's house. They salvaged a few clothes, some books, one or two small items, but fire and water had ruined most of the contents. The house was a wreck, and Simon had already decided to bulldoze the lot and start again . . . unless he was forced to leave here forever. Then John Catton arrived, tired but triumphant, to set the ball rolling again.

"I've been pretty busy," he remarked, lifting his briefcase onto the table in Kleiner's room, pushing a drinks tray aside, and snapping open the locks, "but police work always comes through in the end. It never fails, believe me."

"That's nice to know," Simon said, sarcastically. "Of course, we three have been sitting around here, soaking up a little sun, working on our tans, and otherwise doing damn-all. You make us feel quite guilty. We have three dead friends to account for and nothing on the credit side, so forgive me if I don't applaud your industry."

"Shut up, Simon," Lucia said quietly.

"Go on," Kleiner said. "Just tell us all about it."

Catton opened the case, got out a map of southern Spain, and spread it out over the table. Then he flipped back the pages of a spiral-bound notepad and studied it for a moment before looking up at them.

"I'm very sorry about Lito and Magdalena, Simon . . . and so is Chris. We knew them too, you know. But it's often funny," he continued, "how a solution can be staring you in the face but you just can't see it. If you remember, Jorge Orchoa, the big man in the Cartel, was arrested while dining with friends in a restaurant. Vargas was there, but they had no warrant for him, so he went free. Anyway, I had an idea and asked the DEA man for the name of the restaurant. It's a popular place, on the hill near Mijas, here. You have to book. So I rang up and they remembered the party—the police rushing in with guns to arrest a guest doesn't happen every night—and I found out who booked the table. It was *that* simple. The Cartel's U.K. connection is a major-league London hood called Freddie Bright. He currently lives up in the hills between Puerto Banus and Ronda, here. He's wanted for questioning on a series of bank jobs, where his take currently totes up to something over five million pounds. Freddie is a sweetheart. Shooters are used on all the jobs, and two guards have been killed in the last couple of years. He also runs prostitutes, has a couple of clubs, and, interestingly enough, is also suspected of running in marijuana and heroin. In short, Freddie fits our profile. In addition, Freddie has a boat. He always has had one. That's how he is thought to have brought in the marijuana before he skipped. His current boat is a sixty-foot Riva, which cruises at twenty knots and sleeps six people, maybe eight, if they're friendly. My DEA contact on the Costa del Sol says Freddie's Riva left Puerto Banus about a week ago with six Latin gentlemen aboard. It went into Cartagena to refuel, and was back there again two nights ago. My contact was there asking questions, and he tells me that three men got off the boat. One was hurt, and had to be helped by the other two. In other words, maybe three men were missing, which fits. Rivas are big, flash boats—they attract attention—but they are seagoing craft and could get from Banus to here in two or three days."

"It sounds good. Anything else?" Simon asked.

"Quite a lot, but now for some bad news. The Spanish have released Jorge Orchoa. The Americans are livid, but after Larry Teal was hit, they had no witness for the extradition hearing. Orchoa flew back to Colombia yesterday, and according to my DEA contact, Vargas and three of his minders went with him. That must mean they have set up the European end, got their lab and distribution organized, and are all set to go into business. Anyway, Vargas is now out of my reach."

"When was this again?"

"Yesterday. My theory is that having whacked you here, and with Orchoa safely out of the slammer, they have returned to base to turn on the tap and get the regular shipments of paste flowing into Spain . . . the refinery must be here. Vargas may not know that you escaped, although it's in the papers. If he does know, Vargas may lie low for a bit, and see what we do next. It's hard to tell."

"We'll find him, wherever he is," said Kleiner, glancing at Simon. "We can't have him running around loose, picking us off one by one."

"Well, I have some news about that as well. Let me get back to Freddie Bright. I got all this from Ted Bardsey—he's running scared, by the way, but still denies any connection with Freddie or the Wintle killing. The Iberia printout was no use—they must have booked tickets using false names— but Ted told me that for really heavy work, like a good kicking or maybe a killing, Freddie has been using two tough boys, Eddie Reynolds and Errol Washington. Eddie was once an East End prizefighter, Errol is a Jamaican who also handles Freddie's *ganja* connection. You will remember that the lady at the Iberia check-in told me a black man and a white man checked in together, and Eddie and Errol are mates . . . so?" Catton shrugged. "It's a link."

"Are they definitely down here?"

"I think so. They certainly aren't in London. Everyone on the Met is pulling out all the stops to find out who killed Philip, and the heat is really on. Someone will usually grass on a cop-killer; it causes far too much trouble for everyone to have the Met in full cry. You'd better watch out in case they pitch up here for a second go at you."

"Have you got an address for this Freddie Bright?" Kleiner asked.

"And any photos of him and his heavies?" Simon said.

"Right here," said Catton, handing them over, then scribbling an address on his pad. "I don't know exactly where it is, but I don't think it will be hard to find."

Kleiner glanced at the photos, showed them to Simon, and then put them and the address in his pocket. Then he turned back to Catton. "Well, in that case, I think you can leave the rest to us. Just go home and mind the store while we go over to the Costa del Sol and find Mr. Bright. The less you know from now on, the better."

"I'm not at all happy about that," Catton said. "With this evidence, plus the attack on your house, I could probably get Freddie and his boys sent back to England. I don't think the Spanish would take much nudging on this issue. On the other hand, it may not work, it will certainly take time, it will probably cause trouble for Simon, and Freddie Bright might skip again. He's got enough cash to set himself up very nicely in Brazil, and we have not yet managed to extradite anyone from there."

"Then leave it to us," Simon said quietly. "We'll take care of Mr. Bright. Extradition isn't what we have in mind."

Catton glanced at Kleiner, then returned to his papers. "Don't rush me . . . there is more," he said. "My DEA contact—his name's Gene Hardy—wasn't in Cartagena by accident, or looking for Freddie's Riva—that was just luck. He was looking for a source of cocaine base coming in from South America, and for commercial shipments of ether."

"And what did he find?"

"Wait a moment," Catton implored. "I'm coming to that. Commercial quantities of ether have been imported into Spain through Cartagena within the last two months by a company based in Málaga. Not large quantities at any one time, but bigger than normal, in regular shipments, and to a new company, Despejado SA. Hardy checked the address, and it doesn't exist; it's just a box number. However, the name is interesting. According to Hardy, *despejado* means 'bright,' as in 'bright sunshine.'"

"So it does," Simon said, thoughtfully "That was foolish of him."

"Freddie likes to use Spanish names," Catton said. "His Riva is called the *Mariposa Acera,* the *'Steel Butterfly'*—but you see how it all fits? However"—Catton smiled broadly —"there is even more."

"I take it all back," said Simon, matching his smile. "You have been busy. All this achieved in just the last few days? You're a genius."

Catton shook his head. "Not days, Simon, weeks. You put out feelers, to everywhere you can think of, and sometimes, after weeks of nothing, they all produce results. Then you slot them together in the right order, that's all. As I said, that's police work."

"What's next?"

"My DEA man has been looking at the Customs' copy of the cargo manifests. Within the last three months, Despejado have received regular consignments of what the manifests describe as slurry—that's the stuff that looks like mud which oil crews use to grease their drilling bits. The consignments of mud, or slurry, originated in Venezuela."

"Not Colombia?"

"Definitely not Colombia. But mark this—the bill of lading was drawn up in Cay Dorado. Hardy scrounged a copy from the *aduana* in Cartagena and faxed it to me. Here it is." He took a printed document out of his case and passed it over. The three of them studied the document for a moment, with Simon reading out some of the sections in English.

"Very official," he said at last, "and it looks to be in perfect order."

"I'm sure it is," Catton said. "But my guess is that the drums contain cocaine base. Vargas routes his shipments via Cay Dorado to avoid any keen customs officer getting overly curious, as they would be with ex-Colombia shipments, and so provides a cutout. It's simple, but it's crafty all the same. Cay Dorado is no lily-white place, but the name doesn't scream dope in Europe like Colombia does."

"I'm looking forward to meeting this Mr. Vargas," Kleiner said. "Do you know where he is now?"

"Oh yes," said Catton, smiling. "I know exactly where he is now. He's in Cay Dorado."

"You promised me you wouldn't get involved," Lucia said. "We talked it over, and you promised me."

"That was before they killed Philip, Lito, and Magdalena," Simon said. "You don't know as much as I do about these people, Lucia. They won't leave us alone—once they find out that they missed me, they'll try again. They once chased a man all the way to Budapest and killed him. They'll try again, believe me. We can't even stay here. It's not safe."

"But why do they think you're connected with this? You're not involved," she cried. "It's John's business . . . and Klaus's."

"I know that, but what can I *do?*" he asked. "They have put us all together . . . found out, somehow, that Kleiner and Philip and I are connected. I can't very well write Vargas a letter saying it's all a dreadful mistake and asking him to leave us alone. Maybe we should put an advertisement in the paper . . . Christ! That's it! That's what did it—the paper!"

"Did what? What paper"

"That bloody photograph in the paper . . . the one taken at the party. We were all in it; you, me, Klaus, John . . . that's how they made the connection. Someone set us up. I knew it then, and now I'm certain. Now, Vargas will never believe we're not involved."

"Then we're dead," Lucia said.

"Not yet," Simon said. "Listen . . ."

Back in London, on that very afternoon, the minister for overseas aid was wriggling on the hook, and kept glancing across at Yates for assistance. However, having been introduced to the Cay Dorado high commissioner (*high commissioner!*—for that fly-bitten little island) merely as "my aide," Yates decided to let the minister stew.

"You must see that the position is difficult," the minister said anxiously. "Our funds are not unlimited, and there are problems."

The commissioner, a small, dark Guyanese with beady black eyes, and a manner as sharp as a tack, spread his hands out wide and shook his head. "You keep saying so, Minister, but you don't say why. I can see no difficulties. Last year your government approved the loan needed to extend our runway at Caytown, so that it can handle big 747 and 1011 jets. Now, when the preliminary surveys have been completed within budget and by a British company, you refuse to hand over the money."

"I don't see why you need it," said the minister, blunt at last. "The runway, I mean."

The commissioner sighed. "To improve our trade and tourism, Minister—our links with the outside world. It is embarrassing for an independent state, and especially for one with our strong British connections, to rely on American goodwill. At present, our tourists must transship to smaller aircraft via Miami International, which adds hours to their journey. Also, the Americans harass our citizens and visitors. Our own Chancellor was arrested and detained quite unjustly some months ago. The present situation is quite intolerable."

"Your Chancellor was picked up in a DEA sting operation while accepting half a million dollars from the Medellín Cartel in exchange for allowing the Colombians to transship drugs into Florida via Cay Dorado," Yates put in. "The transaction was recorded on video. The evidence is damning and irrefutable."

"He was released," the commissioner said tartly. "The charges framed by the Americans never came to court."

"He was released because he claimed diplomatic status," Yates said. "That status has now been withdrawn. He won't be so lucky next time."

The commissioner edged his chair around to give Yates his shoulder and leaned across the desk toward the minister, accompanying his words with sharp taps on the desktop. "Minister, we must have this runway. Our economic future depends on it. You are complaining about this loan, but if you do not help us to become self-supporting, we may have to look elsewhere. We look to the British government because you are our friends."

The minister thought this plea over for a moment, his eyes cast down on the desk, raising them to exchange a glance with Yates. Then he turned his gaze on the commissioner, and when he spoke, his tone was businesslike rather than friendly.

"Commissioner, the time has come to speak out. My Government is not happy with Cay Dorado. You are an independent state, but we still retain, at your request, some responsibilities, notably in defense, internal security, and to some extent, foreign affairs. When there were those riots some years ago, we had to send paratroopers and police in to control the situation. Your President then promised free elections, but they have not been held. Your economy is in ruins, yet there are over three hundred banks in Caytown, mainly occupied laundering drug and Mafia money." He raised his hand as the commissioner opened his mouth to interrupt. "No, hear me out. You already have over fifty airstrips around Cay Dorado. Some are littered with crashed aircraft which have flown drugs up from South America. When the Cambridge University examiners were on the island recently, inspecting the schools, they reported back to me that, in answer to the question 'What do you want to be when you grow up?' sixty-four percent of the children gave 'drug dealer' as their first choice. Your island is a disgrace."

"I cannot listen to more of this," said the commissioner, rising. "I shall deliver a formal note of protest to these slanders."

"I think you'd better sit down," the minister said grimly. "We also know you are currently extending hospitality to Emiliano Vargas, who ranks number four in the Colombian Cartel. It is no accident that Señor Vargas has chosen your country for his base, Commissioner. It gives him shelter from the American DEA, easier access to Britain, which he intends to flood with drugs, and, I have to say it, the personal protection of your President. As a prime condition for this or any other loan, you must expel Vargas from Cay Dorado."

"These arrogant demands, which I regard as a blatant attempt at interference in the internal affairs of another country, will be brought to the attention of the Commonwealth Secretariat, and raised at the next Commonwealth Conference, perhaps even at the UN."

"They certainly will," the minister said grimly, "and by us."

"Am I to take it that Her Majesty's government refuse to honor their commitment to our future, and deny us the loan which has already been voted? This is your current position? I think the Opposition will have something to say in Parliament if you welsh on this agreement."

"We cannot consider any further help, Commissioner, until you get rid of Vargas," said the minister, rising. "And that is our current position. I suggest you contact your President and see what he says. If necessary, Mr. Yates here can go to Cay Dorado and see him. And now, Commissioner, I must bid you good day."

When the door had closed, Yates rose, unfolding smoothly from his chair, and went across to the drinks tray, picking up a glass and a bottle.

"Minister, I hope you will allow me to say this: well done! That really put the Cay Dorado situation in a nutshell. Permit me to pour you a sherry?"

"No, Alec, make it a scotch, a stiff one. I need it to wash the taste of that creature out of my mouth."

"What will happen now, do you think?" the minister asked, when Yates returned to his chair. "What will they do about the money?"

"It's hard to say," said Yates, frowning. "My concern, our concern, is really Vargas. He's a problem that won't go away. He has been removing the obstacles that we put in his path, as Catton predicted. He is behind the killings, and he'll keep the pressure on Cay Dorado."

"Can't he and the Cartel simply go ahead with the runway? They are the ones who need it, to fly in drugs directly from South America and out again to Europe, Canada, and the western USA, as we all know. So why don't they simply do it? The Cartel doesn't lack for money."

"Well, first of all, they're mean," Yates said. "Besides, if we do it, then the project has some form of official cover and is not just a naked attempt to build a gateway airport for the Cartel. Hence that claptrap about tourism, although there may be a grain of truth in it."

"Tourism? Rubbish!" the minister snorted. "Cay Dorado has exactly three hotels, and anyone outside the drug business can't even get a room. I've been there, I know. Anyway, they can't have a new runway. The Yanks would go raving mad. They invaded Grenada, a Commonwealth country, mark you, and if Vargas gets a toehold in Cay Dorado, I wouldn't be surprised if they invaded there. I wouldn't blame them."

"The consequences if the Americans invaded Cay Dorado could be far-reaching, Minister. We were not even consulted over the Grenada invasion, and the Opposition made a lot of mileage out of that fact. If it happens again, those sneers about the British bulldog becoming an American poodle will not be too easy to deny."

"I know that, dammit," the minister grunted. "So, what do you suggest? As you requested, I mentioned the possibility that you might go there. May I know why you want to go?"

"Well, if the present government of Cay Dorado has to be overthrown, then I may need to go there to see how it can be arranged. We will have to do it subtly, of course. We can't charge in like the Americans did."

"I didn't hear that, Alec. Those words were never spoken in this office."

"Of course not," Yates said smoothly.

"Does that . . . er . . . suggestion, have approval from down the road, in you-know-where?"

"I really couldn't say, Minister. When we discussed the matter of Cay Dorado the other day, in general terms and quite informally, quite off the record, it was hoped that you might be able to talk some sense into the commissioner today."

"Fat chance of that," the minister snorted.

"Well, nobody thought the chance was very high, given the dependence of Cay Dorado on drug traffic, but no other alternatives were discussed, naturally."

"Naturally."

"However, as I was leaving, the PM did say, almost to herself, that it was not *talk* that got the Argentine forces off the Falkland Islands. I thought that a significant hint, but I could be wrong."

"Do we have any forces in Cay Dorado?"

"Not *in*, no, Minister, but we do have the frigate *Dancer* on the Caribbean station, and she carries a troop of Royal Marines, but they would need a reason to interfere in Cay Dorado's internal affairs. In fact, we would have to be asked. I am thinking about it though. It might be arranged."

The minister got up to pour them both another drink, and spoke over his shoulder from across the room. "I've never known quite what you do, Alec, and now I don't really want to know. Just do what you have to do and keep me out of it. But you will need a very good reason to interfere in Cay Dorado."

"I think we can find a reason, Minister. We must create an explosive situation where our assistance is essential. The ingredients already exist. Cay Dorado has the dangerous Mr. Vargas, but we now have the help of the dangerous Mr. Quarry. I think they will find that killing Quarry's people was a serious mistake."

═══ 11 ═══

A week later, when Lucia could walk properly once again, the three of them flew to Málaga, Kleiner piloting the Lear with Simon beside him in the copilot's seat. Lucia, now smiling slightly, played stewardess, bringing them coffee from the tiny galley, then sitting behind them, one arm resting on Simon's shoulder. It was the first sign of affection in days.

"What do we do when we get there?" she asked. Kleiner was talking on the radio, and it was Simon who answered.

"First, we'll drop in and see my old friend Terry Cockerill, and find out what he knows. Then we do a recce of Mr. Bright's home. We need to find out exactly where everyone is—Freddie himself, any of the Vargas mob who are still around, and especially the two from London who killed Philip. With any luck, they will all be together, though that might be asking too much. We also need to find the coke lab."

"And then what?"

"Then we hit them like a train. What else can we do?"

Kleiner engaged the automatic pilot, and pushed an earphone to one side. "What do we hit them with?" he asked. "Since the Guardia have all your weapons, we are a little short on artillery."

"We'll think of something," Simon replied. "Guns aren't

too hard to find, I'll ask around. Terry will probably know of someone."

It took a little under two hours for the Lear to cover the distance between Palma and Málaga, curving in to the airport, coming down across the sea to thud and rumble along the runway. Kleiner parked the little jet on a hardstand among a dozen other small planes, went into the airport office to fill in forms and pay landing charges, emerging to lead Simon and Lucia out through the airport office onto the concourse. Half an hour after landing, they had hired a car and were speeding west along the Costa del Sol motorway, under the snowcapped bulk of the Sierra Nevada, cruising in heavy traffic through an endless series of coastal developments.

"What a hellhole," Simon remarked from the backseat. "This coast is a tribute to concrete." He jerked his thumb toward the tenth or twentieth series of high-rise apartments, through the towers of which they could get just fleeting glimpses of the sea. "It must have taken a great deal of money to create a hundred-mile-long eyesore like this. I hope none of this is your doing, Klaus?"

"Not guilty," Kleiner said briefly. "Give me credit for a little taste."

"I expect some of them are quite nice inside," Lucia said. "We could even try one for a while, until the house is rebuilt. Not everyone can afford a house and garden, with private grounds, you know."

"Don't be charitable," Simon grunted. "Look, when I first came down here . . . what? . . . thirty years ago, this coast was empty. There was only one hotel between Málaga and Gibraltar—an ex-RAF bloke ran it. It was always full of airline stewardesses. I stayed there for a month, and I didn't draw a sober breath."

"Oh yes?" Lucia said. "Tell me more."

"Ah, memories, memories," Simon sighed. "Well, I was young then. Anyway, if they have to build the coast up, why do they have to ruin it at the same time?"

"Money," Kleiner said. "Everyone chases the fast buck.

Do I turn off here or at San Pedro? I just hope your old friend is pleased to see us when we turn up out of the blue."

It took over an hour and a few stops for directions before they finally bumped up a rutted track to the front door of Terry Cockerill's villa. The house, a long white Andalusian building with a green tile roof, lay dozing in the hot afternoon sun, but two large Alsatians uncoiled themselves from the shade of a tree and came padding over to the car to stand panting, one before each door, their intelligent brown eyes fixed steadily on the passengers inside.

"Terry knows about dogs," Simon said carefully, "so don't get out yet. Just stay put and sound your horn."

One long blast produced a reaction. There was a slight twitch of a blind at an upper window, then a brief pause before the door opened and a short, balding, roly-poly man came loping toward them across the gravel, scowling, hurriedly dressed in just flip-flop sandals and an alarming pair of shorts.

"Wolf . . . get away . . . get back, Tiger! Who the hell are you, eh? Who asked you to—well, I'm. . . . Is that you, Simon? You old *bastard*. You don't half pick your moments. I was just talking Renée into it, and then there was this bloody awful noise . . . I nearly fell off the bed. I was right choked. 'Allo, 'allo, what's this? And who is this pretty lady? Good afternoon to you, my dear. And to you, sir. Any friend of Si's is one of mine. Come on, hop out, never mind the bleeding dogs." Still shaking hands, Terry turned to bellow back toward the house. "Oi! . . . Renée! Look who's here! Your effing boyfriend. Simon, of course—who else? How many bleedin' boyfriends 'ave you got?"

The four of them rolled across the gravel and into the house like a human ball, swamped by Terry's talk, the two Alsatians bouncing along at their sides, barking happily, until Terry booted them back outside, still talking.

"Get out . . . Gertcha! That's Wolf, Mr. Kleiner. He's an intelligent dog, that. Talk about clever? He can do the bleedin' ironing; ask Renée. Where is she?" He turned to bellow again up the stairs, pushing the three of them ahead. "Woman! Get your knickers on. Champagne out on the patio, right? Through here . . . Lucia, Klaus is it? What are you doing with my old mate Simon? Watch him, he's bad company." He flung open the fridge, rattling bottles. "Well, we'll take two bottles and be on the safe side. Here, Klaus, cop 'old of this . . . glasses. Look out, Si, here she is!"

A long shriek from the stairs, like that of an approaching express, announced the arrival of Renée. She came sweeping into the kitchen and gathered Simon up in her ample arms, the pair of them crashing back against the table, while Klaus and Lucia leapt hurriedly out of the way.

"Simon Quarry, you rotten bastard!" Renée cried. "What's this? Not a word for years, and then you turn up with another woman."

"You know there has never been anyone but you, Renée," said Simon, struggling free. "But, alas, you love another. What's a man to do?"

"You lying sod. But don't he talk nice? Hello, dear . . . what's your name? Ooh, I love your eyes . . . ain't she pretty? Terry, get your eyes off. Hello, dear, who are you? Call me Renée. You're all very welcome and you're all staying here, no arguments about it. We've got plenty of room. Tell them, Terry, and get that bottle open. . . . Ooops!"

The Cockerills were unstoppable. The first bottle of champagne disappeared before they had stopped talking, delighted to have an audience and to see Simon again, wrapping Klaus and Lucia in their excess warmth, standing in the kitchen, a tight gaggle of friends.

"So, how long have you known Simon then, Klaus?" Terry asked. "Not long, eh? I've known the bastard for nearly thirty years. He used to be my troop sergeant in the mob. He was a hard, miserable sod . . . not really, only joking. We 'ad some good times, but you've got to watch him. He can get you into all kinds of trouble. I got blown up once, shot once, caught the clap a couple of times." Terry sighed. "Ah, they were the best years of my life. Of course, you're staying here, we won't 'ear different. You can 'ave my eldest's room."

"Oh, but we don't want to put anyone out," Lucia said. "Really."

"You won't be putting him out, dear," Renée said. "He's not here—he's in Parkhurst."

"Oh dear, I am sorry," said Lucia, confused.

"Don't be, dear. It was his own bloody fault. He'll be out in another two years."

It was pleasant, sitting there, even for Kleiner and Lucia, listening to old friends catching up with each other after a few years apart, and letting their hosts make all the arrangements. Terry brought in the suitcases, and Renée took Lucia off for a tour of the house. Later, when they had unpacked and settled in, Renée put the kettle on for a cup of tea. They were all sitting around the kitchen table drinking it, when Simon casually dropped the name. It produced an instant chill.

"Freddie Bright?" Terry said sharply. "Certainly I know him. What do you want with him? He's a right villain, Si. Take my word for it and leave him alone, whatever it is."

"I wouldn't touch Freddie Bright with a pair of tongs," said Renée, shaking her head. "There's villains and right villains, and then there's Freddie Bright. You listen to Terry, Simon, and stay away from him."

"What's the matter with him?" Klaus asked. "I mean, in particular?"

"Well . . ." Terry thought for a moment. "He's a shit, just for starters, and a vicious shit an' all. I expect Si's mentioned my line of work, and God knows I've got up to a few capers in my time, but nothing personal, no violence. Well, no unnecessary violence. But Freddie *likes* violence. I could tell you some things about him, I could."

"Then tell us," Simon said.

"Well, not in front of the ladies. And why do you want to know, anyway?"

"Come along, Lucia," said Renée, rising from the table. "Let's take our tea outside and have a nice natter. I don't want a lovely day spoiled listening to talk about Freddie Bright."

"Well, I'll tell you," Terry said, when the women had gone. "Freddie and me was in the same line of business for a while—banks, vaults, security vans. When I set out to pull my pension, I spent three years, three bleedin' years, setting it up. Got the plans, checked it all careful, laid out heavy money. It went like a dream, and I didn't hurt a hair of no one's head. Freddie's not like that. On the last job, the one that got him here with five mil in his trousers, they got the vault open by boring into the guard's kneecaps with a Black and Decker drill until he told them the combination. Nice, eh?"

"Christ!" Kleiner said.

"Exactly," Terry agreed. "Christ indeed. Freddie's too bleedin' mean and too bleedin' idle to suss out a job like a professional thief, if he can do it the easy way. Then, he's into girls. Renée can't abide him because of that. And he does the protection racket, got yobs beating up Paki shop-keepers who won't pay. I ask you? Now, I hear he's getting into dope."

"Are you sure of that?" Simon asked sharply.

"Oh yes. Me and Renée went to a birthday party up at his place a few weeks back. I don't like the bastard, but why make enemies? We dropped in for 'arf an hour. He had a couple of South Americans there, plus some dago minders, and he took me on one side and tipped me the wink. I told him I wasn't interested. Cocaine isn't my style."

"You mean he offered you a slice of the action?"

"Christ, no! Freddie? No, he was warning me off. I've retired, o' course, but my youngest is still running the family firm back in dear old London, at least until my eldest gets out of the nick. Freddie just wanted to know if there'd be problems if he operated in my manor."

"What did you tell him?" Kleiner asked sharply. "We need to know."

Terry shot a look at Simon before answering. "Well, Klaus, since you ask, I told him I didn't give a damn, but to keep my lads out of it. However, before we go any further with this, what about telling me why you're both here, asking about a turd like Freddie. Frankly, Klaus, Si and I go back a long way, but you just got here. So, tell me, what's it all about?"

On the terrace, sitting beside Renée on the swing seat, Lucia found herself crying. Renée was a good listener when she stopped talking, and suddenly it all came out with a rush, the business in Milan, the killings in Majorca, Philip, Lito and Magdalena, so many things, mixed up with gulping sobs.

"Well, I think you've been a very brave girl," said Renée, patting her shoulder. "Here, have another tissue. I've got a good mind to give Simon the sharp edge of my tongue for getting you into all this."

"It's not his fault," Lucia gulped. "He wasn't there when the house was attacked. He doesn't want any of this, any more than I do, but we can't get out of it."

"Don't you apologize for him, dear. I've known Simon Quarry for nearly thirty years, long before he married that nice wife of his, when he was still in the Royal Marines. He's a hard man if you push him, is Simon. Terry and I did most of our courting on Simon's sofa, after Terry got out of the Scrubs. Simon had a nice business then. He worked hard and made a lot of money, you know. Well, course you do. Then that terrible thing happened to his family."

"What was she like?"

"Who? Eleana? Oh, very nice. A real lady. Very posh, but a real laugh. She and I used to sit in my kitchen, laughing our heads off. When she and the kiddies were killed, I cried for weeks, honest. I just couldn't stop. Simon's changed since then. He's gone a lot grayer, and quieter."

It was easy to talk to Renée. She reminded Lucia of those big, comfortable staff nurses she had met years ago at Guys Hospital, those large, unflappable ladies hiding big hearts behind starched bosoms, who would somehow always find time to chat to the homesick girl from Italy.

"Well, I don't know what to say," Renée said, when Lucia had finished and was wiping her eyes again. "But I can't really say I'm surprised. Simon's a lovely man. I've always fancied him myself, and if it wasn't for Terry . . . who knows? But he's never been what you could call easy. Terry won't have a word said against him, but even he says Simon's a bad man to cross."

"But what shall I do?" Lucia asked. "I can't go on living like this, Renée. I want an ordinary life. That's not too much to ask, is it? But I don't think that's on offer with Simon. It could be so good, but he knows all these dreadful people and . . . it leads to this."

"You'll have to leave him or let him be," Renée said. "You can't change men, dear, not really. Look at my Terry. He's always been a villain, but he's always been a nice man to me. I wouldn't change him even if I could, not really. But I can't advise you about Simon. Come on, let's go and break up that meeting in there. You feel better now, don't you, dear? You really can't beat a nice cup of tea for your nerves."

"Well, it's up to you, of course," Terry said, "but that house of Freddie's is well tooled-up. It won't be easy. You'd better look it over carefully first."

"It smells," said Renée, coming through the doorway with the teacups, Lucia hard at her heels. "That place of Freddie's—what a pong."

"Don't be daft, woman," Terry said. "He was serving curry, so of course it ponged."

"I don't mean the curry," said Renée, from the sink. "Think I don't know curry when I smell it? I mean the other smell, like a hospital. It made me feel quite ill. Like when I had young Steve. Like that."

"Like what?" asked Simon, puzzled.

"Sort of hospital smell," Renée said. "You know what I mean, don't you, Lucia, you being a doctor and all? Like the smell in the delivery room, from those gas and air machines they give you."

"Ether!" said Simon and Klaus together.

* * *

"It makes good sense when you think about it," Klaus said. "Pure cocaine is valuable stuff. Freddie would want to keep an eye on it, especially if it belongs to a nasty piece of work like Vargas. He can't have anyone making off with the stock."

"It's still bloody dangerous to have a lab on the premises," Simon said. "Ether can go off like a bomb. I thought he'd purify the base on some factory estate. Surely that's much safer?"

"Maybe, but then think of the other problems. He'd need security systems, guards, transportation. It would be noticeable. Up at his own house, he can do what he wants. Anyway, I don't suppose the lab is actually in the house. Terry says he has plenty of land up there. If he has air-conditioning and vents the fumes, ether would be safe enough, unless someone puts a bomb in there."

"Now, that's a very good idea," Simon said. "Terry, you used to be a dab hand with the plastic. Got any ideas how we might touch this lot off?"

"Oh, I dunno, Si, it's been years. I've never seen no lab up at Freddie's. I'd have to have a think about it."

"We need to take a look at Bright's house anyway, and find his yacht," Kleiner said.

"The *Mariposa*?" Terry asked. "She's down in Puerto Banus. I saw her coming in there the other night when me and Renée were out to dinner. A couple of Freddie's boys went on board, Eddie Reynolds with Errol Washington, his spade mate from London. It gave me quite a turn when I saw those two coves down here."

"Then that's two more problems solved," Kleiner said thoughtfully. "Are there any more people on board?"

"I dunno," Terry said. "I'd never 'ave noticed Eddie an' Errol, but they got in an argument with some punter. The daft bleeder made some remark in the bar about black bastards, and Eddie and Errol took him out to the carpark and gave him a good kicking. Very touchy boy, our Errol. They went onto the *Mariposa* when they came back."

"That's another thought," Simon said. "It's all useful."

"What is?" Terry asked.

"I'll tell you later. Look, I know you don't like shooters, Terry, but we need to pick up some hardware."

"Now look, Si, I don't want to get involved in all this," Terry said. "I know it's you, an' we're mates an' all, but Renée'd kill me if I got into more trouble, let alone with shooters."

"You're not involved, Terry. We just need a name, a contact. We'll leave you out of it, I promise."

"Well," Terry said reluctantly, "there's a wog in Puerto de la Duquesa, a bit further up the coast. He flogs arms. He's sure to have a few samples about. What d'you want?"

"I don't know . . . a shotgun."

"You don't need him for that. You can buy them in a shop," Terry said. "I can saw it off short for you here. Anything else?"

"Mmmm . . ." Simon thought for a moment. "Just guessing, but a couple of assault rifles. American M-16s would be nice. Then, if we can find one, how about a rocket-launcher and a few rockets, also some plastic explosive, some Cordex fuse, and a box of grenades? Also a pistol and a silencer— I'm a heavy hitter."

"Christ! I'm impressed," said Terry, eyes wide. "Bloody hell! I know they burnt your house down, but what are you two trying to do? Start a war down here?"

Simon shook his head. "Like we told you, the war's been going on for weeks," he said. "We just want to stop losing it."

John Catton was not prepared for what happened, and maybe he should have been. He had been warned repeatedly, and had weakened enough to carry a pistol all the time, though it went against the grain, but he never really believed, in his heart of hearts, that anything would happen, certainly not something like that. Things like that simply didn't happen in England.

He had spent the day with his sergeant, Tom Harris, drafting out his full statement concerning Ted Bardsey. It wasn't a pleasant task, doing the business on a fellow officer, and when the day was done, they both felt like a drink to wash the bad taste out of their mouths.

"With this going on, Tom, we'll not be very welcome in the wet bar or at the Sherlock," Catton said. "So I suggest we get the car, pick up Chris at her chambers, and go and have a drink on the river somewhere. How about it?"

"Good idea, sir. With Chris along, we'll have to find something else to talk about as well. Shall I get her on the line?"

They had picked her up, Tom swapping into the backseat to let her ride up front with Catton, and they were cruising along the embankment, looking for a place to park, when it happened. Christine was kneeling sideways on the front seat, chatting cheerfully to Tom, when the motorcycle came surging up on the outside, the headlight blazing in the side-view mirror, the glare forcing Catton to swerve and brake.

"Bloody messengers," he swore. "Bloody cowboys."

Special Branch cars have bullet-proof glass, but no glass can stand up to concentrated, close-range bursts of high-velocity bullets, a full magazine from an automatic weapon. The first burst glazed the window, the second stove it in, the third took most of Sergeant Harris's head off. Dazed by the noise, the crashing of glass, and Christine's terrified screams, Catton strove to control the car as it mounted the sidewalk and scraped along the embankment wall, scattering pedestrians; he reached across to drag Chris off the seat, pushing her down on the floor as the fury went on, the bike now stopped beside the curb, engine roaring, more bullets slashing through the shattered glass. Only when the car crashed into the steps by Cleopatra's Needle did the bike accelerate away, and Catton, rolling out of the car with his pistol in his fist, did not dare snap off a shot as the riders swerved away through the traffic.

People were running over now, dodging between the cars and trucks to stare at the wreck, the traffic piling up behind in a mass of lights and horns. Catton staggered to his feet, waving people back, and limped over to the open door.

"Chris . . . darling . . . are you all right?"

The pause before she answered seemed endless. "Yes . . . I think so. What about Tom?"

Catton did not need to look into the back. This was a repeat of something that he had been through before.

"Tom's dead," he said briefly. "Try not to look." That done, he put his head down on the roof of the car and began to shake all over.

12

Simon Quarry raised himself slightly on his toes and elbows and began to wriggle forward toward the crest of the hill, moving out into the sunshine from the dark shadows of the trees. Panting, Terry crawled after him. Both were wearing dark shirts and long trousers, clothes that blended well with the rocks and shadows but gave little protection from the rough, thorn-littered ground.

"Christ!" muttered Terry, picking a sharp stone out of his palm. "This is worse than Dartmoor."

"Shut up," Simon said quietly. "And keep your head down, unless you don't want to grow old."

"These rocks are hot, my son—and old is what we're getting . . . too bloody old for this lark."

"Never mind. Is that it?"

They had reached the edge of the steep slope that fell away sharply onto the wide valley below. All around them the green and gold hills of Andalusia shimmered in the afternoon sun, their tops hazy with heat. A small cluster of rocks on the lip of the drop gave them cover and a little shade, while they viewed the group of buildings spread out across the ground below, the usual sprawling villa with pool, and some distance from the house, behind a small hill, a long, low, functional building with a sloping roof dotted here and there with ventilators.

"Yes, that's it," Terry said. "I've never seen that warehouse place though; it's not visible from down there in the garden. Quite like old times this, ain't it? Remember how we used to go on road watch, you, me, and Jim?"

"The old firm's back in business, eh?" said Simon, his eyes still fixed on the buildings below. "Jim is dead, you know."

"No!" Terry sounded shocked. "I didn't know. When?"

"About three months ago. A sniper got him in the head while he was leading a patrol through Crossmaglen. Had just three weeks to go to pension. He should have quit when we did."

"The bastards . . . bloody bastards."

"The world's full of bastards. Here, give me the glasses, I need a closer look."

From their hilltop position, they had a good view of the Bright house and the compound surrounding it. Simon focused the field glasses and began to sweep across the terrain, beginning with the chain-link fence topped with wire on angle-iron posts that surrounded the garden. Halfway through the scan, his eyes picked up something. He fiddled with the glasses to sharpen the focus.

"Hell! See that? That bird? What is it doing?"

"It's a crow. Black ones are crows, white ones are seagulls . . . easy."

"I know it's a crow, you idiot . . . it's what it's picking at. There's something else down there, either a dead fox or maybe a dog. Can't you see? It's a fox."

"How? You've got the glasses, cocker, and my eyes ain't what they were."

"Here, have a look," said Simon, passing him the glasses. "Thing is, it means that the fence is probably electrified, not just the barbed wire on top but the whole lot. So we can't cut our way in. You can't clamp out an entire fence, and there is probably a circuit-breaking alarm . . . tricky."

"So?" Terry put down the glasses and turned to face him. "What now?"

"So, why be tricky? We go in through the main gate. Pass the glasses."

The main way through the fence was a wide gap, the road through it barred by two concrete posts that created a chicane, plus a barrier pole set outside a guard hut. Simon focused on the hut and finally picked up the guard, who was hidden away on the shady side, leaning against one wall. From the hut, the main road ran on up to the villa, a long two-story building with a double garage, a side wing forming a short arm of an L, and at the rear, a wide kidney-shaped pool. The road split before the house, one arm leading to the forecourt, the other leading away around the low hill behind. Between the pool and the house, the rising slope had been grassed; they could see a sprinkler dancing to and fro in the sunlight even now, but from behind the pool the slope rose steeply, bare and open, to a crest that stood much higher than the house, then dropped away sharply for seventy feet or more into an open area, where, surrounded by yet another security fence, stood the aluminum-walled, warehouse-style building. Simon studied this building briefly, noting the spinning ventilators on the roof, the wire-mesh screens on the windows, the marks of tires scored in dust across the fresh black tarmac of the road leading to the double doors at one end of the building.

"Neat," he said. "Very neat."

"Why so?" Terry had made himself comfortable on the ground, his chin resting on his folded arms.

"I'll bet you ten to five, that building there is the coke lab. See the mesh, the ventilators? Freddie can walk there in five minutes from his own front door, but it's concealed by the hill from the main road. Also, if anything should go wrong, the hill protects the house from the blast. Not bad. Not bad at all. How many guards does he keep?"

"I dunno," Terry said. "Maybe a couple of minders and some dagos. I don't know how many. At his party, the place was crawling with coves. I don't know which were Freddie's or this Vargas character's."

"Well, let's watch and see."

It took another hour, frying out there on the hilltop, before Simon was satisfied that he had seen all there was to see. Then they edged back from the crest and crawled away down the hill, not daring to stand up until they were deep in the shelter of the trees.

"I could do with a beer," Terry said hoarsely, dusting himself down. "I'm parched."

"Let's go back to the car and find a bar," Simon said. "I want to think this over before we see Klaus."

They found a bar three miles down the road, pulling off to park the car in the shade, Terry going inside to fetch four San Miguels, returning to knock the tops off the bottles and pass one to Simon through the open door of the car.

"Before we go back," Terry said, "we have to have a word. I'm getting sucked into this caper of yours, and I want to know where we're going. I like your girl, and so does Renée, but that German bloke is a right cold fish. Also, you're working for the coppers, which I can't do. I know Wintle was a good bloke and a mate of yours, but even so . . ."

"It's not just Wintle," Simon said. "Those people over the hill burned my house down and killed two of my people. They would have killed Lucia and me too, if they had had a little more luck, and they will probably try again. It's them or me. I don't have a choice, Terry. If I had any choice, I wouldn't be here."

"That's what you say, but it's not so," Terry said. "You've been at this game before. It's not on, Si. You tell me the IRA killed Jim . . . will you be having a go at them next? So, what's going on, eh? Is gunning for Kleiner your new caper? You've changed, Si . . . you're not the same bloke."

"A lot has happened. I never wanted any of this . . . but I got sucked in and I can't get out."

Terry shook his head, frowning. "Why not just piss off out of sight and start again? That's what I did. I'll help you. I've got connections."

"I wanted to ask you about that," Simon said. "How do you do it? Get right out, I mean?"

"Simple," Terry said. "Make a few plans, then walk away. Take nothing with you but the clothes you stand up in, and never go back. It's like you've died."

"That sounds easy when you say it quick," Simon said,

"but it can't be that easy. You brought that pink, flashy Rolls with you, for example. I don't blame you for not leaving it behind, but it must have been a bit of a giveaway."

"It's not the same Roller," Terry said. "The old one stood outside the house in Bermondsey for three days before the fuzz got anxious and broke the door down. But for the Roller, I'd never have made it. Over the back wall, train down to Portsmouth, ferry to the Channel Islands, over to France, and here I am. Cost of skipping Blighty, one car, and I'll get that back one of these days. You've got to cut and run," he went on. "It's the only way, believe me."

"Well, we'll have to see. Meantime, I need your help on this caper, so are you in or out?"

"I'm in, for a bit of the way, anyway," Terry said. "But have you got it all doped out? What are you going to do? Have you worked out the when, how, and where, just like the old days?"

Simon took a pull at his beer, his eyes fixed far ahead down the road. "I think so," he said at last. "At least, I've worked out how to get in. That's half the battle. I'll go in through the main gate. It's the only way."

Terry whistled, and shook his head. "I didn't think you were serious, but you always had balls. How do you aim to do that?"

Simon grinned broadly at him. "Simple. Didn't you say you knew Freddie well? You are going to drive me in."

Getting tooled up had taken Kleiner most of the day. Finding the Arab and convincing him took until lunchtime, and when they got back to the boat, the Arab insisted on going through the whole social ritual before he got down to business. Kleiner took coffee, declined a drink, admired the boat—which was the size and color of a small naval corvette—and managed to conceal his impatience. Finally, they descended a ladder to the forward hold, where a great array of weaponry was displayed on the benches or on rails around the bulkheads, a lethal warehouse, full of glittering things.

"You see what you want?" asked the Arab, gesturing

toward his stock. "I can get other items, but it will take time."

"Most of what I need is here," said Kleiner, taking the list from his pocket. "I want two M-16 rifles with two magazines to the weapon and, say, one hundred rounds to the gun. I need a twelve-gauge pump shotgun . . . that Winchester 1200 will do fine. I also need a pistol, minimum nine-mil caliber, with a silencer. I'll take this fighting knife. Then, let's see. I want a kilo or two of plastic explosive, some instantaneous fuse, and two or three radio detonators. Finally, I need some RPGs and a rocket-launcher. Can you do all that?"

The Arab's eyebrows had gone up a little during this recital, but he didn't hesitate before replying. "Yes, but some of this is specialized material. It will be very expensive. The rifles alone will cost three hundred and fifty dollars each. Cash."

"I didn't ask about the price. Price is no problem. Can you do it? All of it?"

"Yes. You may have to accept one or two secondhand items, but I can do it."

"And no questions?"

The Arab smiled. "Silence is included in the price."

It was Kleiner's turn to smile. "I've told you not to worry about the price, but I do worry about silence. If you ever feel inclined to ask questions, or even worse, to answer them, remember that I found you once and I can find you again."

"Please . . ." The Arab spread his hands. "This is business. Apart from silence, will you need anything else?"

"Yes," Kleiner said thoughtfully. "I'll need to borrow that Zodiac dinghy of yours for a few hours. Unless you have one to sell?"

"That will be extra. Zodiac dinghies cost money."

"How many times must I tell you not to worry about price?"

Klaus was on the telephone when Simon and Terry returned at the end of the afternoon. Nothing was said until they had both stripped, put on swimsuits, and washed off the dust with a couple of laps in the pool. By then, Kleiner had come out, trailed by Renée and Lucia, and they stood at poolside, waiting until Simon swam over.

"How did it go, Klaus?"

"It went fine, but there is good news and bad news. The bad news is that someone tried to kill John Catton. The good news is that they failed, though they killed his sergeant. . . ."

"Jesus!" said Simon, leaping from the water. "Tell me more."

When everyone had digested the news, Simon looked at the group gathered around the poolside table, chewing his lower lip thoughtfully. "We've got to pull out of here," he said. "It's too risky for Terry and Renée."

"We can look after ourselves," Terry said.

"No, you can't," Simon said. "Vargas knows now that it didn't work in Majorca, and he's got people looking for us. If he finds us here . . . well, there goes the neighborhood. Besides, I think you've done all you can for the moment, except that little driving job. Did you get all the stuff we need, Klaus?"

"Eventually. It's in the garage. The Sons of the Desert can be remarkably cagey. I had to give him references and wait while he checked me out. He put on a real song and dance. Anyway, I have the hardware, and he assures me that anything else we might need will be available for spot cash. I've got you a heavy pistol, an ACP Colt .45, with a silencer. How was it up there?"

"Well, it won't be easy. The place is a fortress. There are at least seven guards. Most of them have pistols, but I saw at least one with a Mac-10. I didn't see Freddie Bright, but his car was there. I'll draw you a map and maybe do another recce, but I have it pretty clear in my mind how we can do it."

Terry shot an anxious look at Renée. "Si wants me to drive him in to see Freddie. What d'you think? Shall I do it?"

Renée's normally cheerful face turned hard as she looked at Simon. "Lucia's been telling me what you are up to here,

Simon. It's not Terry's kind of business, and I don't want him involved."

"I wouldn't ask, but I can't get in without him, Renée. We have to strike at Freddie and then get after Vargas before he gets onto us, and I want to do the job fast and go away. For all our sakes."

"I know Terry will do anything you ask him, the poor bloody fool, but I'd just as soon he didn't. He's all I've got, Simon."

"Come on, woman. If all I have to do is drive the motor, I think I'll do it," Terry said. "Just this once, for old times' sake. I think it'd be a bit of fun."

"Then more fool you," Renée snapped. "If he gets into any trouble, Simon, or anything happens to him, you'll have me on your track."

"Nothing will happen to him, I promise," said Simon, getting up. "Come on, you two," he said to Klaus and Terry. "Let's go and clean our new toys."

"The real problem is where to hit first," Kleiner said. "Or have you worked that out as well? Is it the house or the boat, or both together? I've an idea about the boat."

Simon and Kleiner were cleaning the weapons on a bench at the back of Terry's garage, stripping down the actions, pulling the barrels through with four-by-two cloth, getting the heavy factory grease off. In another corner, Terry, the old commando assault engineer, was making up plastic charges, whistling quietly to himself, stopping from time to time to listen but saying nothing.

"I've got that worked out, up to a point," Simon said, "but there is no point in planning everything in detail, because once it starts, things tend to change. We'll just go in and play it by ear."

"I know that," Kleiner said impatiently, "but where do we start?"

"First, we go for Freddie. Everyone else, except Vargas, is small change, so they can wait. Tomorrow we will go and have another look at his house from the hill, and I'll show you the ground. We will also take a drive to Puerto Banus and check out Freddie's minders and his boat. Then, if everything looks in order, we'll hit them tomorrow. We need to clean that right out, if only for Terry's sake, so Freddie first."

"Are you sure we can get at him? From what you tell me, he has an army up there."

"So what? Terry and I will drive in. I'll play chauffeur and deal with the gate guard. Terry has been there a couple of times and Freddie knows him, so we should waltz in, but if it looks impossible, we'll come right out again. However, if it looks okay, I'll deal with Freddie. Fixing him will put a big crimp in the Cartel's little game. We owe John Catton and Yates that much. Once I have Freddie, you can cut loose on the lab with the RPGs. There is a good firing position on the hill. You can see the house and the lab from there, in easy range. A rocket-propelled grenade or two through the roof should brew things up nicely. Also, if things get tricky, you can fire cover while we pull out. But given surprise, we should manage well enough."

"Right," said Kleiner, wiping oil from his hands. "I can do that. It sounds straightforward."

"When you two say *deal* with Freddie, what exactly do you mean?" Terry asked. "Freddie doesn't make deals. The cops down here aren't too worried about the U.K.'s dope problem. If you give him to them, they'll probably let him go."

"We don't intend to give him to the police, here or anywhere," Simon said. "It's not enough just to short-circuit the Cartel's supply route. We need to show your London colleagues, hiding down here on the Costa del Crime, that working for the Cartel is a risky business. When Freddie gets blitzed, the Cartel won't find it too easy to make another connection."

"Therefore," Kleiner put in, inexorably, "when we have gunned Freddie, and as many of his men as we can, and blown his base to pieces, we are going to roar down to Puerto Banus, kill the two who murdered Philip Wintle, and sink that bloody boat. If anyone gets in our way, too bad. Right, Simon?"

"Correct," Simon said. "It's like a war, Terry. Think of it as a war."

"You can't do that," Terry cried. "This isn't the Wild West, Si. And why do you have to whack Errol and Eddie? Yobs though they are, you just can't do it."

"They killed a friend of ours," Kleiner said, "and there is dirt between us. It needn't concern you, Terry, you can stay out of it."

"This is my bloody house, mate. I have to live here in Spain when you've disappeared off back to Krautland, and Freddie's not the only villain on the coast."

"That's another reason why we have to whack them, Terry," Simon said quietly. "We have to make a clean sweep. You don't have to clout anyone. Just get me into Freddie's place and help blow the *Mariposa* out of the water. Can you do that at least?"

Terry shook his head, wondering how he got into all this. Then he brightened a little . . . explosives were his passion. "Yes. Well, I think so. These shortwave detonators are the problem. Next time you get a book of instructions, Klaus, make sure it's in English. This one's in bloody Arabic."

"I'm sorry," Kleiner said apologetically. "I didn't think to look."

"Well, nobody's perfect. Look, let me show you. You put the detonator in the plastic here, and switch the radio on, tuning sender and receiver, or radio and detonator, if you like, to the same channel—say, ten—see?"

"Okay."

"Right. Then, when you are at a safe distance, you press the switch, and a radio wave ignites the charge—whammo! No boat! Simple."

"So what's the problem?" Simon asked.

"There are two problems, old son. First, I can't read these instructions, so I don't know what the range of the radio beam is—half a mile, two miles? God knows! Second, when I arm the charge and switch the receiver on, I hope none of the radios in the port are transmitting on the same frequency. If they are, the bloody thing will go up in my face. There must be a safety device here somewhere, but I can't find it.

176

Still, that's my problem. You'd better worry about Eddie and Errol. They're a mean couple of bastards who'd stamp on your face sooner than look at you."

"That's what I'm relying on," Simon said.

"You're barmy, both of you," Terry said. "Look, one final question, if you don't mind. Why blow up the *Mariposa*? A beautiful boat like that, it's a bloody crime."

Kleiner looked at Simon before answering. "We are ripping out the entire line, Terry, root and branch. Every link the Cartel has in Europe—labs, transport, personnel, the lot."

"Besides that," Simon said, "Klaus enjoys it."

That evening, Simon and Lucia took a turn around the garden after dinner, Wolf and Tiger cavorting along happily at their sides. It had been a strained meal, Renée grim and silent, Terry giving her anxious glances, making an extra effort to be cheerful. Klaus had taken his coffee and disappeared to his room. The waiting was beginning to tell on them all.

"I've been talking to Renée," Lucia said quietly. "While you were out. I told her everything, asked her advice. She's very sensible."

"Renée's no fool," Simon agreed. "And what did she say?"

"She said that since I can't change you, I must either leave you or accept it . . . live with it."

Simon hesitated. "And have you decided which?"

"Don't you care?"

"Of course I care. But I'm in a bind."

"And then there will be something else, and something else. . . ."

"No, it won't always be like this."

"It will. You know it will." Her voice was flat, resigned. "Yates or Klaus or John will drag you into something else."

"So, what are you going to do?"

"Unlike you, Simon, I do have a choice. Renée pointed it out to me."

"And?"

"Find us a way out of this, and I'll stay. If not, I won't be here when this is over. I can pick up my life again. I'm a doctor, remember? I could go to Africa or India and do something worthwhile with my life. So you do have a choice, Simon."

Simon stopped and turned toward her, taking her hands in his. "I have to see this one through."

"I know that . . . but afterwards?"

"Well, I have been thinking, and Terry has a few ideas. There may be a way. . . ."

"Then find it. Oh, and one other thing . . . Renée thinks we should get married."

Simon chuckled. "She would. She's very proper. Her generation—my generation—thinks this is living in sin."

"She says you are ruining my life."

"She's right," Simon said.

"Then you'd better do something about it."

"I will," he said.

Next morning, half a mile from Freddie's house, Terry pulled the car off the road and put on the brake. Glancing at him from the passenger side, Simon noticed the sheen of sweat on his upper lip, the slight tremor in the hands on the wheel.

"Nervous?" he asked.

"I'm shitting myself. It's been a long time since we went to the wars, Si. Too long, maybe."

"You'll be all right. Do you think Klaus is in position yet?"

"We'll give him another couple of minutes. Who is he, this Kleiner bloke, and what's his game? He gets that mad look in his eyes when he even thinks about Freddie Bright and that Vargas bloke."

"He's got a hard-on for druggies. But it's a game for him as well. He's got everything else and not a lot to do but make more money. Don't ask me. Maybe he's just bored."

"When I get bored, I hop into bed with Renée. He must be bloody mad, that's what."

"I think he probably is," Simon said. "He looks and walks and talks all right, but there is nothing inside but hate. But he can handle himself. He's a very cool hand when the shit starts flying. I've seen him go, and it's most impressive."

"I only hope you're right," said Terry, reaching for the starter. "If he lets us down in there, Freddie will have our balls. And Renée will have yours, if anything happens to me."

"I think we'd better go," Simon said, "before you make me nervous. Hop out, it's time I played chauffeur."

Terry got out and climbed into the back of the Rolls, while Simon shifted across to the driver's side and began to fiddle with the controls, adjusting the mirror and settling into the seat.

"Why don't you get an automatic?" he said. "I haven't changed gear in years."

"I don't hold with them," Terry said. "Not on a Roller. And go gentle, this motor cost me forty thousand nicker. I don't want it scratched."

"Don't worry. If I scratch it, I'll pay for the respray. Pink is a very tacky color, Terry."

"I love it. If you don't like it, bleedin' get out and walk!"

It took them less than five minutes to reach the gate of Freddie's house, Simon swinging the big car around the bends on the mountain road, then putting the car in neutral as it rolled up to the barrier, keeping his eyes ahead as he braked to a halt.

"Over to you," he said.

Terry wound down the window and leaned out, smiling broadly as the guard, a holstered pistol in his belt, came out of the hut and over to the car, frowning.

"Morning!" Terry said cheerfully. "Remember me? I'm Mr. Cockerill, coming to see Freddie. Is he in?"

"Sí, Señor. He is at the house. But is he expecting you?" The man was close now, admiring the car, one hand on the roof, consulting the clipboard in his other hand, running an eye down the list of names. "I do not have you here."

"Naw . . . it's a surprise. I'm not on there. Just give him a bell and tell him I'm here . . . Terry Cockerill. Tell him I've dropped in for a beer."

"Sí, Señor. Momentito." He wandered off, his shoes crunching lightly across the stones. Sitting behind the wheel, looking ahead, Simon watched the man out of the corner of his eye, saw him crank the wheel of the telephone, speak a few words, and then listen, nodding, turning his head to glance at them out of the window.

"We're in," Terry said softly. "In like Flynn."

"Shut up," Simon said. The guard came back, smiling, moving in front of the car to release the chain on the barrier, letting the pole float up as he waved the car forward.

"Go on up to the *casa,* Señor," he called. "Señor Bright says he is getting the *cerveza* out."

"Good," said Terry, winding up the rear window and leaning forward to tap Simon on the shoulder. "In we go, driver."

The man stepped back into the doorway of his hut to let the car roll past, and was standing there, smiling, when Simon trod gently on the brake. As the car rocked to a halt, he picked up the pistol from his lap, leaned out of the window, and shot the guard full in the chest, twice. There was no loud noise, just a soft *phut* from the silencer. The impact lifted the man right off his feet and flung him back through the doorway, crashing down over the table onto the floor.

"Jesus!" said Terry, shocked. "What the hell are you doing?"

Simon opened the door of the car, got out, and walked across into the hut to shoot the man again in the head; another soft *phut,* nothing more. Then he took the pistol from the holster on the man's belt and came out again, closing the door, tossing the pistol onto the passenger seat as he climbed back into the car.

"I'm inside now, Terry," he said, their eyes meeting in the mirror. "You can get out now if you want to. I don't need you anymore, but I do need the car."

"What did you have to do that for?" Terry's voice was wild, shaky. "What had that bloke ever done to you?"

"Nothing. But if we have to get out of here in a hurry, I don't want him standing in the way."

"I don't know what's got into you, Si," said Terry, shaking his head regretfully. "There isn't a war on, man. You need your bloody head examined. This is *wrong,* Simon."

"Correction; there *is* a war on," Simon said, "and if we are going to have an amateur psychiatry session, I'd rather we didn't have it right here. Now, are you coming in or not?"

"Get on with it," Terry said savagely, "and pass that pistol over here."

Freddie opened the front door himself, a beer bottle in one hand, the slightly puzzled smile on his face changing to a frown as he saw Simon getting out of the car behind Terry.

"Hello, Terry. Bit of a surprise you dropping in like this—bit out of order, even. And who the hell is this?" He jerked his head toward Simon. "I wasn't told there were two of you."

"He's a friend of mine," Terry said easily. "Wants to meet you. Simon Quarry, meet Freddie Bright."

Ten feet away, Simon took out the pistol from under his jacket and leveled it at Freddie's navel. "Get back inside, Mr. Bright, and slowly," he said. "Do nothing rash, or this will go off. If you think I'm joking, try me."

Freddie still stood there. *"Who* did you say?" he asked Terry. "What's your game?" If Freddie was afraid, he didn't show it. He kept his hard glare on Terry, and took a swig from the neck of the beer bottle in his hand.

"Do as he says," said Terry, pleading. "He's not joking. He's just killed your bloke down at the gate."

"My name's Quarry," Simon said. "Remember the name? Or Philip Wintle? You must remember him. A couple of your boys beat his head in back in London a while back. Your mob have killed two other friends of mine recently. Now, it's my turn, Mr. Bright, so get inside."

Freddie ignored him, keeping his eyes still fixed on Terry.

"I'll not forget this, Terry," he said. "You'll bleed for this, you grassing bastard, bringing him in here. I'll have your balls for breakfast, see if I don't."

"Get inside," Simon said again. "Or I'll drop you here and now. Put that bottle down, then put your hands up on top of your head. Do it!"

"All right, I know who you are, but what do you want, eh?" asked Freddie, moving back at last. He dropped the beer bottle into the flower pot by the door, and placed his hands, fingers entwined, on top of his balding head, stepping back inside as Simon and Terry came forward. "What's he want with me?" he asked Terry.

Terry shrugged. "You'd better ask him," he said.

"Just for starters," Simon said, "I want back all the stuff your men took from Philip Wintle's flat in London. Where is it? And where are Vargas's boys?"

"You want the stuff? You can have it. It's through here," said Freddie, snarling. "And never mind bloody Vargas, my own boys'll be around soon, you'll see. Come through here, cocker."

Freddie led them down the hallway of his house, lowering one hand to open a door, raising them above the level of the doorframe without being told to, turning as he stepped through. When he brought his hands down again, they were holding a double-barreled, sawn-off shotgun. Simon heard the hammers cock, saw the black holes of the muzzles swinging toward him, heard himself yelling a warning to Terry, flung himself back, and opened fire.

Freddie Bright died game. Simon's first bullet took him full in the chest and knocked him down, but he still got his shot off, once, twice, a deafening boom in the silence of the house, buckshot lashing the walls, shredding the glass mirrors, blasting a huge hole in the front door. Simon and Terry were down in a tangle on the floor, rolling for cover, when Simon got his arm free and fired again. Sitting up in the doorway, the shotgun still held in his beefy hands, Freddie Bright fell back and died.

"That's bloody torn it," said Terry, struggling to his feet, ears ringing from the blast. "Where did he get the shooter from? Are you all right?"

Simon got a grip on a banister rail and pulled himself to his feet. "He had it stashed above the door. Clever. I should have guessed he'd have something like that. Stupid of me. Listen!"

There were shouts from above, footsteps thudding across the landing. Simon ran back down the hallway to the foot of the stairs, glanced up, then leapt back swiftly as a Mac-10 machine gun chattered at him from the upper landing, knocking chips off the banisters, the shot bouncing off the tiles, shattering more of the door glass. Simon snapped two rounds up the stairs and ran back down the hall, full tilt.

"Through here!" yelled Terry, racing ahead. They fled through the living-room door, vaulting over Freddie's body, pistols in their fists, half seeing men outside running hard toward the house from every quarter. There was more shooting, a burst of fire from the hall behind. Terry turned and fired back past Simon, out through the doorway, once, twice, the deep boom of his pistol cutting across the rattle of the machine gun, cutting it suddenly short.

"Jesus!" said Terry, surprised, taking a sharp look at the pistol in his hand. "I hit him."

"Come on, you idiot," urged Simon, pulling at Terry's arm. "Let's get out of here, and fast. Where the hell is Kleiner?"

Kleiner was waiting on the hill. When the shooting started, he had been lying flat on his stomach among the rocks, studying the terrain. Now, he was kneeling, the rifle at his shoulder, sights set, the M-16 sling tight across his arm and chest, braced to open fire. Men were spilling out over the ground below, there were more shots, shouts of inquiry, people yelling to one another; but where the hell were Simon and his fat friend?

They came out of the side door, running hard down the path for the car parked at the front of the house. As they ran, Kleiner saw dust dancing across the bricks behind them, saw a window shatter. He picked out the man firing and killed him with one clean shot in the back. Then he switched his sights and began to shoot down the other men converging on the fugitives. He had hit three before the guards even realized where the fire was coming from. Kleiner saw one man stop and point up the hill, heard a bullet slap over his head into the trees. He aimed at the black pit of that open, yelling mouth, eased the foresight up a fraction, and shot the man right between the eyes.

Simon and Terry were away now, the big pink car racing down toward the gates, the doors still swinging open, tires screaming on the tarmac, a shrill sound above the noise of gunfire. In the open, devoid of cover, the guards had no chance against the rifleman on the high ground. Firing rapidly, shifting aim, Kleiner put more high-velocity rounds into men running about wildly, like ants in the open, quelling any return fire. Then he switched his attention back to the laboratory. Though shielded from the house by the bulk of the hill, the workers inside must have heard the shooting, but only now were men—first one, two, now a third—starting to come out, staring about them, looking up toward the slope, one man pointing up at Kleiner. In the sudden stillness after the shooting stopped, Kleiner could even hear their voices, a rattle of Spanish.

Kleiner put the hot, smoking rifle down, picked up the loaded RPG rocket-launcher, and fired. There was a small sound, a coughing—*stonk!* The first grenade looped away over the hillside down into the valley, and landed just in front of the three men. They had watched it coming, transfixed, and the explosion threw them aside, fragments shredding their bodies. Kleiner grunted and thumbed another grenade into the launcher.

His second shot was better. The rocket-propelled grenade hit the laboratory roof with a sharp clang and exploded. Seconds later, so did the laboratory. Ether is a powerful, volatile gas, and the detonating fumes made a most impressive sight. The roof came off, rising on top of a billowing red fireball, flames licking out around the edge and across the trees. The searing heat forced Kleiner to raise an arm across his face, crouching among the rocks as the roaring impact of the blast swept out of the valley in a roiling mass of dust and smoke and flame and debris. Shielding his eyes, he saw a barrel soar out of the fireball like a fat rocket, curling over his head to explode in the brush behind. Fires started up everywhere in the trees; he could hear branches crackling as the flames raced away through the dry brush, and as the smoke rolled away, he saw that the factory had gone; only a crater still remained amid a scorched and blackened circle of debris. Ignoring the blazing forest at his back, Kleiner put the launcher down, fitted a new magazine into the M-16, and ran down toward the house, picking his way in through the shattered fence. Once in, he moved about quietly and methodically, while the flames licked closer about the trees. He found every guard, dead or wounded, and put a bullet into every head. Only when he was sure that everyone was finished did he climb back up the slope and through the crackling trees to the waiting car. Behind him, the forest began to blaze, the flames driven by the rising wind toward the waiting walls of Freddie's house.

=== 13 ===

Simon Quarry had visited two bars along the quay at Puerto Banus before he reached the one he wanted. In the first, he had a beer to ease a mouth that felt strangely dry. In the second, he had a large Ciento y Tres, taking care to slop most of it over his shirt. Although most of the quayside bars were packed with the early evening crowd, places where people gathered for a drink or two before dinner, the last bar Simon entered was half empty. This fact was not entirely unconnected with the presence, sprawled at a table by the door, of hulking, tattooed Eddie and his big black mate, Errol, who were casting surly looks at anyone attempting to enter, and sharing a large joint. The barman didn't like it much, but over the last ten days Eddie and Errol had frequently demonstrated that they were both quick to take offense, and violent if provoked.

Since neither made any attempt to move, it was easy for Simon to bump into Eddie's legs, exchange a hard look, giving a harder, longer one to Errol, before reeling on up to the bar, knocking over a chair on the way. Eddie and Errol sat up a little straighter in their chairs and glared down the bar after him.

"Gi' me a beer," said Simon loudly, throwing a handful of change onto the brass top of the counter. "Make it a big one."

"What kind? San Miguel, Krönenbourg, Estrella Dorada . . . ?"

"No . . . none of that foreign muck. Sign outside said you had Watney's, so give us a pint of that. Good British beer, that's what I want."

A pint in his fist, Simon propped his elbow on the counter and turned to address the room. "Well, it's nice here . . . I like it. I like it very much. English voices, real ale, and a Sambo in the corner. Just like back home. Bloody España, *por favor,* gets more like sodding Brixton every day." He leered cheerily at the two by the door, and winked at the barman.

"You got a big mouth, white man," Errol said. "Was I getting out of this chair, I might close it for you real good."

"Oh yes?" Simon sneered. "You an' whose army?" He turned his back on the pair and winked again at the barman. "All mouth," he said loudly. "Nig-nogs are all mouth."

"You want to be careful with that pair," said the barman softly, keeping his head down. "They're a mean couple of bastards. I've had trouble with them all week."

"You ought to kick 'em out," Simon said. "Make space for decent people. Give me another one of these—just a half. Don't stand no nonsense from coons, is what I say."

A hand settled on his arm, a big, raw-knuckled hand at the end of a freckled, muscular forearm—Eddie's. His fingers dug deeply into Simon, his face was leaning close, his red-flecked eyes looked mean.

"You are totally out of order," Eddie said slowly. "Racialist, piss-arsed bastards like you need a good kicking, and I'm just the one to give it to you. Keep your trap shut, got it? If you know what's good for you."

"Let it be, Eddie," the barman said. "Can't you see he's drunk?"

Simon tore his arm free from Eddie's grasp and went into his National Front imitation. "You keep your trunk out," he said to the barman. "And you . . ." He turned to Eddie. "You ought to be ashamed of yourself, of your *race,* of being *British,* sitting in front of *foreigners* boozing with a bleeding *coon.* It lets us all down."

"It's a free country," Eddie said, "so why don't you just piss off home if you don't like it?"

"That's just it," shrieked Simon, getting well into his stride. "It's *my* home, *my* home, *your* home! It's not *their* bleeding home, yet it's overrun with nig-nogs. I came down here with the wife and kids to get away from the black invasion, and the first thing I see is you boozing with a bloody spade."

"He don't listen," Eddie said to the barman, shaking his head. "He really wants a kicking, don't he? He's asking for it—straight."

"Not in here, Eddie," the barman warned. "You got anything needs doing, do it outside. I can't have more trouble."

"He won't do nothing," declared Simon, slamming his glass on the counter. "Not him, not a bloke who goes drinking with blokes from Bongo-Bongo Land. Well, I'm not watching. It makes me sick. I'm off somewhere decent."

"You're not going anywhere," Eddie said. "You and me and my mate Errol back there are going somewhere quiet to have a little chat, see?" He prodded Simon in the chest twice with a finger as hard as a rivet, and went back to his table. From there, he and Errol kept their eyes on Simon, waiting. Well, so far, so good, Simon thought. Now, all he had to do was get out of here and bring them hurrying after him. Somewhere quiet they wanted, somewhere quiet they'd get. Quiet as the grave.

"You're in dead trouble," the barman said. "If you like, I'll phone the Guardia Civil and get them to take you out of here. Then you'd better get that wife and kids of yours and push off out of the Puerto. And don't come back."

"I am not going to be pushed around," Simon declared. "We ought to make a stand, and I'm the one to do it."

"You're a prick," the barman said contemptuously. "You're asking for all you're going to get. Just go away, will you?"

Simon pushed himself off the bar and reeled back down the room until he was stopped by Eddie's outstretched legs, braced across the door. Supporting himself with one hand on a chairback, Simon looked down at them. "I've got something to say to you, Sambo," he said, grinning at Errol.

"Is that right?" Eddie said. "And what is it?" The pair of them were grinning up at Simon, Errol slowly stubbing out the joint, Eddie spinning a beer glass gently in his hamlike hands. "It's too late to say sorry now."

"That'll be the day, when I say sorry to the likes of you," Simon said. "I'm going to the carpark to get my motor, and you pair aren't going to stop me."

"Well, you can try it," said Eddie, lifting his legs back. "So why don't you?"

"You called me a racialist back there," said Simon, swaying. "And that's not fair. In fact, the two things I can't stand are racialists and bloody niggers."

That did the trick. Errol rocked forward in his chair and began to get up, while Eddie swiped at Simon with one heavy paw. Simon shoved Errol back in his chair, ducked under Eddie's arm, and stumbled for the door. He just made it. Dodging through the strolling crowds, looking back after a thirty-yard sprint down the quay, Simon saw the pair burst out of the bar and come pounding after him, knocking casual strollers out of their way. He let them follow and keep him in sight, as he ran on into the darkness of the parking lot.

The tall buildings lining the quayside blocked most of the light from the port, but there was still enough to see by as Simon wove his way among the cars. The carpark was full at this hour but quiet, with most of the drivers and their passengers well into their second or third drink at some bar along the quay. There was no difficulty in finding Kleiner, who was leaning against a car near the back fence.

"Is it all right?" Kleiner asked. "Are they coming? Both of them?"

"They are now," panted Simon, nodding. "It got tricky because I couldn't think of any more insults."

"Well, it worked. Here they come. My, but they are a big couple of bastards."

As Errol and Eddie began to circle in toward them, Simon

took the pistol from one pocket, the silencer from another, and began to screw them together before handing the pistol to Kleiner.

"You enjoy this more than I do," Simon said. "So I'll leave this to you . . . it throws high and to the right."

Kleiner turned as the sound of feet grew louder, keeping the pistol by his side as the pair loped up, peering about them in the dim light. They slowed down, grinning, when they saw Simon, sparing barely a glance for Kleiner, Errol straying back to block the entrance, Eddie moving forward toward the pair by the fence.

"You couldn't have stitched yourself up better if you'd tried," said Eddie, wiping the sweat off his face with the back of one arm, the beer glass still in his hand. "This place is just right for a kicking, and Christ, are you in for a kicking." Then, to Kleiner: "If you don't want a share of it, push off now, mate, while you still can."

"No, I think I'll stay," Kleiner said smoothly. "I'd like to watch."

"Eddie," Simon said apologetically, "I admire a bloke who stands by his friend. I'd even like to apologize to Errol for what I said back there. It was wrong and uncalled for, but I just couldn't think of any other way to get you here. And here you are. So . . ."

"What the . . . What's all this Eddie and Errol stuff?" asked Eddie, frowning. "Who the hell are you?" Eddie really was the brighter one.

"We're friends of Philip Wintle," Kleiner said. "Remember him? He was the old man you killed in London a couple of weeks back. That was wrong, Eddie. You have to pay for things like that. Time's up, the bill's due."

Kleiner fired, twice. There was no sound, but Eddie's shirtfront slapped and puckered as the bullets went in, two black holes jetting in the fabric. The impact hurled Eddie back, throwing him against a car to roll off the hood onto the ground, vanishing in the darker space between the vehicles.

"This is one hell of a good pistol," Kleiner said to Simon. "Hits like a mule."

Errol had come forward, missing all this as he weaved

between the cars to stand before them. There had been no sound, so where had Eddie gone? Who were these people? Errol dug in his pockets, fisted out a knife, and snapped it open, the blade glittering as he moved toward Simon, looking about as he approached.

"What you done to Eddie, eh? Where's he gone?"

"Eddie is no more," said Kleiner, raising the pistol. "Eddie has gone to the great kicking place in the sky. Now, it's your turn. Good-bye, Errol."

Errol saw the gun and stopped in his tracks, forgetting Eddie. "I'm getting out of here, man, and you ain't stopping me."

"Want to bet?" Kleiner said.

Errol ran. He whipped around, crashing past a car, and was off across the parking lot, running hard, head back, the knife blade flashing in the shafts of light as he sprinted for the safety of the quay.

"For godsake," Simon said, "get on with it."

"Wait," Kleiner said. He rested the pistol butt firmly in the palm of his left hand, aimed carefully at that jinking form, and fired once . . . twice. A giant hand lifted Errol forward, off his feet, hands flailing, headlong across the hood of a car, smashing into the windshield, before he cartwheeled out of sight, leaving a drift of dust to float up into the slanting shafts of light.

There was a short silence. In the stillness, Simon could distinctly hear the blood pounding in his ears. He watched as Kleiner felt around with his feet for the ejected cartridges, picked them up, and put them in his pocket, easing the hammer forward, before handing the pistol back to Simon.

"You . . . are . . . something . . . else," Simon said at last, spacing the words carefully.

"So are you," Kleiner said. "We both are."

"Maybe . . . but there's a difference," Simon said. He nodded down at Eddie's sprawled body. "You've done that before, haven't you?"

"Several times," Kleiner said. "But not for a long time. Now, it's your turn.

* * *

Seated on a bench halfway down the quayside, Terry had seen Simon go running past, and watched Eddie and Errol pound after him, barging a path through the startled crowd. He listened to remarks about drunken English hooligans, then crossed to a bar and waited there, a beer untouched on the table before him. Surprisingly soon, Simon came back, slipping into the chair opposite, his face pale.

"Well, what happened?" Terry muttered. "Did it work?"

"I'll give you two guesses," said Simon, reaching across the table for Terry's glass. "Do you want this beer? If not, I've got one hell of a thirst."

"Where's the kraut? What happened to Eddie and Errol?"

Simon looked at him wryly. "How long have I known you? You don't really believe any of this is happening, do you? Look, Phase Two is complete. Kleiner is clearing up back there and getting the Zodiac ready. We can go onto the *Mariposa* any time you please."

"Then let's go now," Terry said, "before I puke."

The *Mariposa* was moored, stern on, just down the quay, with no anchor watch, no guard patrolling on the upper deck, the gangway in position. Eddie and Errol were the anchor watch, but they had preferred to do their watching from the bar across the quay. When Simon and Terry stopped at the bottom of the gangway and studied the *Mariposa*, they looked just like any of the other evening strollers, passing the time by admiring a rich man's plaything.

"Have you got your box of tricks?" Simon asked.

"Right here," replied Terry softly, lifting the bag at his side. "What do we do now?"

"We go on board and clean up . . . me first. You stay back here."

Simon leading, they went up the gangway and along the upper deck. The sliding door into the upper cabin was open, and from somewhere below, Simon could hear the voice of someone talking in Spanish, urgently, repeatedly. It must be the radio operator, and from his tone, he had been trying to raise Freddie's house for some time. There was an edge of impatience and desperation in his voice. Simon raised his head and looked across the masts and rooftops of the harbor to where the mountain skyline was glowing from end-to-end with fire. Kleiner had given Freddie a funeral pyre to go out on.

"Wait here," he said quietly to Terry, "and don't go away."

"I'll be here, but be quick," Terry said.

As he reached the bottom of the ladder, Simon took the pistol from his belt and peered around the edge of the drawn-back green curtain that screened off the radio room. With one earphone held to his head, the operator was still talking anxiously into his transmitter. Looking up, his eyes met Simon's in the doorway.

"¿Qué? ¿Quién es?"

Simon fired. The bullet knocked the man off his chair, and Simon left him on the floor as he checked the other cabins, empty now, one with tumbled linen and empty bottles littering the twin bunks. Eddie and Errol were not good housekeepers. In the last cabin, Simon found another man, his hand, chest, and head wrapped in bandages, lying on his bunk reading a book. He looked up in surprise as Simon came in, and he was still looking surprised when Simon fired. This must be the fourth Colombian, one of the killers who had taken part in the attack on his house. Simon stood over him for a moment, suddenly weary, rubbing his eyes, then went back to the foot of the ladder and called up to Terry.

"Keep your voice down," said Terry, rattling swiftly down the stairs.

"Why?" Simon asked. "Nobody's listening. We have the whole boat to ourselves."

Terry glanced in the radio room, at the body in the corner, the crackling radio. "Christ, not another! D'you have to do this? Is it necessary? You're like a bloody plague."

"So it seems. Come on, you have work to do."

While Terry got the deckboards up and began to lay the plastic charges along the keel, Simon searched the boat. He took all the charts from the wheelhouse, a notebook, scribbled notes from the chart table, and a telephone book from the main cabin, riffling through all the books along the shelves. He found very little. Then, opening the cabin fridge to find something to drink, he found the safe. He examined it for a moment, tugging at the handle, turning the combination lock, listening carefully to the soft whirr from the cogs, and then went back to find Terry, who was lying on the deck of the engine room, taping plastic charges onto the ribs of the hull.

"Leave that, and come and see this."

They studied the safe for a minute, Terry patting the steel top admiringly. "Nice job," he said. "Very nice. Putting it inside the fridge isn't a bad touch either. No floor or walls on a ship to fix it to, of course, but still, not a bad idea."

"Can you blow it," Simon asked, "and fast?"

Terry looked at him, amused. "Blowing safes is for the pictures," he said. "I'd need drills, maybe a themic lance, more jelly, and about three or four hours, at least. Also, I'd probably blow the boat to bits in the process."

"So we're knackered? You can't open it?"

"Maybe, maybe not. There's a couple of things I could try."

Terry got up, went over to the ship-to-shore telephone, glanced at it, then came back and began to spin the dial on the safe. "It's a six-figure lock, and you'd be surprised how many people use their own phone numbers as a safe combination. Afraid they'll lock it, forget the number, and have all the goodies stuck inside, I suppose." He tugged the handle, but nothing happened. "Not this time, though. Well, Freddie was never that thick."

Terry sat on his heels and pondered for a moment, then tried again. He spun the dial to and fro half a dozen times, listening, head on one side. Then he grunted, turned the handle, and slowly heaved the heavy door open.

"Second choice . . . Freddie's birthdate. Renée and me went to his birthday party a couple of weeks back, remember? Always worth trying that . . . and we were due for a bit of luck about now."

"You are a bloody marvel," Simon said, admiringly.

"No, my old son, I'm a professional. Turning over safes is

my business, see?" Terry got up, dusted his knees, and went back to laying the charges.

Inside the safe, Simon found useful stuff; a sheaf of passports, Colombian, British, and American, some issued in Cay Dorado, a thick file of shipping documents, airline weighbills and bills of lading, telex copies, another book full of phone numbers, and three kilos of vacuum-packed cocaine. He stowed all this into a bag dredged from under the bunk in Eddie's cabin, and carried it up to the bridge. As he turned on the switch and fired up the diesels, he saw the loaded Zodiac go cruising past, Kleiner at the tiller of the outboard, the contents covered with a tarpaulin, the high bow of the dinghy pointing out to sea.

"Terry!" Simon shouted down the companionway. "Are you ready? I need you up here to cast off the lines. Hurry up. Kleiner has just gone past. Is it done?"

"Just about. I'm going to arm the switches. Keep your fingers crossed. Here goes . . ."

There was no explosion, no violent sheet of flame. Seconds later, Terry came up the ladder, wiping the sweat from his face with a piece of rag. He grinned across at Simon and held out a hand that trembled slightly. "That little job tightened the sphincter. What shall I do now?"

Simon put the engines in neutral and snapped on the navigation lights. "Get down there and cast off those lines. Take your time and look casual. Then get back up here as I back her out."

"Right. Half a mo . . ."

Nobody paid much attention as the *Mariposa* backed into the channel and turned her sharp bow toward the sea. Boats went in and out of Puerto Banus at all hours of the night, for a moonlight cruise, or a fishing trip, or for some other, less innocent purpose. Simon picked up the Zodiac half a mile off the mole, and they cruised on together, the rubber dinghy keeping station fifty yards off their starboard beam, until they were ten miles offshore and the lights of Puerto Banus no more than a thin smear on the horizon, though higher up the mountains were ablaze. Then Simon killed the engines, and Kleiner came bumping gently alongside. They dragged Errol and Eddie from under the covering canvas and down into their cabin on the *Mariposa,* jamming the cabin door shut, while Kleiner lightened the dinghy still further by tipping the two rifles, the RPG-launcher, and all the unused grenades into the sea. Then Kleiner came back and picked up Terry and Simon. The dinghy was half a mile nearer the shore when Terry threw the switch. There was no flash, no big bang, just a solid thump, a tremor through the water, nothing more, but when they circled back to check, Freddie Bright's beautiful *Mariposa* had slipped beneath the surface of the sea.

14

Alec Yates was not normally made very welcome in the offices he visited. The ministers, the ministers of state, the senior staff in their various departments, took care to be cordial enough on the surface, quick to offer him tea or coffee or a glass of dry sherry according to the hour, but there was no real warmth. The reason for this lack of cordiality was suspicion. No one was quite sure where Yates fitted in, what he did, or to whom he was responsible. He flitted between the various offices of state, in particular between the Ministry of Defense and the Foreign and Commonwealth Office, and it was generally supposed that he reported to the Cabinet secretary. He had survived through various administrations formed by both political parties, and knew, or at least had close contact with, almost everyone in that undefined circle of influence that the British call the Establishment. Some said he was MI6, while others murmured that MI5 was more like it. Nobody really knew, yet everyone knew that if there was trouble around, particularly trouble of the violent kind, Alec Yates would have a hand in it somewhere. Alec Yates was in the business of getting things done, and as he was led into the minister's office on this particular afternoon, he knew exactly what had to be done and how to do it. A sense of certainty like that is very useful. The minister didn't really have a chance, but he had to be shifted into position delicately, smoothly, hardly aware of the movement.

"Come in and sit down, Alec . . . tea?" The minister looked worried. "I don't know why this particular baby has landed in my lap, but perhaps you can tell me what is going on. I thought Overseas Aid were in charge. That airport runway is their pigeon . . . milk?"

"Thank you, Minister . . . no milk, no sugar. I suppose you have the ball—or the baby, if you prefer—because you have Cabinet rank and the Cay Dorado islands fall in your remit at Foreign Affairs. However, I can tell you that as far as I can judge, things are going very well."

The minister grunted, moved his well-thumbed copy of Catton's report to one side, and flipped open a copy of *The Times*. "I'm glad to hear it. Since you tell me that is so, I must accept it, but have you seen the papers? 'A huge forest fire is raging above the Costa del Sol, causing some loss of life and great damage to property . . . believed to originate after an explosion above San Pedro d'Alcantara, on the property of Freddie Bright, well-known figure in London's underworld . . . et cetera, et cetera.' Also, right here in the next column, please note, a short paragraph saying that Bright's luxury motor yacht sailed from Puerto Banus and has disappeared, and underneath that, a note that the police are still seeking witnesses in the murder of Commander Wintle. To that we can add yesterday's front-page headlines on the attack on John Catton. I see today the IRA have denied involvement. Who planted the idea that they did it in the first place? But an interesting juxtaposition of articles, eh? The reptiles have nosed out that something is going on."

Yates smiled. "Well, an inspired leak at such a time can be useful, but let me assure you, Minister, that no one on the Costa del Sol, especially Freddie Bright, is in any position to talk to the press. His yacht is at the bottom of the Mediterranean, and the contents of his safe are under lock and key here in London. Quarry had them sent up yesterday in the diplomatic bag from Gilbraltar. When we have finished, we will have all we need to silence the Opposition, if it ever comes to that. The evidence we have assembled could be very useful."

"Even so," the minister grunted, "we approved the Catton scheme on the understanding that Philip Wintle, a man of known standing and the highest discretion, would be in charge—then he is killed, and now we have this." The minister rapped the newspaper. "Fires, boat thefts, shootings. It is making a noise, Alec. Someone is bound to notice, and then what?"

Alec sighed slightly. "Minister, insofar as it is obvious at all, it is obvious only because you and I know where all the pieces fit. To everyone else, all these events, from Wintle's murder on, are just an inconclusive jumble of unrelated incidents. Besides, first we have Catton, and then Kleiner and Quarry as two cutouts. As a third, you have me. You are completely in the clear."

"Up to now," the minister said sourly. "Only up to now. What all this is leading to is overturning the government of a friendly state. If that leaks, the UN and the Commonwealth will go mad. The government here will certainly fall, and that ought to make even you nervous. It scares the hell out of me."

Yates laughed lightly as he rose to add hot water to the teapot before refilling their cups. "It shouldn't scare you, Minister, but even so, I think you will feel happier if you know nothing about it . . . although I need your approval, of course."

"How can I approve if I don't know the details?" sighed the minister. "Let me hear the worst."

"Well, you can approve the principle, but leave the rest to me. It is essential that the arrangements appear to be a series of fortuitous events, a happy conjunction serving all parties. We must also be asked to intervene in Cay Dorado."

"That will be a nice trick if you can pull it off," the minister said.

"I think that can be arranged," Yates said smoothly. "There will now be a short delay, perhaps a week. This is to enable the various pieces to move into position, and the final planning stages to be completed. In my role as an aide from overseas, I shall fly to Cay Dorado in a few days' time for detailed talks about the proposed loan for the runway. That is the closest the government will come to any of this, and that loan has parliamentary approval. No one can make anything of that."

"I'm glad to hear it," the minister said. "And then?"

"Well, from this point on, the less you know, the better. However, I would ask you to stand by on a certain date to approve certain assistance under our security treaty with Cay Dorado from one of Her Majesty's ships."

The minister's eyebrows rose. "To do *what?*"

"One of our frigates, HMS *Dancer,* which is currently on station in the Caribbean, is starting a series of courtesy visits, beginning in Miami. She will be there for two days. She then sails directly for Cay Dorado. *Dancer* is also carrying a troop of Royal Marines from L Company of 42 Commando, which is currently stationed in Belize."

"Phew!" the minister exclaimed. "The plot thickens."

"Slightly, but it's all quite legitimate, Minister. Anyway, the scene now shifts to Cay Dorado. HMS *Dancer* arrives and begins the usual round of events surrounding a visit to a foreign port. There will be a captain's cocktail party for the local dignitaries and leading citizens. The President will be there with his Cabinet, as will I, and few people refuse an invitation from the Royal Navy. There will be a football match between the lower deck and the town team, a children's party, and as part of our defense and assistance program, the Royal Marines will address themselves to smartening up the island's defense force—drill, weapons training, and so on. Part of this training will include a night-raiding exercise for the entire defense force on a small cay some twenty miles by sea from Caytown. It will be conducted by one junior Royal Marines officer and a sergeant, leaving a captain of marines and thirty commandos on *Dancer.* The island's defense force consists of one rifle company of about a hundred men loosely affiliated to the West Indian Regiment, and we need them out of the way.

None of the participants knows anything about the wider issues. It's all SOP, standard operating procedure. On that night, I shall be dining with the President to finalize the loan. So, Minister, now you see the position. The defense force is miles away, I am dining with the President, and Vargas, I hope, is in his house waiting for the outcome of our talks. There are one or two other elements I won't trouble you with, but if all goes well, by the time the dust has settled, Cay Dorado will be both shaken and stirred."

When they returned from Puerto Banus, Kleiner thought that they should leave at once for Cay Dorado. Simon wouldn't hear of it. "We have to stay put," he said bluntly. "We got Terry and Renée into this mess, and the least we can do is stay here and look after them. Vargas won't let this go by . . . he's got too much time and money involved, and he'll hit back for sure."

"Then we should hit him first," Kleiner said patiently. "We know where he is, so why don't we go after him?"

"And how do you propose to get onto Cay Dorado? It's an island, man, and if we get on, how do we get out again? Cay Dorado is run by Vargas and his goons, and the President and police force are in his pocket. We'd never get off the airport."

"There will be a way," Kleiner said stubbornly. "There always is."

"I'm sure there is, but meanwhile we wait . . . and lie low," Simon said. "And that means you. You're the famous face around here, and if anything will pull Vargas down on us, it will be someone spotting you. So stay here and relax, while Catton sets up the next stage with Yates. Cay Dorado is Yates's problem. It's his move."

Kleiner was still restless, and took to long walks in the hills, returning late in the evening, covered in dust and torn by thorns. On other days, he would play long games of tennis with Lucia, or vanish across the mountains to Coin or Antequera to telephone his offices from remote pay phones. It was during one of these days, when Terry and Simon were sitting by the pool, playing chess, that the phone rang, and Terry, his eyes still on the board, picked up the receiver and answered it.

"Hello . . . Terry Cockerill . . . Who?"

There was a long silence, while Terry listened, his eyes on Simon, the startled expression on his face changing to one of amusement.

"Well, that's very kind of you," he said at last. "I remember it well . . . two coves and a girl . . . shouldn't be too difficult. No, I'd rather you left it to me, been enough trouble. No . . . I'll phone you . . . all right, you phone me. Have this on the house. Natch . . . right. And the same to you . . . 'bye."

He put the phone down and looked at Simon, grinning. "'Ave a guess . . . 'ave two."

"Vargas," Simon said. "Who else?"

"Fuck," said Terry, his face falling. "How'd you work that out?"

"You've met; at Freddie's party, right? He needs another connection. You have a firm in London. Maybe you're not interested, but it's a start. Right?"

"Wrong," Terry said. "Well, half-right. He said he had a business proposition, but right now he needed to find some people who were being difficult—a Mr. Kleiner, a Mr. Quarry, and a girl. Said he'd pay heavy money for a tip-off. Just think . . . I could probably have picked up fifty grand. Anyway, to stop him looking elsewhere, I said I'd be happy to look around . . . as a gesture of goodwill like. You're running out of time, Si. He's going to gun you, if he can."

Simon nodded, brooding. "I know . . . I also know that we ought to get out of here. It's too risky for you. On the other hand, it's safe as long as we lie low. When the Cartel are after you, there aren't that many places to hide."

"I don't mind for me," Terry said, "but there's Renée. He said he'd phone again in a couple of days. What'll I tell him?"

"I'll talk to Kleiner," Simon said. "Maybe we can lay a few fake trails . . . maybe we can lure Vargas out of Cay

Dorado. He may be after us, but we're after him, remember. All we have to do is tidy up a few loose ends."

Ted Bardsey was a loose end for the Cartel. If everyone else had not been so busy after the attempt on John Catton, someone might have thought about it and either sent Ted somewhere safe or at least offered him protection. The snag was that nobody really believed that the sort of thing that comes with cocaine, things that happened every day in Miami or Bogotá, could possibly happen in England. The fact that it had already happened to Wintle and Catton didn't alter this perception. After all, Bardsey was still a serving and senior officer in the Metropolitan Police. A suspended, even discredited officer perhaps, one under investigation by CIB2, but a serving police officer for all that, and therefore fireproof.

Bardsey spent most of his time at home these days, behind drawn curtains, slumped in front of the television, staring bleakly at the flickering screen for hours on end, working his way steadily down a bottle of whisky. He felt awkward in the streets, felt people were staring, while down at the golf club the atmosphere at the nineteenth hole grew increasingly stiff. The only relief from gloom came in the periodic visits from the CIB2 officers, probing into his affairs. In spite of all they were doing to him, taking his life apart, their visits were almost welcome, so when the doorbell chimed that afternoon, he hauled himself out of his chair and lumbered willingly toward the front door, bumping into his wife as she came out of the kitchen, wiping her hands on her apron.

"Oh not again," she said. "Shall I . . . ?"

"No, I'll get it, love. It'll be the Nosy Squad back again. You just put the kettle on, and I'll let them in."

When Ted saw the young men on the doorstep, his first thought was to take them for Mormons or Jehovah's Witnesses out on a mission. He had half closed the door again with a "Sorry, not interested," when they rushed him, carrying him back before them into the hall. That was when he tumbled to who they might be and what they could do.

With all his faults, Ted Bardsey had guts too. He yelled to his wife to run while he held them off, but she came rushing into the hall to see what was happening. One of the young men leapt forward and caught her as his companions dragged Ted down. She was strong and she fought back, but he held her, stabbing her twice, stifling her screams by stuffing her apron into her mouth, covering her face as he cut her throat. It was a slaughterhouse in there, but at least she died quickly. Ted was not so lucky. Vargas had told his hit men to teach Ted a lesson. It took both of them to cope with Ted as they dragged him, eyes bulging, through the kitchen out toward the garage. Later on, when the news got out, people wondered how the killers knew he had kept a chain saw out there.

That evening, Catton joined the small number of people admitted to Alec Yates's flat. He made his way there by various routes, skipping on and off subway trains, hopping a bus down Oxford Street, and finally dodging through the traffic to cross Piccadilly and wait impatiently for admittance, his eyes urgently scanning the street behind.

"You are quite sure you weren't followed?" asked Yates, taking his coat. "That business with Bardsey this morning was disgusting . . . what kind of people are we dealing with?"

"That's not all," said Catton, accepting a stiff brandy. "Vargas is hunting Quarry and Kleiner. Fortunately, the person he contacted was this villain that Quarry knows. Listen . . ."

When Catton had finished, Yates shook his head decisively. "Well, they can't. Absolutely not."

"Why not? It's a good idea," Catton said. "Quarry has used himself as bait before, and with a little luck this might get Vargas out of Cay Dorado."

"I won't . . ." Yates paused. It went against the grain to reveal his hand, but there was no alternative. "Look, it's all set . . . and it all depends on getting Quarry into Cay Dorado, not getting Vargas out."

"But why?"

When Yates had told him, Catton's face was grave. "Even if they get in, I don't think they have a cat in hell's chance of getting out again," he said, "and I think you know it."

Yates shrugged. "Whether they succeed or not is not important," he said. "The important thing is that in trying, they create a situation I can exploit. At the worst, they will do that, and that will be sufficient."

"And what about them? What about Kleiner and Quarry?"

Telling the truth can be catching. Yates rolled the words around his mouth for a moment, savoring them. "If you want to know the truth," he said, "Kleiner is hoping to hold the government to ransom, and Quarry has caused me personal embarrassment in the past. Frankly, I don't give a damn what happens to Quarry and Kleiner."

On the same afternoon that the Cartel's hit men dismembered Ted Bardsey, Simon Quarry and Lucia Fiori got married. The ceremony was held in secret under special license by the registrar of Gibraltar, and considering all the circumstances, it was a happy affair. Terry Cockerill was best man, Klaus Kleiner gave the bride away, and Renée Cockerill, in a wide and outrageous hat, stood behind Lucia as matron of honor. There was confetti, presents, and later, back at the Hotel Puente Romana, even a cake. Terry insisted on giving a reception, and the vast amounts of champagne he ordered kept things rolling on merrily until the couple decided they had had enough and left the dining room to take the elevator up to their suite amid a long round of ironic cheers from the other three guests.

Simon checked the room, finding a plastic bucket full of confetti positioned over the bathroom door and the apple-pie bed. Lucia found the whoopee cushion under the mattress.

"Remind me to strangle Terry in the morning," she said. "I *hate* practical jokes. At his age, it's ridiculous, and he ought to be careful and not draw attention to himself. With Vargas still on the loose, being best man at our wedding is a high-risk occupation."

"Well, it was Renée's idea, after all," Simon said, "and if we ever get the house rebuilt, we'll ask them to stay and celebrate properly. You can even give another party."

"Oh, I like them, especially Renée, and I know Terry's a dear—a villain, but still a dear. Anyway, what shall we do now?"

"Well . . ." Simon said, "it is traditional . . ."

"We did that last night," Lucia said. "Twice."

"So? It's different when you are married," said Simon, unknotting his tie. "Haven't you heard?"

"Really?" Lucia said. "I wonder why. Anyway, you will have to wait . . . I'm taking a shower."

When Lucia came out of the bathroom ten minutes later, wrapped in a towel, she caught Simon putting down the telephone, his face thoughtful, his eyes following her as she went across to the dressing table.

"Who was that?" she asked warily. "Not Terry hoping to come up and join us for a romp, I hope."

"No. It was John . . . John Catton. He sends his love."

"How is he? Is anything the matter?"

"He's fine . . . but there's a little problem in London. He sends his congratulations. Look, Lucia, the game's on again, so listen. Klaus and I are to meet him in Miami on Friday. Meanwhile, you go to London. Someone will meet you at Heathrow and take you to Christine's. Stay there until I call. Chris will stay with you, and some help will always be on hand. As soon as we have finished with Vargas, I'll phone you, and we'll make our move . . . everything else is set."

Lucia wrapped the towel around her legs and swung around to face him. "You'd better tell me," she said wearily, lighting a cigarette. "It's more trouble, right? What's happened now?"

Simon slumped into a chair by the window, his hands in his trouser pockets, and stared across at her. "It's counterpunching time again," he said. "Vargas is clearing the decks. He's done a Larry Teal on us and had Ted Bardsey killed. They killed Bardsey's wife too."

Lucia came over and settled down on the bed, one arm

behind her head, blowing a long plume of cigarette smoke toward the ceiling, saying nothing. Simon got up, poured them both a scotch, took the glasses over to the bed, and sat beside her.

"We've got to hit him," he said. "I know how you feel, but it's him or us."

"You seem very sure you can succeed against Vargas," said Lucia, taking his hand. "I just hope you are right."

"I'm right," he said. "And if it can be done, I can do it. Besides, this time I have Kleiner, and he's a one-man army in himself."

"Klaus is different, that's all. You only see his bad side."

"That's true," Simon admitted, "but even with his good side, he's still a killer in a camel-hair coat."

"I know," said Lucia, sighing. "Don't let's quarrel about Klaus . . . suggest something. Change the subject."

"All right," said Simon, rising. "I will. I suggest we behave as much as possible like any other married couple. Drink up, and then I shall pour us a glass of Terry's champagne. Then we shall climb into the bath together and splash about. Showers are for single wimps . . . baths are for lovers."

"You can scrub my back," Lucia said thoughtfully. "It makes up for a lot."

"I certainly can. If I've ruined your life, scrubbing your back is the least I can do."

Kleiner ran his eyes down the list of points on his pad, shifted the telephone more comfortably into his shoulder, and ticked off the last one. "That's all I have," he said into the mouthpiece. "The most important concerns the Rottepunkt business. Crédit Suisse may wish to charge up to three points over the odds for the money. Don't budge over two . . . if they stick, raise the rest from Chase—we have a long line of credit there still untouched."

The voice was doubtful. "If you were to see them in Zurich . . . talk to them even, we might get it for one or one-point-five. It does get very difficult when you are never around, Herr Kleiner."

"Rubbish," Kleiner said. "I am in contact every day . . . if my directors can't cope without me, what am I paying them for?"

"Well . . . that may be so, but you do have personal engagements. We—you—are sponsoring a performance of the Kirov at Covent Garden in three weeks' time. There will be a gala performance . . . a member of the Royal Family is coming . . . your absence might be interpreted as a snub. There are invitations here to functions at the Guggenheim, the Elysée Palace . . . even from the White House. If you fail to turn up, there will soon be talk in the papers. . . ."

Kleiner pondered, tapping the notepad with his pencil, turning it over and over, running up a score of little marks on the paper, thinking.

"Very well," he said at last. "Give me two weeks, then accept one engagement, the more public, the better, in London, Paris, New York, and Washington. . . . We'll have a party—book some suites at Gstaad—move the yacht. Where is she?"

"At the moment? I think Santorini . . . you loaned it to Stavios."

"I *chartered* it to Stavios. Make sure it is totally shipshape when we get it back. He's to pay for every cigarette burn."

"Very well . . . About this money for Miami—fifty thousand in cash, in the safe deposit . . . not simply at the bank?"

"No . . . in cash. I don't want to cash checks. Put it under one of the nominees. Keep my name out of it at either end. No one is to know where I am. Do not attempt to find me. I shall be in regular contact."

"Very well . . . ah, that reminds me. A small thing . . . Mr. Quarry's lady . . . his wife? She has moved all the money from our trustee fund—several millions."

"Really?" Kleiner looked thoughtful. "I wonder why. Where did it go? Do you know?"

"Since I thought you might ask, I have checked. Some—about three million—went into bearer bonds. Half the rest went into gold, deposited at the Swiss Bank in Zurich. The rest . . . who knows?"

Kleiner thought this one over. Bearer bonds belonged only to the bearer—the person who had them in hand. Gold was movable . . . the metal stayed put, the value traveled about on slips of paper. It looked as if Lucia was planning to disappear . . . interesting.

"Well," Kleiner said at last. "It's her money. Keep me posted if you hear any more though."

When the contact had rung off, Kleiner sat on at his desk for a moment, stretching his body back in the chair, arms over his head. Then he got up and went out onto his balcony, looking down across the blue sparkle of the swimming pool far below, and across the golf course. Simon and Lucia were walking back toward the hotel from the golf club, Simon with one arm round Lucia's shoulders, swinging a putter in his other hand, their heads close together. They are up to something, Kleiner thought . . . and I think I can guess what it is. Smiling, he picked up the telephone and began to dial again.

"John . . . I'm returning your call. What's the matter?"

Alec Yates believed in hedging his bets. In his world, everything could be useful, every scrap of information turned to effect. The news of Quarry's marriage, relayed to him by Catton, was another item that he might slot in somewhere. It took him less than an hour to work out where, and only a phone call to put the wheels in motion.

"Mrs. Wheeler? . . . Alec Yates. How are you? Good. Listen, I have another snippet of information I'd like you to plant . . . like the last, but it must make the international press and the Spanish papers. Oh very juicy, I assure you. All the world loves a lover. You know that Quarry's house was attacked and his staff murdered? Well, lead with a résumé of that, and add the following . . . ready? I'll speak slowly." Yates picked up his notes and read aloud:

"Yesterday, though still in hiding on the Costa del Sol, Simon Quarry married Lucia Fiori at the Registry Office in Gibraltar, with international tycoon Klaus Kleiner in attendance. Also present was alleged East End mobster Terry Cockerill, whom Scotland Yard wish to interview in connection with the Heathrow Bullion robbery—strange company for respectable businessmen. I can now reveal that, since the attack in Majorca, Klaus Kleiner and Simon Quarry have been living at Cockerill's house near Mijas."

"Have you got that? Polish it any way you like, but get it in. The check's in the post."

When he had put down the phone, Yates linked his hands behind his head and sat back in his chair, smiling. "That should bring Vargas down on Quarry's friends like a ton of bricks," he said aloud. "I wonder what the agile Mr. Quarry will do about that."

When he saw the clipping in the *Herald Tribune,* Simon did nothing . . . Kleiner took charge. Within ten minutes, he had a helicopter away, clattering across the hills and the high-rise flats, whisking Terry and Renée, the latter quietly furious, down to the airport at Málaga, where Kleiner's jet was already warmed up and ready to go.

"I'm going to wring your bloody neck when this is over, Simon Quarry," she said. "And I'm not getting into that thing . . . it's not safe."

"It's a lot safer than staying here," Kleiner said. "Inside two hours, you'll be somewhere even safer. I have an island in Greece, you're going there—make yourself at home . . . use the yacht. I have guards there, and it's very secure. Stay there until all this is over. It won't be for long, I promise."

"Well . . ." Renée relaxed a little. "If you insist. It'll make a change, won't it, Terry? I only hope the food's all right."

"I have a French chef," Kleiner said.

"I can't abide French food," Renée said. "If I have a French meal, I rush home for a bacon sandwich."

"He'll cook anything you want," Simon said urgently. "Now, for godsake, get on that plane."

"What about Lucia?" Terry asked. "If it's not safe for us, where is she going?"

Simon stared at him. "She's already back in London, don't worry about her. She'll be well taken care of, and kept under guard. Except for you two, everything is under control."

"You must be joking," Terry said. "Lucia should come with us, or maybe I should stay here with you, lend a hand."

"We're not staying here either; we're going after Vargas. Now, for the last time," said Simon, raising his voice above the roar of the jet engine, "will you get on that plane. We need it back here in twelve hours . . . now go!"

That much at least seems real. The question is...

15

John Catton arrived in Miami two days after Quarry and Kleiner. He found Pete Sinker waiting outside the "Arrival" doors, a cigar jutting from his teeth, his hands jammed in his jacket pockets, his face frowning. The frown only eased a little as Catton came through the crowd toward him, holding out his hand.

"Pete! It's good to see you. Are you the one meeting me? Look, I brought you a box of cigars, all the way from London, England, but I didn't think I'd see you so soon. How are you?"

Sinker rolled his cigar to the other side of his mouth and stuck out a hand. "I think I'm fine, John. Don't waste your time looking for your two buddies. They ain't here. I didn't pass on your message. I think we have to talk." There was ice in his tone.

"Fine. What about?" They were outside the airport concourse now, dodging across the traffic into the carpark, heading toward Sinker's battered car.

"About what the hell is going on. The word is that Vargas is on the rampage. I hear one of your guys back in London got seriously hit. Or did he just cut himself to pieces accidentally with that chain saw?"

"Now how did you hear about that?" asked Catton, coming to a stop. "Bardsey is our second casualty; they also hit a friend of mine and had a go at me. I should have listened to you a while back, but, well . . . I didn't. We have to move quickly, or we won't move at all."

Sinker was groping for the car keys. "Cutting a British cop to bits . . . it even made the *Miami Herald*. They keep an eye on the druggies—good stories, stuff like that. So, the Cartel has come to London . . . very nice. Don't say you weren't told. Who was the other guy?"

"I'll tell you later. Look, do you feel like a late lunch, or even a cup of coffee? I could chew a crab—airline food is just disgusting."

"Why not? Then we can talk, and I know a little place . . . well, so do you, right? We went there before. Besides, like I say, you and I have to have a little heart-to-heart."

They drove across town to the Stone Crab Restaurant and Bar, which was dark, cool, and, in midafternoon, half-deserted. There they took a table at the back, ordered drinks and two covers with a bottle of California Chablis, and sat back, eyes adjusting to the gloom, looking each other over.

"All right . . ." Catton took a drink of iced water and put the tinkling glass back on the table. "Come on, I can see something's wrong. What's on your mind?"

"Well, I'll tell you a story," Sinker said. "Couple of months back, a nice Britisher comes into my office all the way from Scotland Yard, and asks for help—official. I take him in, fix his problems, show him around. I thought we got on real well. Anyway, he goes home, sends me a postcard from London, soldiers in red suits, very British. Then things start to happen I don't know about. It seems to me that I got into a one-way trade back there, and I don't like that. This is my territory, and right now there are two European gunnies sitting up there in the Omni Tower telling me how high to hop. And they can do this because you, my friend, passed them on to me . . . and they also carry heavy heat from the DEA in Washington, D.C., and London. I'm chewing my cigar here, taking this shit, and I look out the window this morning and what do I see coming down the slot but a great big British destroyer with a whole company of Marines on deck. We're being invaded, yet. And then I hear, on the street, that the next port of call for that warship is a little island a hundred or so miles south of here, which I would like to see taken off the map. I connect to this because yesterday I get a basketful of telexes from Langley on a certain pain-in-the-ass island, telling me to sit tight and smile. So I ask you, just one time only, either you tell me what's going on, or I pull the plug on cooperation, and you and Langley can both kiss off."

Catton heard him out, watching his face, keeping his own expression serious, waiting for Sinker to run down, switching from the water to the chilled California Chablis, pouring them both a glass. Finally, Pete Sinker stopped and lit up another cigar.

"Your ball," he said.

"All right," Catton said. "I'll tell you all you want to know. You'll have to take my word for it that I only found out about some of it myself this morning . . . about the frigate and the Marines, and that's why I'm here. You want it long or short, simple or complicated?"

"Short and simple."

It didn't take long to tell the story. Sinker listened, putting in a question now and then, cracking his crab and picking out the meat, nodding. When Catton had finished and was attacking his own dish, Sinker sat back and sipped his wine for a while, thinking.

"That is one hell of a tale," he said at last, "but it all seems to hang on those two guys. Can they do it? If it goes wrong, you will have your balls in the wringer back home, and those two guys will be very, very dead. What do you think?"

"I think you may be right, but it's still worth it. Someone must do something about Cay Dorado. Besides, the political risk is really very small. Look, Kleiner is well known to be semi-insane on the subject of drug dealers. Two years ago, he even offered to pay off Bolivia's entire foreign debt if they would pull out of the cocaine trade. The *narco-traficantes* outbid him, and Kleiner didn't like that. Quarry is already listed on every intelligence dossier as a hit man—a pity, because he's not really like that; he just looks after himself

—but what the hell! I have discovered that the CIA once actively considered assassinating a hundred and fifty of the world's top traffickers—and their list included foreign ambassadors, heads of state, film stars, celebrities—you name it. Our method is on a much lower key, with low risk and high gain."

Sinker shook his head, marveling, and lit up another cigar. "Maybe, but not for Quarry and Kleiner. Remember that video? And look what happened to what's-his-name . . . Barley? . . . in London."

Catton shrugged slightly. "Bardsey. They know the risk. Anyway, most of this is Quarry's idea. This is his game. If it goes well, they simply fade away. If not, they lose. We have a dead German industrialist and a lone Englishman, so who's to care? Even if Quarry and Kleiner get the chop, they will have stirred up enough noise to justify British intervention in Cay Dorado, and that's all we need. Anyway, that's Yates's affair. My business is to keep the Cartel out of Britain."

Sinker sucked on a crab claw, thoughtfully. "You're a tough dude, y'know that? I always thought I was the hard bastard around here. I half thought you liked these guys . . . you said they were friends?"

"I do," Catton said. "Well, I like Quarry. Besides, who knows, he may pull it off, but this is business. Now, finish your drink and let's get over to the Omni. Do you have the stuff from Langley? Did the CIA actually come through?"

"They actually did," Sinker said. "It's in my car."

Simon Quarry had a room on the tenth floor of the Omni Tower, with one floor-length picture window looking out onto Biscayne Bay, across the top of the *Miami Herald* Building; Kleiner had the one next door. They didn't go out much, and they never opened the door anyone knocked at—they had opened the communicating door between their suites and always emerged from farther down the corridor to pick up messages, let in Room Service, or welcome callers. Most of the staff thought they were a couple of successful, and therefore cautious, dope dealers, though since these guys were heavy tippers, they kept that thought to themselves.

With Catton along to referee, the meeting with Sinker went smoothly. Sinker emptied the Langley packet out on the carpet and spread the contents across the floor. The CIA had done a good job. Here were maps, photographs, a stack of mimeographed reports—everything they needed to know about Cay Dorado. Kleiner chatted to Catton while Quarry and Sinker set out all the information on the floor, starting with a map of the island, leading on through streets plans of Caytown to photographs of Vargas's house, and the inside and outside of Government House, both from street level and surveillance satellite. Here too, there was a detailed floor plan, filched from the files of some old Colonial architect. It was all very thorough. Glancing up and out of the window to the gray warship moored across the bay, Pete Sinker began to think it might just work, after all.

"You two tell me what else you want, and you've got it," he said. "Vargas and his friends have been screwing me for years, so I'd like to help you screw them back a little."

"Well, I've got a list of the stuff we need right here," Simon said, "but we might need to add to it when we've had a closer look at the situation on the ground. How much do you know about Cay Dorado, Pete?"

"Never been there," Sinker said, "but we have a guy down there under heavy cover. He works at the Nelson Hotel . . . here, right in the center." A nicotine-stained forefinger tapped a blown-up satellite photo and a CIA checklist. "It's the only decent place in town. He picks up a lot of useful juice from the diners, because only druggies can afford the prices. The President lives here, up the street, in the old Governor's Mansion . . . he's added a couple of wings. The cops are here, according to the spooks. They call it a police station, like you do in England—eight patrolmen, constables, a sergeant, and an inspector, all locals, all owned by Vargas. Their basic pay is less than five thousand dollars a year, so what do you expect? The schmucks have to live."

"Where does Vargas live?"

"Here, down by the edge of the harbor." Sinker consulted a photograph, the list, and the street map. "It used to be the Finance and Administration Building back in the good old days of empire. All that's gone over to the President's palace, because he or his relatives run the show, and he likes to keep any spare cash handy. Vargas has a suite—very ritzy from what my guy says—on the top floor . . . it's a three-story building. There are maybe thirty Colombian guards there at any one time. He has a dock here, at the end of the garden, couple of boats, a helicopter pad . . . see here? Keeps a Bell Augusta on it. Lots of cars . . . if you take a closer peek, you can pick out the stretch limo. Also has a plane, DC9, at the airport. It has Air Dorado markings, but Vargas is the only one who flies in it. Plenty of shipping here in the harbor. Small planes go in and out all the time, mostly dope, money, all kinds of shit. Now, they want to extend the runway for big jets, but you know all about that."

Quarry nodded and picked up the photo of Vargas's mansion and studied it, rubbing his chin, glancing at the map. "Mmmm . . . big! How do we get in, I wonder? Any ideas?"

"Christ knows," Sinker said. "I'd worry about getting out, if I were you—it's a fortress. The guards have automatic weapons, and they will outnumber you fifteen to one. And better they kill you than catch you. Don't you worry about that? Just a teeny-weeny, itsy-bitsy bit?"

Simon rubbed his ear, sitting up on his heels on the carpet among the maps and photos. "No, not really. Look, if we could afford an open assault, I'd ask for odds of three to one on our side, but since we have to be sneaky, two is more comfy—we can be sure anyone else is an enemy. With a bit of luck and a bit of craft, we may even get them shooting at each other. I hope so, anyway. It might help whittle down the odds."

Kleiner got out of his chair and came over. "How is it going?" he asked. "Is there anything I can do? You seem to have enough stuff there."

Simon was still brooding over the large-scale map. "You could get me a cup of coffee," he said slowly, "but otherwise, no."

"You're the boss," Kleiner said. "I'll ring down." And he went away toward the telephone.

"How do you get on with the kraut?" Sinker asked quietly. "Rich guy like that, messing in all this. It don't seem right."

"I get along with him all right," Simon said, "but I've given up wondering about his motivation. It's cheaper than polo, and he can handle himself in a tight corner, you can believe that."

"If I had his money, I'd find myself something better to do. I'd lie on a little island, fishing rod between my toes, letting naked models light my cigars with fifty-dollar bills, that's what I'd do."

"Well, he does what he does," said Simon, smiling. "Now, if you mean what you say about helping, let me give you a list of what we are going to need. Given the right stuff, I think I can see how we do it."

"You know what you're going to do?" asked Sinker, surprised. "So soon? Just like that? Just by looking at a dumb map?"

"More or less," said Simon, getting up, dusting his trousers, his knees cracking. "You see, I've done this sort of thing before."

"Okay, let me see. You want Cuban fatigues and a Mac-10 each, plus four mags to the gun? You want grenades, two RPG-launchers plus shells and belts, not Uncle Sam's . . . Russian, Czech, Chinese, whatever? Nice . . . I like it. You want a pistol with a silencer? I can do you a Colt .45 ACP, if it's what you want, but a silencer is tricky. Still, leave that to me. I got a friend can gussy it up for you. You want plastic, electric detonators, knives? Knives! Okay, knives. You want Mace, teargas, a twelve-gauge pump shotgun? You want to start a war?" Sinker's eyebrows were reaching his receding hairline.

Simon ignored that. People had been saying that almost

daily for the last couple of months. He pointed at the list. "All this stuff must be both well used and traceable to Cubans here, or one of the resistance groups or, even better, taken in from Cuban *narco* gangs operating against the Colombians here in Miami. If this can look like a gang squabble, so much the better. Every little bit helps our cover. The *narcos* will know who really hit them, but that's no problem. We want them to know what they are into if they push against the U.K."

"There aren't any Cuban *narcos* left," Sinker said. "It's the Colombians who control the coke trade in Florida. All the *Cubanos* are either bobbing about on the bottom of Biscayne Bay, or look like chopped liver."

"You said the Cubans dabble in dope to finance anti-Castro groups," Catton said. "Half the pushers in the malls are Latinos."

"Sure they are, but it's nothing heavy. They deal on the street, or push grass. The Colombians would turn very mean if anyone screwed around in their serious shit."

"Even so, that will do," Simon said. "We are trying to build up layers of cover. The story John here will put out—or someone will put out—is that Cay Dorado, that well-known drug haven, is the scene of a battle between rival *narco* gangs of Cuban and Colombian *traficantes*."

"Well, it's neat, I'll say that," said Sinker, nodding out of the window to where the slim gray shape of HMS *Dancer* lay beside the dock far below, her superstructure now illuminated with colored lights. "That's one hell of a prop you've got down there. It could fool me. Going in like this has class. Most people would just hop on a flight."

"Getting out of Miami with the artillery would be as nothing compared to getting it into Cay Dorado," Kleiner said. "Vargas owns the place, and you can bet he keeps a very close eye on visitors."

"I can see that," Sinker said. "Thing is, having all that help on hand is no good unless Spurling folds and asks for it. If not, you are in deep shit, friend. You may get in without help, but you'll need help to get out."

"For that, we have to rely on the diplomatic end," Catton

said. "On your old friend Yates, Simon, who loves you not at all."

"Friend Yates could be setting us up," Kleiner put in. "I'd lay odds he planted those press leaks. Getting rid of you, me, and Vargas in one go is neat work and would certainly amuse him; save the government trouble and money. All he has to do is hold his hand for a while after we go in."

Simon shrugged. "It's too late to think about that," he said. "It's too late anyway. Look, Pete, can you get this stuff, plus some service rucksacks to put it in?" Suddenly, Simon looked tired, turning heavy eyes on Sinker. "As soon as possible, without attracting attention."

"Sure, tomorrow afternoon, or whenever you want it."

"Tomorrow is fine, but I'd like to check it over. Then maybe we can crate it and get it onto the *Dancer* by midnight. She's due to sail sometime tomorrow night, as soon as we board."

"Can do," said Sinker, nodding. "Most of the stuff is held in some government warehouse, and it's no sweat to get some loose if I jerk the CIA's chain. I'll gather this stuff in over at the airfield beyond Hialeah—plenty of hangar space out there—full of engine crates. Better we crate it up ourselves, right? Fewer in on this, the better. I'll get a hammer, some nails."

"Right again," said Simon, nodding. "This is our secret, and it had better stay that way."

The next day was busy. Catton, Quarry, and Kleiner took a taxi across to the dockyard and had a short meeting with the captain of HMS *Dancer,* a quiet, noncommittal naval officer. He had already been ordered to cooperate in the affair and ask no awkward questions. His orders for Cay Dorado, marked TO BE OPENED ONLY ON RECEIPT OF A SIGNAL FROM MOD LONDON, were already in the cabin safe.

"Naturally, I shall do all I can to help," he said, offering them pink gins, "and my officers will be discreet. They don't call us the Silent Service for nothing, you know. I have told the crew you are media men researching for a television series, so do remember to ask a few questions about where they come from and so on, and make a few notes."

In the afternoon, they joined Pete Sinker in a hot, airless hangar at an airstrip in the Everglades, where they cleaned and test-fired the Mac-10s, primed the grenades, learned how to use the gas, the detonators, and the grenade-launchers. When the stuff was checked and stowed into two small crates, Sinker went to the telephone. Half an hour later, a small truck took the crates, now labeled VIDEO AND CAMERA EQUIPMENT, down to the dockyard, where six ensigns from HMS *Dancer* manhandled them gently aboard, remarking on the weight. That done, after a drink and a shower at the Omni, they went out to dinner, driving in Sinker's car to Christine's, down Miami Beach.

"This is on me," said Pete Sinker, opening the menu. "When you get back here, it'll be your turn. I'll be happy to help you celebrate."

"One or two last little things," Simon said. "If anything does go wrong, can you clear out our rooms at the Omni? We've kept them on because we'd like people to think we are still there. It's another layer of cover. But if we don't get back, just clear them out, pay the bill in cash . . . and suddenly it's like we never existed. Can you do that for us, Pete? John will be in Caytown by then, or I'd ask him. There are funds in this envelope."

"Keep it," Sinker said. "The DEA will pick up the tab."

"You'd better take it," Simon said. "Kleiner's telephone and telex bill alone would bankrupt your budget . . . believe me."

"Well, I have a business to run," Klaus said mildly. "I have to keep in touch with my directors."

Sinker shook his head. "You can run a business with this going on?" he asked.

"A man needs a hobby," Kleiner said. It was the closest he had come to a joke. "And that reminds me." He reached into the pocket of his jacket and handed an envelope across the table to Catton. "Take this," he said. "But only open it if things go seriously wrong."

"What's in this?" Catton asked.

"An offer you can't refuse," Kleiner said. He handed the other envelope to Sinker. "Nothing mysterious in this one, Pete, but it will cover the bills."

"You just take care of yourself over there, you hear?" said Pete, putting the envelope in his pocket. "Don't you give the bastards an even break, you promise? They sure as hell won't give *you* one."

"We will," Kleiner said. "I mean, we won't . . . we do."

Sinker glanced at Kleiner briefly, then turned back to Simon. "You figured out how to get in?" he asked, dropping his voice.

"I think so," Simon said. Suddenly, he looked tired again. In the candlelight from the table, Sinker saw the lines etched on his face, the pouches under his eyes.

"Uh-huh . . . and how to get out?"

"I never think that far ahead. It's not worth it."

"And when do you hit them?"

"The day after tomorrow, about eleven at night, more or less. About then, anyway. It's not up to me. We go when it's set."

"Uh-huh . . . and that's it?"

"That's it," Simon said. "Look, can we order? It's getting late, and Klaus and I have a ship to catch."

On the stroke of midnight, HMS *Dancer* slipped her lines and began to back away from the quay, an anchor watch of sailors lining her sides, those officers not engaged in working the ship exchanging formal salutes and cheery waves with their American counterparts on the quay. The frigate swung into the channel and then began to move out to sea, sliding smoothly away in the dusk, gaining speed until soon only her running lights revealed her position to the watchers still waiting on shore. When even those lights had faded, Pete Sinker threw his cigar butt out of the car window and reached for the ignition.

"I feel kind of flat," he said to Catton. "I'd feel better if we could be over there helping those guys."

"So would I," John said. "Suddenly, it all seems impossible, and I can't believe it's actually going to happen. But then, Quarry always says that the waiting is the worst part."

"I like Quarry. I know he's a gun and all that, but he's a nice, dependable guy. Kleiner . . . ? I think he's a flake, but I wish them both luck in this thing. You too. If it goes wrong, they won't be in line to take the blame."

"Quarry was quiet tonight," Catton said thoughtfully. "That's not like him. He's normally rather cheerful, and the tougher it gets, the more cheerful he is."

"Well, he's got a lot on his mind," said Sinker, turning on the engine. "There's heavy weather ahead . . . a lot to think about. Let's go get ourselves a drink."

"Maybe that's it," said Catton, glancing out to the fading lights of *Dancer,* "but I think he has thought it all out already. In fact, I know he has. I just hope it works, that's all."

An hour later, flat on his bunk, fingers linked behind his head, Simon Quarry lay staring at the bottom of Kleiner's mattress, a foot or two over his head. He had stopped thinking about Cay Dorado. There comes a time on these capers when it does no good to think about them anymore. You just have to do it, do the best you can. Simon knew that and turned his thoughts to other things, to the future and Lucia. He was still thinking of her when Kleiner spoke.

"Simon . . . are you awake?"

"Who could sleep?"

Kleiner chuckled. "It's not easy, I grant you. Maybe we should have brought a few glasses down from the wardroom and had a party?"

"What have we got to celebrate?"

"Well . . ." Kleiner's voice was careful. "I could celebrate the fact that you are still here. I don't think I could handle this on my own."

"You couldn't," Simon said. "That's why I'm here. That, and for Renée, and Terry, and Lucia . . . and all the other poor bastards you and I are connected with."

"Will it work?"

Simon's bunk creaked as he shifted in it. "With a little luck . . . otherwise it might be tricky. We need a little luck."

"Napoleon said a good general had to be lucky," Kleiner said. "Incidentally, I know what you're planning for afterward. I think I'm lucky you stayed on this far."

Simon's bunk creaked again. "We'll need more luck than that," he said.

"I've made a few arrangements in case our luck runs out," Kleiner said. "I've made an offer to John over KSI . . . just in case we don't get back. It was in the envelope."

"Well, that makes sense," Simon said. "With Philip gone, you'll need some help there, and it must pay better than the Yard."

"The offer includes you, if you want it."

"Include me out," Simon said.

16

Steaming at an economical fifteen knots, HMS *Dancer*, a Type-22 Royal Navy frigate, could have reached Cay Dorado from Miami in twelve hours. In the event, it took thirty-six hours, because the ship diverted to one of the deserted out-islands so that the officers of the commando troop could carry out a reconnaissance for their forthcoming night exercise with the Doradan Defense Force. The main island came up on the ship's radar screens at four o'clock on the morning of the second day, and just after dawn, with the white buildings on the green terraced hillsides above Caytown in full view from the bridge, the captain sent his yeoman to fetch Quarry and Kleiner from their bunks. When they entered the day cabin, he was sitting behind his desk, examining a package taken from his safe.

"Good morning, gentlemen," he said, waving them into chairs. "Sorry to get you up so early, but Cay Dorado is in sight. May I ask you to look at this package? Please note that the seals are intact. Agreed?"

"Agreed."

"Good . . . initials here, please. Now I don't know what is going on, and I don't want to know. I only need to know what part my ship, and my ship's company, have to play. My first instruction is to ask you to show me an envelope. Which one of you has it?"

"I do," said Simon, producing it. "Please note, still sealed. May we have your note to that effect?"

"Noted," the captain said. "I have received a signal from London telling you to open it. You may now proceed."

Simon tore open the envelope, took out the single sheet of paper, and showed it to Kleiner. "It's on," he said. "This is just the official go-ahead for it. Our part, at least." He looked at the captain and passed over the note. "As you see, we are permitted to go ashore as planned, sir."

"Well, so far, so good," said the captain, folding the note. "Though why all these games are necessary, I really can't imagine."

"It's a cutout, a fail-safe," Kleiner said, "though I'd like that note back. Not that anyone could have stopped Quarry and me going ahead and carrying out our task."

"Really?" The captain smiled, raising an eyebrow. "First, you would have to get off my ship. I carry thirty armed Marines, who might slow you down a bit. It's no accident we are tasked with carrying you both to Cay Dorado, Mr. Kleiner, that much I do know. And no, you can't have this note back. I am instructed to destroy it."

Simon gave Kleiner a wry glance. "Yates," he said, "covering his ass, as usual. We're on our own the second we step off this ship."

"Well, we needn't press the matter," the captain said. "Now, before I open my sealed instructions, you, Mr. Quarry, will have to tell me—I quote—'the name of our mutual friend.'"

"His name is Philip," Simon said.

"That's the name I was given," said the captain, as he began to crack the seals. "Now, let's see what they have planned for me."

By the time HMS *Dancer* sailed out of Miami, Cay Dorado had long been one of the Western world's top centers for cocaine trafficking. It was virtually the island's only industry. Everything else had been let go. On Cay Dorado the *narco-traficantes* could break-bulk and transship cocaine from large ships into fast "cigarette boats" for the short crossing to Florida. Propeller-powered cargo planes from Colombia and Bolivia screeched hurriedly to a halt on the island's short World War II airstrip (Spurling had sent the first loan for the runway extension direct to his private account in the Turks and Caicos Islands), and local laborers transshipped the white stuff into Pipers and Cessnas, flying it in to airstrips deep in the Florida Everglades. Cocaine was the most efficiently run, and by far the most profitable, of all the island's industries, but very little of the profits got past Spurling to the island people. Twenty-four years after independence, the Doradans had changed— they were a sullen crowd now, and who could blame them? Their diet was minimal, unemployment had sapped their willingness to work, their children, uneducated, roamed the streets, begging or robbing the few tourists who still came by. The island had rotted into despair, but without the safety net—as Spurling might see it—of apathy. The people's resentment now centered on his person, so that he stayed in power only with the support of the *narcotraficantes* and their gangs of armed men. Even so, his rule was precarious, and everyone knew it. Given the right spark, there would be an explosion that might well blow Sir Lancelot Spurling off his throne forever. As he welcomed Alec Yates into his opulent presidential office on that sultry, subtropical evening, that spark was coming south upon the sea.

Spurling came around the desk to greet Yates, hand outstretched, smiling broadly. He was in an expansive mood. He had set himself up for this meeting by snorting two or three lines of 95 percent pure Colombian *périca* in the presidential bathroom, and was higher than a kite. He ushered Yates into a chair, offered him a brandy (just restraining himself from suggesting that they share a snort or two of snow), and led off the interview with a glowing account of the island's prosperity, political stability, and opportunities for investment.

227

"Well, Mr. President," said Yates, when Spurling had finally slowed down, "as one of our Great War generals used to remark, 'I've heard different.'"

Spurling raised an eyebrow. "Can you deny we are prosperous? Cay Dorado is awash with money. Look at the banks, at the yachts in Cay Harbor. We are a financial center for the Central Caribbean, and everyone knows that Cay Dorado is the pearl investment in the area. We are turning offers down every day."

Alec Yates could bullshit with the best of them, but this was really too much. "Look, Mr. President, let me be blunt. I'm here to represent my government because, like it or not—and mostly not—we have an Aid and Defense Treaty with you, God help us, and you want money. Please don't waste my time and yours in telling me things we both know simply are not so. Let us get down to business."

"You are here to discuss the loan," said Spurling, ignoring this, "and how it is to be paid over. I am glad your government has finally decided to honor our agreement. I was a little concerned, but now . . . Well, no problem, Mr. Yates. My government has prepared a detailed program for the airfield work. I can have it here in a moment. All we need is the money."

"There will be no loan," Yates said shortly. "Or rather, no money. We have given you money before, and we are still wondering what you did with it. If we agree to the runway extension, *we* will commission the contractors and fix the budget directly. Opportunities for local graft will be quite minimal, I can assure you of that."

Spurling smiled broadly. He didn't care what Yates might say—sticks and stones may break my bones, et cetera . . . The British were going to build the runway, that was the important thing. Vargas would be delighted, the Colombians would stay, his people could be controlled, and the Americans could go take a running jump. They wouldn't risk an invasion with the British investing in the islands. And if Yates seriously thought he couldn't cut a slice from the contractors' cake, Yates was stupider than he looked, which was encouraging. Had he never heard of a payroll level, or a tax on cement? Why, the opportunities were endless.

"However," Yates continued, "there are still some questions. First of all, if you are so well off, why don't you finance the runway yourself, or get all those banks to cough up? Why are the British being honored? Your speeches on the local radio and at the last Commonwealth heads of government meeting in Vancouver were not, well, full of brotherly love for my country."

"Whatever our political differences, I admire British energy and craftsmanship," Spurling said brightly. "Besides, we have historical links. I am prepared to forget the past, and let bygones be bygones. The British will always have a place in these islands, and in our hearts." Spurling rather liked that last bit. He would make a note to use it in his speech of thanks the next time the Queen had him to dinner on the Royal Yacht . . . but what was this irritating civil servant saying now?

"Why not ask the Americans?" Yates continued. "They have unlimited amounts of get-up-and-go, much technical expertise, and are just over the horizon. It's a lot easier and cheaper than hauling cement in from Britain and paying expatriate rates to our contractors, wouldn't you say?"

"I might as well tell you," said Spurling frankly, lighting a cigar, "we did ask them to tender, but they said no. I can't think why. Jealousy, perhaps. For all they say, they hate to compete."

"Well, I can give you a couple of other reasons," said Yates, moving in for the kill. "Firstly, they don't want to give you any more money. It tends to disappear. Secondly, they fear that the airport, if improved, will simply make Cay Dorado an even more efficient center for drug distribution. Thirdly, if you asked them to tender, which I rather doubt, you'd still prefer that we do it, because you need a British presence here to keep the Americans off your back and stop another Grenada—right? To put it frankly, Mr. President, you and your South American friends need our skirts to hide under while you flood America with dope. And now we hear that there are plans to do the same thing in

Britain . . . a Señor Vargas has been mentioned, and the Colombian Cartel."

Spurling suddenly wished he could make another trip to the bathroom. "Really, Mr. Yates! This is CIA nonsense. I have to tell you that they, and the American government, are trying to destabilize my government because of my support for liberal regimes and revolutionary freedom fighters in Central America. I *insist* you retract those remarks. As for this Señor Vargas, I have never heard of him."

"Really? Now, that *is* passing strange," said Yates, smiling broadly, "because his house is right over there, just across Independence Square, and two of his men are sitting outside your office door at this very moment, clutching machine pistols. Your secretary had to ask their permission to let me in. Please don't fence with me, Mr. President."

"Oh . . . you mean *that* Señor Vargas," Spurling said. "It's a very common name here, you know. Señor Vargas is a good friend of this country, and of my government, a heavy investor in this country, a businessman, nothing more. His guards are here because my men are not really efficient. That's all."

"Vargas is a doper," Yates said. "No, Vargas is *the* doper. Your high commissioner must have relayed our request. Señor Vargas must be expelled."

"Absolutely not. This is a free country," said Spurling, slapping his hand on the desk. "Our liberties are hard-won, and not negotiable. Now can we discuss the airport extension, or is this interview at an end? I will not tolerate any interference in our internal affairs. So shall we move on, or not?"

Although he would never have put it so bluntly, Yates didn't give a damn about Spurling's internal affairs. He was simply going through the motions. There was not the least intention of giving Spurling the loan, so Yates could negotiate for hours—it hardly mattered. What did matter was that he—and Spurling—would be able to provide a convincing reason for his presence here when the Big Story broke. Besides, he needed to get back here, into Spurling's office, for the penultimate stage of the drama. Yates let his gaze drop and his shoulders slump. It didn't come easily, but he managed it. He would get his chance later.

"Very well, Mr. President . . . if that is your final answer. I can tell you that you will get the loan. We will build the runway. I must refer our conversation back to London, and I would like to rest and freshen up a little. Could we meet again—say, after the cocktail party on the warship? I suppose you will be attending the party? Shall I see you there?"

"Of course." Spurling was all smiles again. "Tomorrow evening I intend inviting the officers to dinner here. I am available this evening, but why can we not meet later today? Then we could celebrate our agreement at the cocktail party."

"Well, naturally I have to report back on this preliminary meeting to my minister, and with the time difference between here and London . . . you know how these things are. But I think you can take it that everything will be settled tonight. We can hardly let Señor Vargas spoil our traditional friendship. Now, if you will excuse me . . ."

"I'm very glad to hear it," said Spurling, rising, "and I am sure the outcome of our talks will be positive. And now, Mr. Yates, before you leave, how about that brandy?"

Yates knew the man was there before he opened the door of his room. He could smell the cigarette smoke out in the corridor, and the smell grew stronger as he slipped into his room and closed the door. The man was sitting in the dark, his back to the far wall, only the sudden red glow from the cigarette revealing his presence. Yates continued on into the room and bent over the lamp on the center table.

"Don't put on the light," the man said. "Not yet. Better not at all."

"I won't, if you wish," said Yates, pulling up a chair, moving closer and sitting down. "How did you get in here? When did you get out of jail?"

"Yesterday. I came up the back stairs. My brother works here, and he sneaked me in. They let me out last night—

maybe in honor of your arrival. I have to report to the police every day, and we have to be careful."

"We will be, don't worry," Yates said. "Does Spurling suspect anything? Are you being watched? It's important to keep everything very low-key for at least another few hours."

"I'm not worried about Spurling," the man said. "Vargas is the one to worry about. Vargas owns Spurling, don't you know that? And they are not watching me, they're watching you."

"Are they now?" Yates said thoughtfully. "I wonder why."

"You're a stranger, from London, a British government man, and Vargas is cautious. Why wouldn't he have you watched? Anyway, is it all set at your end?"

"I think so," Yates said. "The ship arrives this morning, and my people will act tonight. After that, it depends on you. Can you get your people stoked up and out on the streets? If you can do that, then I think we can pull it off."

"To think is not good enough. If I bring my people onto the streets, I need a good reason, and I must be sure of your support. We will only get one chance, for the *narcos* have guns they will certainly use. If what you *think* doesn't work, we will have a bloodbath here. Tell me what is arranged about Vargas."

Yates told him. It went against the grain to tell anyone anything, but he told him. Not all of it, naturally. Just what the man needed to know, and it seemed to be enough to convince him.

"That's fine," the man said at last, his dark face briefly illuminated by the match as he lit another cigarette, "as far as it goes, but can you rely on these people? Now listen, tonight we have a union meeting in the Labor Hall—our first this year—to celebrate my release from detention. With you and the Royal Navy here, Vargas won't dare rock the boat by sending his goons in to break it up, as they did last time. I'll see there is plenty of free rum at the buffet, wind them up with a speech, and once the shooting starts, we'll hit the streets. But if your people don't nail Vargas,

we won't move. And if we don't move, you won't budge
Spurling."

"I know that, but we need a really good riot," Yates said
earnestly. "A big one, enough to convince the press and the
UN that it's popular, well supported, and serious. A bit of
yelling and stone-throwing won't do, not if we are to get rid
of Spurling. So don't pull your punches."

"We won't . . . you'll have your riot," promised the man,
jerking his thumb toward the window. "There is a lot of
anger to tap out there. But once Spurling goes, you British
will definitely stay until we have elections. Is that clear? You
won't rat on us like last time and let the *narcos* back in?"

"You have our word," Yates said.

HMS *Dancer* came into Caytown Harbor as a British
man-of-war should, the crew lining the decks, her single
4.5-inch gun firing a steady salute from the foredeck, the
Doradan flag at the truck and her bugler exchanging notes
with the band of the defense force drawn up on the quay.
Once the lines had been secured and the gangway lowered,
the usual round of visits began. The Caytown mayor and the
harbormaster came aboard for drinks in the captain's cabin,
the football team departed for its needle match with Dorado
Rovers (and lost 5–2), while the Royal Marines Commandos, in full fighting order, fell in on the quayside and
doubled off to the defense-force barracks, a solid bunch of
khaki topped off with green berets. Apart from the default-
ers and the officers' servants, who were kept on board to
prepare the quarterdeck for the officers' cocktail party, the
rest of the crew went ashore for a happy afternoon's
whoring, under strict orders to return on board, stone-cold-
sober, not later than nine o'clock. Anyone failing to return
on time would be skinned alive at a later date. The crew
grumbled at this curtailment of their night ashore, but saw
nothing odd about it in the circumstances. That was just the
bloody navy for you. As the last sailor hurried out of the
dockyard gates, Alec Yates came strolling through, climbed
the gangway onto the *Dancer*, doffed his Panama hat to the
quarterdeck, showed his pass, and was led to the captain's

cabin, where the local dignitaries were just taking their leave, faces flushed by several large pink gins. Yates introduced himself to the captain, and they chatted of this and that until the other two arrived.

"As far as I am concerned, all is in order," Yates said. "The captain tells me that Vargas will be coming to the party, so you can get a close look at him. After that, he will be at his house; he rarely leaves it. I'll be with the President. Everything is as ready as it can be, so it's up to you two to open the ball at . . . shall we say twelve? Would that be convenient, Simon? . . . Klaus?"

Kleiner shrugged and glanced at Simon. "What do you think? It's your show."

"Why not?" Simon said. "The witching hour will do nicely."

"Then let's all have a drink," the captain said. "And the best of British luck to you both. I don't know what you are up to, but I think a little luck might come in handy."

The officers' cocktail party went off rather well. The President inspected the guard of honor and praised their turnout, the men looked efficient in their tropical rig, and the officers were, as always, perfect hosts. The fairy lights twinkled, the drinks flowed, the conversation became animated. From their vantage point on a wing of the bridge, Simon and Kleiner watched Vargas arrive, immaculate in a white dinner jacket, climbing lithely up the gangplank, leaving two squat bodyguards waiting on the quay. They got a good look at him before returning to hide in their cabin while the officers took the guests in small parties to tour the ship. At eight-thirty, one of the Royal Marines officers departed to change into his working gear for the night exercise, and by nine the captain was looking anxiously at his watch. The party was a roaring success, but would the blighters ever leave? he wondered.

Fortunately, the sudden arrival of the bulk of the ship's company, singing and smelling of strong drink, plus an outbreak of activity around the ship's boats, gave enough people the hint. By nine-thirty, all the guests had gone, and the fairy lights had been extinguished. The Doradan Defense Force came marching down the quay at ten, and by ten-thirty the boats were streaming out of the harbor in line ahead. Simon and Kleiner followed last in the *Dancer*'s little Zodiac, staying with the other craft until they were well out to sea before killing the outboard and letting the small rubber boat drift, driven toward the beach by the onshore breeze. In that dark hour, no one saw it coming, no one heard the soft thud as the round hull bumped gently into the side of Vargas's yacht. It lacked ten minutes to midnight. They had done it the simple way, coming in where no walls or gates or wires could keep them out. They had come in up Vargas's escape route. They had come by sea.

=== 17 ===

There was a sentry on the dock, but Kleiner killed him. It wasn't difficult. The man was well down a joint, his head full of colored lights as he strolled along the planking. Kleiner followed the smell of marijuana, edging along the jetty waist-deep in the water, tracking the man like a shark on a blood trail, reaching up out of the sea to drag him into the water. He held the man under until he had stopped kicking, then let him go. Simon came wading in past the floating body, pulling the Zodiac behind him. They unloaded the stores in the shadow of the dock, wading out again to fix charges to the hulls of three of the boats, then climbing onto the dock to open the fuel cocks and let gasoline spill out into the sea. They even found a drum of fuel and sloshed that about as well, until the air reeked with fumes. While they were doing that, another sentry wandered up, curious, sniffing the air, so they killed him as well, with one silent shot in the head from Simon's pistol. As he squeezed the trigger, he wondered briefly if the muzzle flash would set the whole kit and caboodle off, but nothing happened. Kleiner took that man's Mac-10 machine pistol, slung it over his shoulder, and dumped the man into the sea, off the end of the jetty. Two down already. Then they picked up their heavy rucksacks and weapons and headed across the soft, sandy beach toward the house. In spite of the strolling guards, getting there was easy. There was plenty of cover among the trees and bushes, plenty of deep moon-cast shadow, no sound from the soft marram grass as they flitted across the lawns. Besides, this was their game, one they had played before. It was easy to dodge the occasional wandering sentry.

Because he knew about aircraft, Kleiner dealt with the helicopter, slipping across to fix a charge to the fuel tank while Simon lay back in the shadows ready to fire. When that part went all right, they edged up to the big limousine parked outside the half-open double-fronted door of the mansion, and put another charge on that. By half a minute to midnight, they were as ready as they would ever be. Back in the trees, Kleiner snapped the cover back from the luminous dial of his wristwatch and leaned over to grasp Simon's hand, his eyes a white gleam in his grease-blackened face.

"Ten seconds," he whispered. "Good luck."

Simon counted five and hit the switch. The big yacht by the jetty practically leapt out of the water as the first charge went off. Then another explosion rocked the craft alongside, sending a deep, rolling crack bouncing around the hills. The gasoline went up with one vast *whooosh,* and a great, cracking roar that lighted up the night sky and rattled windows halfway up the mountain behind Caytown. On the bridge of HMS *Dancer,* the captain smiled, put down his binoculars, and pressed the alarm bells. Back in the grounds of the Vargas mansion, Simon opened fire.

As bits of boat and jetty came raining down across the garden, the guards were suddenly everywhere, spilling out of the front door like bees from a hive. Simon drove them back inside with a couple of bursts, watching out of the corner of his eye while several of those pinned outside crawled to elusive safety under the limousine. When they were packed tightly behind the wheels, he changed channels on the transducer and hit the switch. The limousine went up in the air, crashing back to burst into flames. The return fire from underneath the vehicle stopped. One man went racing out across the garden, his clothes on fire, a human torch running across their front, so that turning to shoot him down was almost a kindness. A few yards away, Kleiner was cutting loose with the RPG-launcher, lobbing his first shells into the upper story of the house and starting a fire, rising to his knees to send one or two more across the outer wall into one of the black windows of Government House, just across the square. The second grenade landed three rooms down the corridor from the President's office, the blast throwing Yates and the shocked President Spurling off their chairs to the floor.

"Jesus Christ!" cried the President, down on all fours, looking toward the window as noise swelled up from the streets. "What's going on? Is it a riot?"

Yates, that student of history, remembered that Louis XVI had asked the same question, and couldn't resist giving the same answer. "No, sir," he said smoothly. "It's a revolution."

Out in the streets, the revolution was well under way. The meeting at the Labor Hall had been going on since nine o'clock, in a growing tide of excitement fueled by rum punch and set alight by fiery speeches from the platform. Two minutes after the shooting started, a drunken mob surged out of the hall into the streets, trying to find out what was going on and take advantage of it. The three Colombians they met outside, men who were sprinting down the street toward the square, should not have run away. Running away made the mob chase after them. They should certainly not have drawn pistols and fired back at their pursuers, for although they hit two, that only made things worse. The enraged mob simply ran them down and tore them to pieces. Then the rioters got down to the serious business of the night, overturning cars, smashing windows, looting shops, starting fires, beating up anyone who got in the way, years of pent-up fury and frustration spilling out at last. A small group went off to besiege the police station, attacking it with stones and blasts from shotguns. Others, somewhat wiser or more sober, simply went off to hide until the storm passed. The firing from the Vargas house went on, and the heart of Caytown gave itself up to death and destruction.

Simon and Kleiner were surrounded now. The odds against them were too great. They were pinned down in the thick bushes before the house, heavy automatic fire cutting the air above their backs, the cordon about them tightening slowly. They forced it back with short bursts, hardly daring to fire back, in case they revealed their position. When the first rush came, a dark wave of men screaming out of the trees behind, they rolled over and beat it off, red flames jutting at their hips. The last man fell within touching distance. They beat off another rush with a burst from Kleiner's Mac-10 and two aimed shots from Simon's pistol, but they couldn't live much longer out there. The cover of the garden was working against them, and a grenade would finish them off.

"We've got to get into the house," yelled Kleiner, rising, changing magazines. "Come on!" He was halfway there, leaping for safety across the forecourt, pouring fire into the deep shadow of the open door, when the bullet took him. It hit him in the back of the right leg and went right on through, smashing the bone, spinning him around. Another hit him on the shoulder, then another, and another, their impact flinging him hard against the wall. Then it was not just a death, it was an execution. Coming forward from the trees, Simon heard the roar of weaponry and saw the jerking body, the bullets flailing Kleiner, the brick dust dancing from the wall. Kleiner was dead long before Simon cleared cover and made his own bid for the elusive safety of the house.

"I think we should go ashore, sir," the Captain of Marines said urgently. "The men are drawn up as ordered, and I have detailed off a landing party from the crew and issued riot gear, but we can't do anything from here. There are fires in the town center . . . it's getting out of hand, sir. Listen to that shooting."

"We can't interfere in another country's affairs without being asked, Charles," the captain said, "and stop pacing about, it's making me nervous. So we'll just sit here and wait until somebody brings the President of this hellhole to his senses."

Down on the floor of the President's office, crouched under the President's desk, Alec Yates was attempting to do just that. It was safer down there, for two ricochets had already whistled through the windows, there was smoke seeping under the door from the fire down the hall, and one of the buildings across the square was already well ablaze. Outside they could hear the howling of the mob, but the President was still proving stubborn.

"I will not resign!" he screamed. "Never! And you can't depose me. I am the President of Cay Dorado for life. The UN will protest. I shall appeal to the Commonwealth, to the Queen."

"You can't *not* resign, Spurling," said Yates, raising his voice above the din from outside. "You've bloody well had it. Can't you see that, man? I've got a suitcase full of evidence against you. The UN won't lift a finger . . . when do they ever? Your people are on the streets. Vargas and his company can't help you." He clawed an envelope from his pocket and pushed it toward the President. "Vargas is probably dead by now. Sign this resignation and request for our assistance, and I'll get you to the *Dancer* . . . but hurry! If that mob gets in here, they will lynch you. It's all over, can't you see that? Think, man, for once in your life. It's your only hope."

"You fixed all this," the President snarled. "You did this, you bastard. You English bastard!"

"You're bloody right I fixed all this," said Yates, thumping the carpet with his fist. "And I enjoyed doing it. So sign, blast you, or die in your own dunghill."

Spurling signed. Crawling out from the cover of the desk, Yates reached up for the phone.

Simon made it to the house. One bullet hit the rucksack over his shoulder with the force of a mule's kick, but he still made it. The guards were still picking over what was left of Kleiner, shooting his body to rags, and Simon was in the house before they had time to switch aim. He burst through the door, almost fell over a body, and exchanged a burst with a man at the foot of the stairs, cutting him down before his machine pistol clicked empty. Suddenly, briefly, there was a silence, just the odd shot from outside, the crackling of flames from above, and the distant roar of the mob. Simon tossed the machine pistol onto the hall table and dragged the shotgun out from under the straps of the rucksack, cocking it with one smooth clash of metal, and turned toward the stairs. There came the sound of feet from above, and he stepped back into the stairwell, waiting until the stairs shook and creaked under pounding feet. Then he fired up through the woodwork, once, twice, blasting a hole, the muzzle flashes setting the wood alight. He was halfway up, vaulting the sprawled bodies, stepping across the smoldering, splintered gap, when the first of the guards rushed in through the outside door. A blast of buckshot threw that one back across the mat, with half his head missing. While the other guards hesitated, thinking that one out, Simon worked another shell into the breech and climbed on up the stairs, taking them three at a time.

The house was on fire, smoke licking along the ceilings, swirling waist-high along the corridors. He could hear the crackle of flame more loudly now above the shouts and occasional bursts of gunfire from outside. He climbed on, past the second-floor stairwell, the steps afire and sagging, littered with plaster and grenade fragments, the shotgun ready, held at the high port across his chest as he came out onto the upper landing. A wounded man was lying up there, his leg shattered by RPG fragments but alive and just conscious. Simon lifted his chin with the muzzle of the shotgun, and pressed the muzzle against the man's throat.

"Where is Vargas?" he asked. "The Big Boss . . . hey?"

The man stared up at him, eyes blank and filled with pain. Simon tried again. *"¿Donde está el Jefe?"* he asked, pressing the barrel into the man's neck.

The man screwed his head away and nodded toward the end of the corridor, grunting with pain at the effort of turning his head.

"Allá . . . en el gran despacho."

Simon turned his head and looked down the shadow-filled corridor to the double doors at the far end. Vargas was in his office, where else? Waiting until the firing stopped, sticking close to his loot, letting the others in his pay do their jobs and take the heat, looking after *numero uno*. Meanwhile, time was running out. His men were on the stairs below Simon now, coming up slowly, past the fires and the damage, firing long bursts ahead as they climbed. Simon got up and began to run down the corridor, faster and faster, firing one round, and then another as he came on, full into the door ahead, shattering the wood and the lock, putting the full weight of his body into the charge, bursting into the room, the doors slamming back against the walls on either side.

Vargas was in there, in smoke-stained evening clothes. Vargas made a fight of it, moving about the room, snapping three fast shots at Simon from a long-barreled revolver, but a shotgun is better for that sort of work, and Vargas made one big mistake. He missed. Skidding to a stop, Simon fired twice, placing his shots just behind or in front of that dodging figure, careless of the return fire, watching splinters leap up as the buckshot ploughed into the bookcase, seeing it send a great white cloud of pure cocaine leaping from a pile of one-kilo bags stacked high on Vargas's desk. With his third shot, Simon put a full charge into Vargas's chest and saw the impact shred him away against the wall, smearing the paint as he slid down, out of sight. Suddenly, it was quiet, and in that brief silence he felt the weariness again, sagging into a chair by the door, resting his head in one hand for just a moment, the shotgun barrel hot across his knees.

It was almost over now, and there could only be one end to it. Everyone else had already gone. Philip, Kleiner, Ted Bardsey, Freddie Bright, Lito, Magdalena, good people and bad, and a lot of others who were just unlucky enough to get in the way or be in the wrong place at the wrong time. Simon could hear the guards coming. They were already on the last flight of stairs, a dozen of them creeping up carefully around the fires. He shook his head, clearing thoughts of Lucia from his mind, then rose and began to walk back down the corridor toward them, pushing the last few cartridges into the magazine of his shotgun.

EPILOGUE

Most of the fires were out by daylight. A damage-control crew from HMS *Dancer* were still ashore and hosing down the embers of one burned building, and the Royal Marines had driven the rioters off the streets and imposed a curfew. The ex-President-for-Life, Sir Lancelot Spurling, had appeared briefly on breakfast television to announce his resignation, reading from a prepared statement, and posters were already going up in windows all over Caytown, announcing new elections, to be held under British and UN supervision. In spite of the smell of ashes and gunfire, there was a hint of hope in the air.

Alec Yates came on board HMS *Dancer* just before noon, his face heavy and tired, his clothing dirty, and went directly to the bridge, past the long lines of sailors leaning on the rail, watching the last thin lines of smoke whirl up from the wreck of Vargas's mansion in the trees across the dockyard.

"Well, any news?" the captain asked. "Anything to report to MOD? I'm getting signal after signal from the U.K., but what do I tell them? And when do I get my men back?"

"Fairly soon. A Commander Catton from Scotland Yard will arrive here in an hour or so to take over the police and public-order duties for a while. He was in Miami, fortunately. How is our ex-President?" Yates collapsed into the captain's chair and looked about for coffee. "I imagine he's feeling pretty depressed."

"Not at all. He's very perky. He's taken over my day cabin and is down there now, reading *Country Life*. He was asking about the prices of property in the home counties. Apparently, he wants something about an hour's drive from London but near a golf course. Surrey sounds about right. Wentworth or Sunningdale perhaps? Any sign of my other guests?"

Yates shook his head. "They didn't make it. I identified what was left of Kleiner in the garden over there . . . not a pretty sight, I'm afraid. A wounded Colombian told me they had another gringo pinned in the house while it burned down. That would be Quarry, but of course we'll keep that quiet. Fortunately, Vargas didn't get out either. It's funny . . . I never really liked either of them, Quarry or Kleiner." Yates wiped his face with a crumpled handkerchief. "And yet I wish they were here. Somehow, it shouldn't have ended like this."

"You need a drink," the captain said firmly. "I think they knew what they were doing . . . what they were getting into. Can you explain what happened to Kleiner? He's a very well-known figure, and the press will be here this afternoon."

"We can provide a couple of explanations; perhaps he was here trying to get the runway contract. But if they don't buy that, and they probably won't, we shall tap our noses and remind them that Kleiner has been a relentless campaigner against the international drug trade, of which Cay Dorado is a base, and so on. After that, they'll make it up. That's what they usually do anyway. As to the rest, I suppose they did know the risks they were taking," Yates said. "But yes, I'd still like a bloody big scotch."

"So that's about it, Minister," Yates said, "and all in all, I think we can regard it as a most satisfactory conclusion. We have tidied up Cay Dorado, given the Cartel a bloody nose, and as a little bonus, relieved ourselves of a most expensive personal obligation to Klaus Kleiner. And useful though he has been from time to time, Simon Quarry is no loss."

The minister scratched his jaw quietly, then picked up a

piece of paper from his desk, studying it for a moment before raising his eyes across the desk. "Well, Alex, I hate to spoil your day, but I'm afraid I have some different news. Did you know that Catton is leaving the Yard? No? We offered him Bardsey's slot in Major Crimes, but he turned it down. It appears he has obtained a large shareholding in Kleiner's KSI. I'm also afraid that our security deal holds good. A Miss Christine Hitchcock, or Mrs. John Catton, as we must now learn to call her, has reviewed the arrangement, and apparently our contract was with KSI, not Kleiner personally, and rock solid. Catton will probably make a fortune in the next few years."

Yates pursed his lips and shrugged at the yard. "Well, no doubt he'll earn it, Minister, and he may be no loss at the Yard. He was getting much too friendly with people like Simon Quarry."

The slight smile on the minister's face broadened into a grin. It was not often anyone had the chance to stick the knife into Alec Yates, but here was a chance to do that and then twist it.

"Well, that's another thing, Alec. Didn't you report that Quarry had been killed on Cay Dorado?"

"That's confidential, Minister. Nobody knows officially that Quarry was even on Cay Dorado, and thank God, the press are far more interested in what happened to Klaus Kleiner. No one knows or cares about Simon Quarry."

"You didn't see the body . . . ?"

"No, Minister, the house was gutted. May I know why you are asking me this?"

The minister's smile broadened a little further. "It's never that easy, Alec. Kleiner's death is all over the front pages, but I did happen to notice a little item inside, in the social column. I have it right here. You'll never guess who turned up yesterday at John Catton's wedding!"